WHAT PEOPLE ARE SAYING ABOUT

DESIRING DRAGONS

Desiring Dragons is unique in its examination of the creative processes involved in writing fantasy and account of their value. Kevan shows that rather than being a mode of escapism, writing fantasy is grounded in shamanic and visionary traditions. The process of exploring otherworlds and returning with stories is healing and empowering for writer and reader alike. Kevan's extensive knowledge of mythic literature and personal experience of the magic of Bardism underlie a book which uncovers fantasy's deep roots and provides a treasure horde of practical advice for fantasy authors.
Lorna Smithers, poet

Following in the footsteps of Blake, Coleridge, and Tolkien, Kevan Manwaring invites us on a quest to find our grounding and meaning in the often arrestingly strange, far reaches of the human imagination. His *Desiring Dragons* is an invaluable resource for Fantasy writers wishing to hone their elfish craft, or for anyone seeking to understand the creative process that produces the still largely misunderstood genre of Fantasy.
Dr Charlotte Hussey, poet *Glossing the Spoils*

Desiring Dragons

Creativity, Imagination and the
Writer's Quest

'Let the Revels Begin', by Tom Brown

Desiring Dragons

Creativity, Imagination and the Writer's Quest

Kevan Manwaring

COMPASS BOOKS

Winchester, UK
Washington, USA

First published by Compass Books, 2014
Compass Books is an imprint of John Hunt Publishing Ltd., Laurel House, Station Approach,
Alresford, Hants, SO24 9JH, UK
office1@jhpbooks.net
www.johnhuntpublishing.com
www.compass-books.net

For distributor details and how to order please visit the 'Ordering' section on our website.

ISBN: 978 1 78279 583 4

A CIP catalogue record for this book is available from the British Library.

Design: Lee Nash

Printed in the USA by Edwards Brothers Malloy

CONTENTS

Disclaimer

What This is Not:
***Desiring Dragons* is not another 'How to Write...' book**

Writers, please – don't follow instructions; follow inspiration! All that follows can be taken with this pinch of salt. As the poet Vernon Watkins wisely said once: 'There is no theory however strict that a work of genius cannot contradict.' So, even if you are not a genius (and who is, in all humility? It seems to be a term applied only posthumously, which doesn't help us here) you should at least bear Watkins' edict in mind, (to use a deeper definition, *speak from your spirit*) as well as the following 'non-commandments':

The author encourages you to...

- Step *on* the grass and stray *from* the path.
- Learn to trust your writer's instincts.
- Ignore everything except your vision.
- Begin your quest right away – don't let anyone or anything put you off.
- Dare to dream. You are the hero – the dragon is waiting for you to win its treasure.
- Start this book at any part. Dip in and out. Find something useful and have a go.
- Use anything in the book in any capacity – workshops, writing programmes, etc. (just cite the author).
- Blast yourself out of the genre ghetto. Don't think in genre, think in original ideas.
- Write as though someone has a gun to your head. Make it good, make it count.
- Pass the book on. Others might desire dragons too.

The Words to Bring Dragons

Curled up in my bed,
crouched in sweat,
around the tome of imaginary deeds,

I fly with lances, build palaces in the
space around my head.

You showed me what space there is to fill.

We all love stories,
but to a storyteller,
the master's voice speaks to pupil through

dark marks, thoughts' traces
on yellow, thin leaf:
the code of dreams.

Sent out, a message in a bottle,
stored, reactivated.

I know what you mean when you say 'magic'.
I feel it too,
what my teachers have awakened.

You built my refuges,
stout castle walls,
taught me the words to bring dragons,
made me face pain.

I am the knight of cups,
the crippled knight,
holding the chalice steady, lest it spill.

Water is not rare,
teardrops are as common as raindrops.
I belong by the water.

At fifteen, my test of manhood.
I received my gift and my trial:
the story and the sickness.

Here I find anew the old self,
quiet wisdom that is free to the seeker,
the peace to heal.

My burden, too long carried,
I make ready to birth you,
story that was never meant for myself alone.

Magic conceals as it reveals,
I will hide in plain sight.

Who will guess what magic means?
Only you,
for whom I wrote this,
unknown comrade,
pure heart,
pupil to my teacher,
sharing our dream
through the web of minds.

Anna Rubin

Preface

A 'How to Write Fantasy' book is perhaps a contradiction in terms – for Fantasy, by its very nature, is about imaginative writing. If you need a book to tell you how to use your imagination, you are perhaps not Fantasy writer material. Unfortunately, not many are – even those who see print. A lot of what is published under the Fantasy banner often shows, if anything, a dearth of the imagination – Nth generation rip-offs of Tolkien et al; or thinly-veiled movie treatments, inspired by other movies (showing the author's malnourished literary imagination) – junk-food Fantasy*. When Fantasy is good, it stands its own in the world of classic literature – *The Lord of the Rings; Gormenghast; His Dark Materials; The Mists of Avalon; The Master and Margarita* – these writers have drawn from the source, not merely other writers in the field, indeed some of them were pioneers, actually creating the genre we know today. And so this book does not want to share some 'formula' for writing Fantasy fiction – the very anathema of imaginative writing – instead, it invites you to consider the journey, the actual creative process and our motivation for undertaking it.

To liken the experience of writing to an heroic quest might be seen as romanticising an activity which can be literally prosaic. No doubt some will see this book in that light – and I fully acknowledge this.

Let it be said from the outset – at the end of the day, writing simply comes down to sitting down and getting on with it until it's done.

Nevertheless, there is something Herculean in the task – certainly redrafting and editing can feel like clearing out the Aegean stables, again and again. It takes considerable effort to get to the stage Orwell talks about when he declares: 'Good prose is like a window pane.' Before the pane, the pain.

The reasons why we undertake such a task, and inflict such potential torment are various and mysterious. In this book I attempt to explore some of them – not to be prescriptive, but to invite you to reflect upon your own motives. Perhaps you'll find a mirror here; or your own reflection cast in a new light. It can be reassuring to know that where you are venturing others have ventured before – *and have made it through*. There are many maps between, and the terrain is slightly different for each of us. However, there are some commonalities – which suggest a mythic structure to the experience, which I sketch out here, knowing that it is just one take upon it. By no means, the Writer's Quest is meant to be the definitive blueprint. That would be to set in stone the nebulous process of the creative act.

For each writer, the reason why they write is different. Yet it is wise to reflect upon our motives as we embark upon such an endeavour.

Orwell, in his classic essay, 'Why I Write' lists four:

1. Sheer egoism
2. Aesthetic enthusiasm.
3. Historical impulse.
4. Political purpose.[1]

He admitted the first three were prevalent – certainly in his early writing – although the latter became his defining trait as a writer. Yet, although he believed a writer's 'subject matter will be determined by the age he lives in', nevertheless, before he even puts pen to paper, 'he will have acquired an emotional attitude from which he will never completely escape.'

The writer might not be able to shake off these formative factors – and nor should they – but they can rein in their influence: 'It is his job, no doubt, to discipline his temperament and avoid getting stuck at some immature stage, or in some perverse mood: but if he escapes from his early influences altogether, he will have killed his impulse to write.'[2]

This notion is important – certainly Tolkien's early influences drove his urge to write – his 'desiring dragons' from a young age.

'I first tried to write a story when I was about seven. It was about a dragon. I remember nothing about it except a philological fact. My mother said nothing about the dragon, but pointed out that one could not say 'a green great dragon', but had to say 'a great green dragon'. I wondered why, and still do. The fact that I remember this is possibly significant, as I do not think I ever tried to write a story again for many years, and was taken up with language.'[3]

Clearly, this early catalyst provided the grit in the oyster of Tolkien's fledgling imagination, setting him off down the Road of Words.

However, we should not see in Tolkien's pathology a clue for our own. The key incident of anyone's creative journey will be as idiosyncratic as they are. To try and devise a unifying theory of creativity will be fool-hardy in the extreme, as neurologist Alice W. Flaherty suggests: 'The kaleidoscope of reasons why writers think they write remains hard to fit into any one theory, although all fit the needs theory of self-expression to some extent.'[4]

And so, all that follows is coloured with my own predilections and foibles. If I see things through 'mythic goggles' it is because I am a storyteller. Such metaphoric filters are my stock-in-trade. And so my analysis of the mysterious alchemical process of writing imaginative fiction is undoubtedly going to be coloured by this.

If we do not write about what obsesses us, haunts us, taunts us, and delights us, then what is the point?

What motivates us as writers, and what keeps us going – these are two key questions I shall be exploring in this brief raid into the Underworld of the creative process. Let us venture into the dragon's lair – risking all – and hope to return with the treasure of insight, bringing light to an endarkened place.

The book is divided into two main sections. The first, 'Desiring Dragons', is an essay on Fantasy – its origins, evolution and application. Tolkien's approach is foregrounded throughout (the book takes it title from him after all), although other authorities are also cited. There is no attempt to be encyclopaedic here. Rather than be considered the 'final word', it is hoped that the essay will prompt further discussion. The writing and reading of Fantasy is an ongoing research project for not only scholars and authors, but also fledgling writers, students, and, of course, readers. The territory continues to expand – with every innovative book, film, graphic novel, play and computer game – so an exhaustive charting of it would quickly become redundant. All that can be provided is an entreport.

The second section is a breakdown of what I call 'The Writer's Quest', based upon the Old English poem, *Beowulf,* one of Tolkien's chief influences. In this, the creative process of writing is explored in the context of the 'journey of a novel', and as such can be applied to all genres of writing. At the end of each chapter there are 'questings' – suggestions for follow-up activities.

The appendices comprise of 'The Dragon's Hoard: Other Essays', the spoils, as it were, of the first two.

This split-brain structure is to reflect the Theory and Practice (I use the word 'theory' warily – such things are as elusive and evanescent as fairies. I merely share what I have caught in my butterfly net). There will be inevitable bleed-through – as with the hemisphere of the brain. To paraphrase the poet Edward Thomas, this is no mere case of left and right.[5] The creative impulse is more mysterious than that. This book does not attempt a definition of what is territory as idiosyncratic as each author, but a spirited foray into a relatively unknown region – normally left out of creative manuals. It is a curious visitor's first impressions, rather than a 'Google Earth' attempt at virtual omniscience. Somewhere it'll always be cloudy.

Writing Fantasy is a kind of leap of faith – the author as Fool, stepping off the precipice, hoping his invisible Art will keep him aloft. Certainly, the reading of it is – the act, not merely a willing suspension of disbelief, but a spirited swinging over the abyss. We leap into the void *because* it is perilous, *because* it is dark and mysterious and deliciously other.

So, in an attitude of Fool-like unknowingness, and fool-hardy bravado, let us follow that gruff, donnish magician into the Perilous Forest – the glow of his pipe in the gloaming our only guide.

May *Desiring Dragons* help to light your way as you embark your quest.

Kevan Manwaring, Stroud 2013

* There is, however, good stuff out there. For a selective list of contemporary Fantasy, see **Further Reading**

Introduction:
The Fascination of the Worm

'Even today (despite the critics) you may find men not ignorant of tragic legend and history, who have heard of heroes and indeed seen them, who yet have been caught by the fascination of the worm.'
JRR Tolkien[6]

Twentieth Century Professor of English and novelist JRR Tolkien, who perhaps more than any other single author has brought alive worlds of Fantasy in his vast Middle Earth sequence of stories, as a child 'desired dragons with a profound desire':

> 'Of course, I in my timid body did not wish to have them in my neighbourhood. But the world that contained even the imagination of Fafnir was richer and more beautiful, at whatever the cost of peril.'[7]

If we read this as a yearning for Fantasy, (that is, the experience of such, as opposed to the genre – although we will dignify both with the capital in the hope that one will encourage the other) then I do not think he is alone in this, as the huge popularity of Fantasy in books, films and computer games prove. There seems to be an endless appetite for it: *The Lord of the Rings, Dr Who, Star Trek, Star Wars, Harry Potter, The Twilight Saga, Avengers Assemble,* and no doubt more 'franchises' await to hit the big or little screen. Despite a distinctive post-9/11 trend for 'real life stories', gritty realism, and tales of hard luck and 'winning through adversity' (spawning shelves of 'misery lit'; or 'trauma memoir') the world, it seems, is hungry for Story, especially of the fantastical kind.

Why is it so many seem to 'desire dragons', as Tolkien did? What purpose, if any, is there to Fantasy? Is it just make-believe for grown ups, or does it serve a more profound function? This brief excursion into Fantasyland endeavours to explore, if not answer, these questions, and perhaps the very act of *asking questions* – curiosity, or the quest for knowledge – is at the root of all this ultimately. The desire to know has led humankind from the cave to the moon. Wishing to know what lay over the next hill, and the next, beyond the borders of the familiar, over the sea, over the horizon – following the journey of the sun, our constant companion of consciousness, throughout the day, into the unconscious of night – this has driven humanity on, and fuelled most of its fantasies. The unknown provides a vacuum for the subconscious, for the Shadow, the Id, the other. We populate the night with our own.

And we probe the shadows with a thrill of fear and a desire to know.

Tolkien, in a witty reply to a letter in *The Observer* (16 January, 1938) signed by someone calling themselves 'Habit', requesting more background about 'the name and inception of the intriguing hero of his book', (*The Hobbit*, published 21 September 1937) responded thus:

> 'Sir, – I need no persuasion: I am as susceptible as a dragon to flattery, and would gladly show off my diamond waistcoat, and even discuss its sources, since the Habit (more inquisitive than the Hobbit) has not only professed to admire it, but has also asked where I got it from. But would not that be unfair to the research students? To save them trouble is to rob them of any excuse for existing.'[8]

Despite Tolkien's claiming not to 'remember anything about the name and inception of the hero', he gave a typically conscientious and erudite reply. His letters show the fathomless quality of his learning (his scholar's mind akin to the Mines of Moria) and provide a plethora of portals to explore – enough for a lifetime, and thus he has not robbed research students of their existence, but thrown a gauntlet down to 'curious Hobbits', who are intrigued by the mysterious origins of such wonders, in what smithies were they forged, and whether the alchemical secrets of the wordsmiths trade can be gleaned, used, and passed on.

I must disclose my own interest in this realm of the imagination – with my five-volume epic, *The Windsmith Elegy*[9], I could be categorised as an author of Fantasy, although I prefer the term 'Mythic Reality' (for that is how it feels to me – more of which we will discuss later). As a writer of 'Fantastical Fiction' (as it once used to called) the genre, as a whole, holds an obvious appeal to me, but more so the mysterious impulse that drives us to write and read it, and beyond that, the act of creation itself.

The central thesis I would like to forward here is that the roots of Fantasy go deeper than sometimes the genre suggest – that there is more to it than mere 'Sword and Sorcery', and the endless rehashing of Tolkienesque tropes. What if Fantasy is not merely a form of escapism (although that in itself is not 'wrong'), but a way of exploring imaginative possibilities?

In the purest expression of Fantasy, something more fundamental is at work. Could Imagination serve as a gateway to other realms, other possibilities – a kind of 'Quantum TV' – with different bandwidths showing glimpses of 'that which does not exist, but could', and sometimes does, in our imagination?

Many beginner writers who attempt to write Fantasy do not seem to understand the genre. They copy the shadows on the cave wall; without having a full gnosis of what drives their creation (as someone who has taught and assessed creative writing since 2003 I can wearily attest to this – although I am occasionally astounded by what my students produce). There is often a gulf between idea and execution, which is frustrating. It feels as though I am receiving a poor signal from a distant land.

The craft provides the Transatlantic cable, but I do not wish to lay it down here – many others have done that. Rather than simply provide a list of techniques, I believe it would be more useful (and better for the writer) to explore the 'biology' of Fantasy, and our motives for writing it.

- Where does the impulse to write Fantasy come from?
- What takes place in the act of writing, i.e. the creative process – specifically in the creation of works of Fantasy?
- What benefits are there, if any, for the writer, as well as the reader?

And so I begin this essay with these questions in mind – and a sense of unknowing.

A quester, armed with his question, is a good place to start.

Part One

Desiring Dragons

1

Defining Fantasy

'This is a regrettably true tale such as no correct thinking person ought to regard seriously.'
James Branch Cabell[10]

To define something as nebulous as Fantasy is to perhaps attempt an impossible task – the kind of thing a hapless heroine will be forced to undertake in a fairy tale: to sort rice grains from wheat, needles from straw, the false from the true.

As a genre, it is notoriously difficult to pin down – like an over-sized worm in a fairy tale; it has a tendency to wriggle away. In *The Encyclopaedia of Fantasy* (1999) John Clute gives voice to this, saying that Fantasy is: 'a most extraordinarily porous term, and has been used to mop up vast deposits of story which this culture or that – and this era or that – deems unrealistic.' He cites Brian Atteberry's notion that Fantasy is a 'fuzzy set', which can best be described through 'prescriptive and exploratory example'.[11]

Yet, to avoid this quest slipping through our fingers, we need something solid to hold onto, to guide us. A phial of Elendil to light our way, or a Sting-like blade to glow blue when we encounter an ugly untruth.

One could argue that *all* fiction is imaginative to a lesser or greater extent, but in Fantasy the imaginary is emphasised. In fact, perhaps the only sustainable definition of the genre is that *it is only limited by your imagination.*

However, it is wise to begin with the familiar, the reliable, before venturing out into more chancy territory. The good old 'Strider' of a guide, the OED (the fit-for-the-wilderlands concise version), defines it as the following:

Fantasy (n): *the faculty or activity of imagining improbable or impossible things.*
2. a genre of imaginative fiction involving magic and adventure

The latter is the popular perception of the term, but the primary definition remains obscure – as though an etymological version of *The Man in the Iron Mask* has occurred, with one definition locked up in an oubliette, while the other basks in the glory. It is time to release the lesser known aspect (the Faculty; as opposed to the Genre) from the dungeon — a key aspect which is often sadly lacking in Fantasy fiction.

It is important to distinguish between those immortal twins, Science Fiction and Fantasy, although this is notoriously difficult. Arisen from the same gene pool of the imagination, they have been raised in very different ways, and encountered wildly divergent fates – yet they are often conjoined in bookshops under the 'Science Fiction and Fantasy' category. Sometimes firstborn Fantasy is even subsumed under its later sibling – all books of a fantastical nature lumped under 'SF' – who Set-like wishes to slay his brother. But Fantasy rises Osiris-like, in the Underworld of the Subconscious, where he resides – the archetypal judge of all our endeavours. It is the source of all invention. Fantasy is the Nile, from which a vast delta of subgenres has been generated. At best, Science Fiction might be classed as the 'Lower Nile' – but that makes it no less important than its older sibling, even if he may carry some dream-silt from more ancient lands.

But, perhaps we need a less poetic analogy, or demarcation – to stop the Nile of Fantasy from flooding all the lands of minds and men.

Robert Silverberg has a crack at it, in his introduction to *The Fantasy Hall of Fame*, but admits 'the impossibility of making any of these definitions stick: 'Science Fiction is that branch of Fantasy which one generally deals in extrapolations of the consequences of technological development, and which attempts to stick fairly rigorously to known or theoretically possible scientific concepts. Fantasy is a much broader field of fiction that is less firmly bound to the tyranny of fact, and for the purposes of any given story is permitted to assume nearly any idea as plausible, though it is desirable for the author to elicit a suspension of disbelief through the plausible development of a basically unlikely notion.'[12]

For the record, my working definition is that Science Fiction has, at its core, a rationalist/scientific explanation of the universe; while as Fantasy offers a magical or mythic explanation. Of course, there are always exceptions to the rule, and with new discoveries in science (quantum physics especially) the boundaries between science and mysticism are blurring (territory authors such as Philip Pullman explores in *His Dark Materials* trilogy).

JRR Tolkien is perhaps the greatest Fantasy writer of all time; certainly he is incredibly influential and possibly the most emulated author in fiction (i.e. endless Sword and Sorcery pastiches). He disliked the use of allegory (unlike his fellow Oxford inkling, CS Lewis), and liked to describe his stories as Fairy Stories in the truest sense, that is, set in an Otherworld: 'most good fairy tales are about adventures of men in the Perilous Realm'. He argues that the successful writer of 'fairy stories' is one who: 'makes a Secondary World which your mind can enter. Inside, what he relates is 'true': it accords with the laws of that world.'[13] It has an internal logic – consistency, causality and an ecology of its own (often sharing some laws with our own world, i.e. gravity, night and day, hunger, sleep).

In an exploration of several famous Secondary Worlds, *Realms of Fantasy*, Edwards and Holdstock say: 'The writer must not cheat: the laws governing the invented world may be different from our own, but they must be applied consistently.'[14] Essential qualities are Realism and Conviction – the author has to totally believe in their world, and if they do so thoroughly and skilfully enough, they may make the reader forget that it is invented, or at least willingly suspend their disbelief.

Not all Fantasy is set in a Secondary World, but it is by far the most common trope. A Secondary World Fantasy: 'takes place in an invented world, which may or may not have some doorway into our own.'[15] A general survey of different kinds of Secondary Worlds include: Stories set in the ancient past; Stories set in present-day lost worlds; Stories set on other planets; Stories set in the distant future; Stories set on Fantasy Earths quite separate from our own but with affinities to it. Notice that many of them tread in Science Fiction territory, but it all depends on the 'explanation' behind the Way Things Work, as well as language, or tone, e.g. there is a world of difference between William Gibson's *Neuromancer* and Michael Ende's *The Never-Ending Story* (both imaginative fiction of the Eighties).

Fantasy is the means by which we may imagine and enter into other worlds. It is closely associated with Imagination – it provides a gateway. However, Tolkien goes to great lengths to elucidate on the difference between Fantasy and Imagination. Firstly, he defines the latter as 'the power of giving to ideal creations the inner consistency of reality.' Having established this, he then goes onto to tease out the quintessential difference with Fantasy:

'The mental power of image-making is one, or aspect; and it should appropriately be called Imagination... The achievement of the expression, which gives (or seems to give) 'the inner consistency of reality', is indeed another thing, or aspect, needing another name: Art, the operative link between Imagination and the final result, Sub-creation.'

For the purposes of his essay, 'On Fairy Stories', Tolkien sought a word which embraced: 'both the Sub-creative Art in itself and a quality of strangeness and wonder in the Expression, derived from the Image.'[16] This quality, essential, to fairy-story, he sums up as 'Fantasy'. He cites one of its chief effects as 'arresting strangeness', and although he acknowledges some people bridled at this ('They dislike any meddling with the Primary World, or such small glimpses of it as are familiar to them'), he refutes their misconception – that Fantasy is mere idle dreaming. He argues that true Fantasy is 'difficult to achieve'.[17]

To create a world so convincing that it 'commands or induces a Secondary Belief'[18] is something Tolkien says requires the art of elvish art of enchantment: 'To the elvish craft, Enchantment, Fantasy aspires, and when it is successful of all forms of human art most nearly approaches.'[19]

We will look at this in more detail in later chapters, but for now, let us end this brief examination by citing Tolkien one last time, who declares: 'Fantasy is a natural human activity. It certainly does not destroy or even insult Reason; and it does not either blunt the appetite for, nor obscure the perception of scientific verity. On the contrary. The keener and the clearer the reason, the better the Fantasy will it make.'[20]

This last caveat is a critical one. Any who venture into the twilight realms of Fantasy need a sharp sword and a keen eye, to avoid being mired in the swamps of soft-focus whimsy, mazed in the caverns of cliché, or assailed by the plague of plagiarism.

At its best, Fantasy forges something of beauty and substance so real, so alluring we want to step into it and live there.

CS Lewis describes coming across a copy of *Phantastes*: 'The glorious week end of reading was before me. Turning to the bookstall, I picked out... Phantastes, a faerie Romance, George Macdonald. That evening I began to read my new book.... I met there all that already charmed me in Malory, Spenser, Morris... But in another sense all was changed.... It was Holiness.'[21]

Fantasy creates imaginary, magical worlds that do not exist, but so skilfully, that we wish them to do be true, at least for a little while.

And this is the definition will shall use.

2

The Cottage of Lost Play

> *'There is a place called 'heaven' where the good here unfinished is completed; and where the stories unwritten, and the hopes unfulfilled, are continued. We may laugh together yet.'*
> JRR Tolkien[22]

Tolkien ostensibly wrote *The Hobbit* for his son, Christopher, but I suspect he was ultimately writing it for himself – for his own 'inner child' – for the project extended in effort and scope far beyond a bed-time story for his little boy. This is not to say his Middle Earth magnum opus was merely dabbling in 'childish things' – for he approached it with all the powers of his professorial mind, genius as a writer, and gifts as a philologist – but there is perhaps an element in all Fantasy writing which is a yearning to return to the 'garden of lost innocence', whether that be of childhood, early human evolution, or an Edenic pre-lapsarian state.

In writing Fantasy we are all trying to get back to the garden – in one way or another, whether we imagine Secondary Worlds of arboreal splendour, medieval feudalism, deep magic, or assassinatory sang-froid: it is all playing dressing up in the attic of our imaginations, or hide and seek at the bottom of the garden.

Tolkien (jnr) became literary executor of his father's estate, and published posthumously a 12 volume *History of Middle Earth*. Amongst those, he edited a 2-volume collection of JRR Tolkien's fragmentary or unpublished stories called *The Book Of Lost Tales* (2002). One of those is 'The Cottage of Lost Play'. The basic storyline is that a traveller named Eriol comes to a fairy land by ship. He wanders to the centre of a great island and weary, looks for shelter for the night in a small cottage in the village at the center of the island. The name of the house in Elvish is 'Mar Vanwa Tyalieva' or the Cottage of Lost Play. Lindo and Vaire are his hosts. With them are many of their kin as well as friends and children of many ages. Eriol hears a summoning gong. Vaire calls the room to which they go the 'Hall of Play Regained'[23]. It is where tales are told and is filled with children and people of all ages. Here is an extract of the poem Tolkien wrote about it:

The Little House of Lost Play

(Mar Vanwa Tyaliéva)

We knew that land once, You and I,
and once we wandered there
in the long days now long gone by,
a dark child and a fair.
Was it on the paths of firelight thought
in winter cold and white,
or in the blue-spun twilit hours
of little early tucked-up beds
in drowsy summer night,
that you and I in Sleep went down
to meet each other there,
your dark hair on your white nightgown
and mine was tangled fair?

Here the liminal state necessary for entering such otherworlds is suggested in phrases laden with yearning such as: 'the paths of firelight thought' or 'the blue-spun twilit hours'. These are akin to Yeats' 'when moth like stars are all alight' – when Wandering Aengus lights a fire, glimpses his 'glimmering girl', loses her and ultimately finds the binary opposites alluded to in Tolkien's 'dark hair on your white night gown/ and mine was tangled fair' in the 'silver apples of the moon, the golden apples of the sun'. It seems we need these polarities to navigate by and between, like the clashing rocks of the Symplegades. Whether they are the hemispheres of the left and right brain; the subconscious and superconscious; the Qabalistic pillars of Mercy and Severity; the Apollonian and Dionysian; or the Divine and Diabolical – between such extremes we find our doorway.

Lindsay Clarke, in his essay 'Imagining Otherwise',[24] explores this notion through the ancient symbol of the *vesica pisces* – which he sees a 'locus of … collision' between the inner and outer world. He writes that: 'it is through the meeting of opposites that something new appears.'

Yet the challenge is holding these polarities in balance long enough for something of wonder to slip through. Clarke articulates this creative tension: 'the proper exercise of the imagination is an energetic process of negotiation between the outer world and the inner world through which we strive to hold together their often contradictory pulls.'[25] Reality is always threatening to transgress the fragile borders of Fantasy – a threat which gives such polders (to use Grant and Clute's use of the term) as Narnia, Middle Earth or Neverland an evanescent fragility and poignancy.

This is epitomised by Tolkien's poem about him and his brother, 'The Little House of Lost Play' – a lost Arcadia of childhood innocence and imagination. The poem paints a scenario so fey and whimsical it is doomed to corruption – an Eden we must be exiled from to gain Knowledge. Yet, here worlds were born.

Tolkien and his brother were not unique in forging worlds of Fantasy from the gardens of childhood. The Brontë sisters created their own world, two imaginary islands called Gondal and Gaaldine, (was Tolkien's Gondor indirectly inspired by these?) which they populated with knights and damsels, emperors and princes. This was the nursery of their imaginations, and from this cutting of teeth in a mutual story world came the authors of *Wuthering Heights, Jane Eyre* and *The Tenant of*

Wildfell Hall. It is worth looking at this juvenilian world-building in detail for the insight it gives into fledgling fabulists.

All the Brontë children (Charlotte, Anne, Emily and Branwell) were involved from fairly early childhood in writing the chronicles of imaginary countries in elaborate detail with great gusto. Mr Bronte's return from Leeds with a box of wooden soldiers for Branwell on 5th June 1826 first released this extraordinary imaginative energy. Each child chose a soldier and determined his name and character, and these characters became actors in a series of games that grew steadily more elaborate as more characters were invented and the actions in which they were involved grew into complicated serial stories. Written out meticulously in a neat and tiny hand, the stories form an extraordinary collection of miniature home-made manuscript books. The surviving Brontë juvenilia have been carefully examined by Fannie E. Ratchford and discussed by her in her book The *Brontës' Web of Childhood* (The title of the book comes from Charlotte's poetic account of these literary activities, 'We wove a web in childhood'). Her conclusion is that the little booklets are a closely connected series of stories, poems, novels, histories, and dramas having a common setting and common characters, written through the sixteen years between 1829 and 1845: 'They are the epic cycle of an imaginary world in which the four young Brontës lived, moved, and had their being, into which they projected themselves and all that they knew of life from narrow experience and wide reading.'[26] The surviving work is mostly Charlotte's; she and Branwell developed their cycle of Angria; while the stories of Gondal, which were developed independently by Emily and Anne, have not survived. All that we have to indicate the nature of the Gondal cycle are poems by Emily and Anne spoken by Gondalian characters at critical moments in their history and a very few prose fragments referring to the progress of the stories or identifying a place or a character.

However, we have a precious insight into the weaving of this 'web of childhood'. On 24th November 1834, when she was sixteen years old, Emily captured a vivid vignette of creative life at Haworth parsonage:

> 'Taby said just now Come Anne pilloputate [peel a potato] Aunt has come into the kitchen just now and said Where are your feet Anne Anne answered On the floor Aunt. Papa opened the parlour door and gave Branwell a letter saying Here Branwell read this and show it to your Aunt and Charlotte. The Gondals are discovering the interior of Gaaldine. Sally Mosely is washing in the bock kitchen.'

And there we have that enticing phrase: 'The Gondals are discovering the interior of Gaaldine.' The completely matter-of-fact way in which this remark about the progress of the Gondal epic is inserted into the account of ordinary household affairs indicates the degree to which the events of this imaginary world were taken for granted by Emily as an integral part of the world she lived in. Gaaldine, as other clues indicate, was conquered and colonized from Gondal. Anne added in pencil to the list of proper names at the end of the family's of Goldsmith's *A Grammar of General Geography* a list of Gondalian place-names which provide some important clues for reconstruction of the stories. 'Gaaldine, a large Island newly discovered in the South Pacific' comes immediately before 'Gondal, a large Island in the North Pacific'. We know from the poems that Gondal had a climate and landscape like that of Yorkshire, while Gaaldine had a landscape of tropical luxuriance.

It is a curious fact that Tolkien's own mythos alludes to a similar Atlantean 'lost island', Numenor, and he was haunted all his life by a recurring dream which filled him with a dread of inundation. He puts this into the mouth of Faramir, in *The Return of the King,* who describes his vision of a 'great dark wave climbing over the green lands and above the hills, and coming on, darkness unescapable. I often dream of it.'

Primal fears and desires seem to be the pistons and petrol in the engine of the imagination.

David Daiches, in his introduction to *Wuthering Heights* (1965), observes: 'The most impressive and passionate of Emily's poems are Gondal poems, and even though they obviously reflect her own deepest emotional needs they are on the surface dramatic utterances by characters. Some of these characters, and some of the situations in which they find themselves, remind us vividly of characters and situations in *Wuthering Heights*...Emily Brontë's strange and powerful novel thus sprang from a lonely but well-stocked imagination.'[27]

Many other writers were inspired by formative experiences, from childhood games of make-believe and the personal cosmology of their neighbourhood – the world on their doorstep, and what lay beyond. We all start off with an imperfect knowledge of our vicinity, and how the world works – and fill in the gaps.

Alain-Fournier, a French author killed in action in 1914, wrote a single classic novel, *Le Grand Meaulnes,* (1912) whose title, although referring to the daring young protagonist, can be translated as 'The Lost Domain'. The novel is paean to the magic of childhood, when the borders of one's world were still being probed, crossed, regained. The schoolboy hero 'borrows' a powerful horse and carriage, in a Phaëton-like act of bravado and folly. He goes missing for three days and returns with an intriguing dream-like account of an adventure into a 'mysterious domain', which he strives to return to for years, in search of the lost trail that will lead him to his sweetheart – a quest that leads to a bitter awareness: 'I'm sure now that when I discovered the nameless domain I was at some peak of perfection, of purity, to which I shall never again attain. Only in death, as I once wrote you, can I expect to recapture the beauty of that moment…'[28]

In his memoir of reading, *The Child That Books Built,* (2003)

Francis Spufford explores the evolution of his imagination through the childhood classics which influenced his development. In describing his experience of reading a book he says: 'You never came out the way you came in.' Each talismanic book was a rabbit hole of possibility, of unexpected transgression and transformation.

Fantasy author Robert Holdstock suggests the conversations and behaviour of adults eavesdropped upon by children create a psychic landscape of larger-than-life characters, heroes and villains – what Carl Jung termed 'archetypes,' the psychoanalyst's phrase for 'primordial images': conscious representations of eternal principles; representations that can vary a great deal without losing their basic pattern. 'They are without known origin and they reproduce themselves in any time or in any part of the world.' [29] For Holdstock, the stuff that archetypes are made of – mythic images – inspired his neologism 'mythagoes'. These emerge from the symbiotic interaction between his characters and a remnant of ancient woodland, Ryhope Wood, in his 'Mythago Wood' cycle of novels. It is suggested the 'mythagoes' are plucked from a deep and ancient part of the protagonist's brain – a mysterious process which seems a mirror of Holdstock's own creative process:

'All things are known, but most things are forgotten. It takes a special magic to remember them.'[30]

The gateway of Ryhope Wood (a classic example of 'Threshold Fantasy' – what Farah Mendelsohn might call 'Portal-Quest' or possibly 'Liminal', for it has elements of both)[31] seems to be an amalgamation of an actual remembered landscape from childhood, and imagination, as Holdstock describes:

'There was a Roman villa on the hillside behind my house. I have no idea how old I was – four perhaps – when I began fantasising about the Roman ships coming up to the harbour there. That's where Romney Marsh is now, but in Roman times it was under the sea.'[32]

Thus, Holdstock's storyworld was formed from his own 'lost island' – the reclaimed land of Romney Marsh in Kent, 'reclaimed' by his imagination, that might one day be reclaimed back by the sea again if Global Warming persists. And similarly our own precious outliers of imagination (suffering the islandisation of 'mature' materialism, which insists such toys be put back in the box so that we can get on with the serious business of living) are threatened with engulfment and oblivion – by the tides of mundanity and commerce, or the marine transgressions of the mainstream.

The storytellers told themselves stories before telling the world. They began by desiring dragons – that is, creating Fantasy worlds – and we became infected with their feverish enthusiasm, because the longing is inside all of us. Later, it may be channelled into something more practical or at least attainable (motorbikes, mountains, obscure records or books) but for a time-being we are all united in the garden of lost play:

'In one thing only were all alike, that a look of great happiness lit with a merry expectation of further mirth and joy lay on every face.'[33]

This quality is perhaps the secret drug we look for in all Fantasy writing – although it might be buried beneath a myriad of masks, sub-genres, styles and tone. It is the *hiraeth* for this which makes us return again and again to the shelves, looking for the book that will act as a portal to the place we once experienced (or wished we had) and yearn to return to, forever exiles in our sensible adult world. It is this deep longing we will look at in the next chapter.

3

Sehnsucht and the Art of Writing Fantasy

'I idly turned the pages of the book and found the unrhymed translation of Tegner's Drapa *and read,* 'I heard a voice that cried, Balder the beautiful Is dead, is dead.' *...I knew nothing about Balder, but instantly I was uplifted.... I desired with almost sickening intensity something never to be described....'*
CS Lewis[34]

The writing and reading of Fantasy is often driven by a deeper longing than a simple nostalgia for a lost childhood. It can be motivated by deep dissatisfaction with daily life – which can manifest as a form of grief, a long-term depression, or even illness – pervaded by a heartbreaking longing for 'something other'. Modern life can seem unbearable to some – its ugliness, its tensions and dysfunction. Faced with Climate Chaos, financial meltdown, terrorism, geopolitical conflict, religious intolerance, etc. – alongside our personal struggles in work, home, heart and health – it is small wonder that some turn away from the world, yearning for another life, another way of being.

This goes beyond merely wishing for another career, partner, body, or neighbourhood.

Those with this chronic malaise long for worlds wildly different to our own – for Wonderland, Narnia, Middle Earth, Perelandra, Pandora, Barsoom, a 'galaxy far, far away', or the Final Frontier – the more exotic, the more alien, the better (although not so alien that we cannot relate to it, or have a protagonist we can identify with). Like Tolkien,[35] they do not want an allegory (which, in Fantasy fiction, is a bit like going on holiday overseas only to find that it is really 'just like home') – even if ultimately it is hard to escape any allegorical allusions[36].

What many fans of the genre hanker after is a sense of other-worldly adventure.

The push/pull factors which drive this – as described above – are summed up in a unique German term: 'sehnsucht'. A notoriously elusive word to translate or pin down in a single, neat definition (a fact which makes the very word seem like some kind of novum, introduced from another reality) 'sehnsucht' is a German noun translated as 'longing', 'yearning', or 'craving', or in a wider sense a type of 'intensely missing'.

Sehnsucht is a compound word, originating from an ardent longing or yearning (*das Sehnen*) and addiction (*die Sucht*). However, these words do not adequately encapsulate the full meaning of their resulting compound, even when considered together. George Tabori, stage director and author, called 'sehnsucht' one of those quasi-mystical terms in German for which there is no satisfactory corresponding term in another language.

Sehnsucht represents thoughts and feelings about all facets of life that are unfinished or imperfect, paired with a yearning for ideal alternative experiences. It has been referred to as 'life's longings'; or an individual's search for happiness while coping with the reality of unattainable wishes. Such feelings are usually profound, and tend to be accompanied by both positive and negative feelings. This produces what has often been described as an ambiguous emotional occurrence.

It is sometimes felt as a longing for a far-off country, but not a particular earthly land which we can identify. In this respect it relates directly to Fantasy.

Furthermore there is something in the experience which suggests this far-off country is very familiar and indicative of what we might otherwise call 'home'.

Sehnsucht took on a particular significance in the work of author CS Lewis. Lewis described sehnsucht as the 'inconsolable longing' in the human heart for 'we know not what.' In the afterword to the third edition of *The Pilgrim's Regress* he provided examples of what sparked this desire in him particularly: 'That unnameable something, desire for which pierces us like a rapier at the smell of bonfire, the sound of wild ducks flying overhead, the title of *The Well at the World's End*, the opening lines of 'Kubla Khan', the morning cobwebs in late summer, or the noise of falling waves.'

It is this almost intangible quality (perhaps captured in the evocative title of John Barry's 1999 album, 'The Beyondness of Things'; and in the soundtracks by Howard Shore of *The Lord of the Rings* movies) which drives the reader and writer of Fantasy on.

Many writers over the centuries appear to have been sufferers of sehnsucht – out of place, out of time, their work reaches beyond their paradigm, charged with this unbearable yearning. Richard Jefferies was one such soul, ill-at-ease in his life, the period of history (late Victorian) he was born into. In his spiritual autobiography, *The Story of my Heart*, he describes the awareness of 'something beyond' and his deep longing for it:

'...I have only just commenced to realise the immensity of thought which lies outside the knowledge of the senses. Still, on the hills and by the seashore, I seek and pray deeper than ever. The sun burns southwards over the sea and before the wave runs its shadow, constantly slipping on the advancing slope till it curls and covers its dark image at the shore. Over the rim of the horizon waves are flowing as high and wide as those that break upon the beach. These that come to me and beat the trembling shore are like the thoughts that have been known so long; like the ancient, iterated and reiterated thoughts that have broken on the strand of mind for thousands of years. Beyond and over the horizon I feel that there are other waves of ideas unknown to me, flowing as the stream of ocean flows.'[37]

Like the poet in WB Yeats' 'The Lake Isle of Innisfree', who feels the call in his 'deep hearts core' to leave the world for remoter shores, Jefferies felt the heart-wrenching pull to explore these unseen horizons: 'Let me launch forth and sail over the rim of the sea yonder, and when another rim arises over that, and again and onwards into an ever-widening ocean of idea and life.' 38

Jefferies notes, that, with the venturing forth, pulled by the 'subtle power of the great sea, there rises an equal desire.' The desire works both ways. A transfusion is called for: 'Give me life strong and full as the brimming ocean; give me thoughts wide as its plain; give me a soul beyond these.'[39]

In Jefferies' sehnsucht for a 'soul beyond these', he mirrors the soul-sickness which in shamanic cultures is cured by a medicine man or woman singing the soul back into the body. The sufferer is enduring 'soul-loss-ness'. Not finding a home in their body, family, school, neighbourhood, friends or colleagues, the sufferer sends their soul into other realms. Sometimes these realms are identifiable, and in the modern age often commodified, hugely popular, and amusingly prosaic – The World of Warcraft; Downton Abbey; Hogwarts; the Marvel Universe; etc – or they might remain inchoate and mysterious. The 'soul' of the sufferer is buried, like the heart of the queen in The Maiden Tsar[40]– a Russian folk-tale – within an egg, within a duck, within a hare, within a trunk, within an oak tree.

English folk musician Nick Drake was another sehnsucht-sufferer. His oeuvre of beautiful, melancholic music is pervaded by the quality, as epitomised by the posthumously-released song 'Magic':

I was born to sail away
Into a land of forever
Not to be tied to an old stone grave
In your land of never.
(Drake)[41]

A 'dream-brother', in spirit at least to Nick Drake was Jeff Buckley, who tragically followed his father, Tim Buckley, to an early grave. Drowning in an apparently freak accident, Jeff Buckley seems to have heard the same 'Song of the Siren' as his father:

> Should I stand amid the breakers?
> Should I lie with death my bride?
> Hear me sing, 'swim to me, swim to me, let me enfold you:
> Here I am, here I am, waiting to hold you
> (Buckley, Beckett)[42]

For Nick Drake, Jeff Buckley and other kindred of the doomed, there was sadly no cure ... in this life. It is a malady which only the purest strain of Fantasy can assuage. Lesser versions do little to ease the suffering – indeed, they can increase it. Poor scripts, acting, Special FX, or OTT soundtrack can set the teeth on edge. Supposed enhancements to the cinematic blockbuster (ever in search of the Next Big Thing) such as adapting a single book into a movie-trilogy, smothering everything in 3-D, or filming in 48 frames per second, can actually break the spell. They become another symptom of The World – trying to colonise our dreams and exploit them shamelessly.

The condition of sehnsucht is remedied not by the unimaginative regurgitation of Fantasy tropes – as the countless derivative novels, TV shows and films attest – but by the quality of the 'Sublime'. This is defined as: 'of such excellence, grandeur, or beauty as to inspire great admiration or awe' (*OED Concise*). It is seen in the works of William Blake; John Martin; the Symbolists; the Pre-Raphaelites; German Expressionism; Surrealism; master novelists (Bulgakov; Tolkien; Angela Carter; Pullman; Holdstock; Gaiman; George RR Martin, etc) and movie-makers (Jean Cocteau; Andrei Tarkovsky; Francis Ford Coppola; Wim Wenders; Terence Malick). There has been an emergent trend in cinema – post 9/11 – for awe-inducing visual spectacle, often of a catastrophic nature (*The Day After Tomorrow; The New World; The Return of the King; Apocalypto; The Road; The Tree of Life; John Carter; The Hunger Games; Oblivion; Thor: The Dark World; Star Trek: Into Darkness; Oblivion; After Earth; World War Z*). This trend – especially for post-apocalyptic fiction, has become hugely popular, especially in the Young Adult fiction market (*The Hunger Games Trilogy, The Passage,* ad nauseam). Like a pair of gloomy Goth siblings, adolescent angst fits neatly with doom-laden prognostications. For a teenager, it always 'the end of the world'. Yet their doom-mongering fever is catching. The slew of zombie movies, TV dramas and books seems to be rabid by-product of this catastrophising tendency. The nihilist doctrine, which such fodder advocates, is the ultimate abnegation of responsibility – if the world is ending, you do not need to sort it out. Survivalist fantasies are just another consoling fiction – shadows on the walls of your doomsday shelter – and humanity's end-game is big business.

Such *panem et circenses* seem to have captured the zeitgeist.

Yet nothing is new under the (dying) sun. This trend was foreshadowed by a movement in the Romantic Tradition as the 'apocalyptic sublime', best epitomised by the Ragnarok-like landscapes of John Martin. Martin, like Blake, drew for inspiration from The Book of Revelations – one of several 'Bad News Bibles' that prophecy apocalypse (e.g. the Elder Edda).

Although the sublime can easily become ridiculous (when massive budgets are not matched with excellent scripts) this ravenous desire for spectacle does not want to go away. Our sehnsucht might not be satiated by such fodder, (junk food for the imagination, as opposed to a feast) but it will graze upon it – continually. Perhaps it is an addiction to longing itself – and thus can never be satisfied.

4

Once Upon a Time...

Beyond the woods, beyond the seas, beyond high mountains lived a frightful dragon.
Chuvash traditional story opening[43]

Stories are as old as human time, and have been shared from when our ancestors told the earliest stories around the first fires – nurturing the frail flame of consciousness in the endless dark, giving shape to the shadows and keeping fear at bay... explaining the unknown or unknowable through the language of myth. Tolkien said, 'To ask what is the origin of stories ... is to ask what is the origin of language and of the mind.'[44] Author Robert Holdstock concurs with this. In an interview with Stan Nicholls in *Wordsmiths of Wonder* he says: 'I'm interested in the origins of story, in the beginning of our need of stories for entertainment, and you can use the actual tools of story to explore story itself.'[45]

Certainly, by studying Fairy Stories – that most efficient of all narrative arts – a writer can learn the essentials of fiction (Character; Setting; Line of Desire; Conflict; Structure). Beneath virtually ever modern narrative – be it a film, a TV drama, a play, an opera, ballet, computer game, novel, or comic book – there is a Fairy Story: the skeleton in the attic of all forms of tale. It is wise to study them – for in their simple folk magic lies the secret of storytelling – the magic ingredients that have made them last for centuries. The German poet Schiller wrote: 'Deeper meaning resides in the fairy tales told to me in my childhood than in the truth that is taught by life.'[46]

Humans are storytelling creatures. It's how we make sense of the world, the universe, and each other. Fairy stories are a relatively recent addition to the canon of stories passed down by the oral tradition since time immemorial. Many of them started in this way, were passed on and worn down like smooth coins from teller to listener, the lingua franca of the common folk – until finally written down by collectors, or perfected by writers in the 18th and 19th Century after a long and inkless journey. The Brothers Grimm, Hans Christian Anderson, Charles Perrault, Jean de La Fontaine, and others brought them to a wider audience and made them fashionable in the courts and palaces. Seemingly crystallised in these forms, they have been with us ever since, but in a sense they have always been with us, for they are hard-wired into our very beings. EM Forster says: 'The story is primitive, it reaches back to the origins of literature, before reading was discovered, and it appeals to what is primitive in us.'[47] Because story has this primal power, it pushes our buttons. Archetypal characters and situations haunt our dreams, reoccurring throughout our lives. With their disquieting and sometimes shocking imagery, fairy tales talk to us in the language of dreams, or as scholar of fairy tales, Marina Warner puts it: 'a language of the imagination'[48] Although fairy tales shouldn't be completely explained away[49] – for their power lies in their enchantment, which evaporates in the cold clear light of rational reality – understand how fairy tale works, and you have the foundation of all fiction, for the same universal figures, tropes and patterns haunt all stories.

William Gray, from the Sussex Centre for Folklore, Fairy Tales and Fantasy says of them: 'They often take place at twilight, between worlds. They evoke the idea that we all carry within us traces of an older, more primitive, way of being, in which we take what we want, when we want it – a part of ourselves we must give up.'[50]

In fairy tale and in most folk tales, myths and legends, key motifs occur again and again – and these have been categorised and catalogued exhaustively by Victorian collectors obsessed with putting things in neat 'display cases' (the late Imperialistic tendency to put the world in a museum) – identifying and auditing story motifs like pinning butterflies to a board. Yet beyond this (sometimes useful; sometimes denuding) labelling, there is a commonality of structure and tropes. In fairy tale, the basic ingredients of all stories can be seen in their quintessence: a beginning, middle and end; a setting; hero/heroine; villain; conflict; quest; change; punishment/reward; resolution. Campbell said all these can be boiled down to the Monomyth: the essential story at the heart of all stories, mirrored in culture myths the world over: 'A hero ventures forth from the world of common day into a region of supernatural wonder: fabulous forces are there encountered and a decisive victory is won: the hero comes back from this mysterious adventure with the power to bestow boons on his fellow man.'[51]

Holdstock, whose oeuvre has an archetypal quality to it – exploring as it does the creation of story through its many-layered metanarratives – takes up this notion: 'I am attracted to the idea of all stories coming from one first story, that in fact there is a monomythic idea that surfaces in every writer. We all have different belief systems deep down, we just take different routes by which we came to them. We might come to them through a canvas, through music or writing a book. We are touching something very much in common, but expressing it in different ways.'[52] He talks of each personal 'little dream' in relation to the universal 'big dream'. There's an overlap, a shared territory and iconography: 'The shared pattern recognition binds us all.'[53]

That 'shared pattern' is a kind of map, and as such fairy tales are maps of the human soul. American theologian Thomas Moore wrote: 'Storytelling is an excellent way of caring for the soul. It helps us see the themes that circle in our lives, the deep themes that tell the myths we live by.'[54]

One could say that all characters in a story are aspects of the author, fragmented and seeking wholeness. The journey of the story can be seen in Jungian terms as a process of individuation[55], of integration, a kind of mandala of narrative. EM Forster again: 'Stories are nourishing, reassuring, they re-establish a kind of cosmic order.'[56] That is why their simplicity and their happy endings are so satisfying. Chicken soup for the soul indeed: they offer the original 'story medicine', which alludes back to their possible shamanic origins, when the shaman would perform for the tribe, and re-enact for them the magical healing journey of his vision, there and back again.

Yet, for there to be a Mythic Return (echoed by Campbell and Tolkien) there needs to be a sense of exile. Tolkien argues that Man has been removed from the world of Faerie: 'Our fates are sundered, and our paths seldom meet. Even upon the borders of Faerie we encounter them only at some chance crossing of the ways.'[57]

This sense of dislocation is often extrinsic in the plot – a child is sundered from its parents and brought up by step-parents; or orphaned; or denied its inheritance, name or home – but is often present in the tone. Things are not quite what they seem – it is as though the membrane of the dream will be punctured at any moment; as the innocence of childhood inevitably must with the coming of age. Maturity can feel like the ultimate disillusionment – a hormonal breaking of the spell. Tolkien is at pains to point out that the genre is not inherently one for children. The Victorians relegated these tales of the nursery, with their cult of childhood, but they have something to offer to all of us. (Tolkien lists the prime value of fairy stories as: Fantasy; Recovery; Escape; Consolation, which are discussed in more detail later). Fairy tales can offer us an illuminating 'look back over the shoulder' at what we have lost in the rush to 'grow up' – not only as individuals, but as a culture. Precious things have been cast away – priceless soul wisdoms, which can help us in daily life. By understanding how narrative works, we can glean a perspective on our own and perhaps change it. These 'fateful tales' can help us to wake up in our own, seize the sword and defeat the sorcery that has bound us for so long.

Ironically, fairy stories rarely feature fairies – although by the power of enchantment which many of the characters who feature in them are under, the 'People of Peace' make themselves known. With a gentle jab of his pipe Tolkien suggests: 'Most good 'fairy-stories' are about the adventures of men in the Perilous Realm or upon its shadowy marches.' Clearing her throat (or coughing at the pipe-smoke) Marina Warner points out, etymologically, the word 'fairy' is related to fate, and the stories invariably revolve around meeting it or changing it. Therefore, if fairy stories can be reconsidered as 'the Stories of the Fates', then this would account for the absence of fairies, and also for their often fatalistic quality. The characters are trapped by their fate; a fact that A.S. Byatt feistily subverts in her story: 'The Story of the Eldest Princess.'[58] An 'Old Woman' tells the protagonist: 'You had the sense to see that you were caught in a story, and the sense to see that you could change it to another one. And the special wisdom to recognize that you are under a curse – which is also a blessing – which makes the story more interesting to you than the things that make it up.'[59]

The extraordinary company pause in silence to ponder this profundity. A log spits in the grate, a stray spark nearly setting the rug alight until someone stamps it out.

In fairy tales everything is metaphor. The smallest action is charged with significance, because fairy stories are not called so because they feature fairies, but because they are set in the Otherworld of the Faerie, the Perilous Realm, where one must be careful what one eats, drinks, speaks, or how one treats others. It is a kind of karmically-accelerated zone, where characters get their comeuppance very quickly, again shortening the distance between set-up and pay-off, and creating a satisfying sense of justice being done, as wrongs are righted. Bruno Bettelheim ruminates: '...fairytales carry important messages to the conscious, the preconscious and the unconscious mind, on whatever level each is functioning at the time. By dealing with universal human problems, particular those which preoccupy a child's mind, these stories speak to his budding ego and encourage its development, while at the same time relieving preconscious and unconscious pressures.'[60]

Fairy tales are often about exploring boundaries and suffering the consequences for breaking taboos, and in that sense they are instructional rites-of-passage ritual tales. Marina Warner in *From the Beast to the Blonde* says: 'fairy tales exchange knowledge between an older voice of experience and a younger audience ... they draw social outlines around boys and girls, fathers and mothers...'[61]

Yet the morality is only a side-effect. Their main power lies in their enchantment, which will be looked at next. Warner adds: 'Fairy tales often claim the moral ground, but their spell-binding power lies within the enchantresses and giants, the magic, the wonders, the mishaps and the good fortune they relate.'[62] She suggests two essential qualities in them are: 'Pleasure in the fantastic, curiosity about the real'[63].

Fairy tales often involve metamorphosis, most elegantly in Ovid's *Metamorphosis*, a collection of Greek Myths transposed to the Roman pantheon. And they change themselves through time, as each teller gives the plot-embryo their own style or twist. Italo Calvino, Angela Carter, A.S. Byatt, Carol Ann Duffy, Philip Pullman and others have done this superbly in their fiction and drama. Many movies update them, milking them in endless variations, far removed from the raw full-blooded source texts. Rarely, a film such as *The Company of Wolves* (1984) Neil Jordan's eerily lyrical adaptation of Angela Carter's wolf stories, or even Terry Gilliam's *The Brothers Grimm* (2005), captures something of their dark spirit, a million miles from the anodyne animations which most people know them by. While as *The Princess Bride* (Reiner, 1987) was the first mainstream Hollywood movie to really approach fairy tales in a post-modernist way, (screenwriter William Goldman adapted it from his own 1973 novel) it was Pixar's *Shrek* (Adamson; Jensen, 2001) which started the current spate of fairytale reworkings. In the early Twenty First Century there has been a rash of revisionist fairy tale films, including *Red Riding Hood* (Hardwicke 2011); *Mirror, Mirror* (Tarsem, 2011); *Snow White and the Huntsman* (Sanders 2012*); Hansel and Gretel: witch-hunters* (Wirkola, 2012*); Jack the Giant Slayer* (Singer, 2013). They often attempt to subvert the 'victim' mode of the protagonist – stuck in his or her 'fate'. Yet they seem less interested in the psychological truths of such tales, as their availability as copyright-free plot concepts. After years of contemporising myths, legends and fairy tales – Hollywood screenwriters seem to have decided to revisit the sources and give them a new spin. Yet the material contains this permeability without drastic structural shenanigans. For the 'originals', if there can be any such thing with oral stories that exist in numerous versions, have been described as: 'a huge theatre of possibility' by Marina Warner. Like all imaginative fiction, they revel in the 'What if...?' They 'disrupt the apprehensible world in order to open spaces for dreaming alternatives' (Warner again, wanting the last word). By playing with them, and working with them in our own lives, we can 'rewrite our own narratives' and perchance give ourselves a happy ending. In the way the characters in a fairy tale change their lot, so can we, by the power of the imagination.

5

These Things Never Happened But Are Always

'The imaginary is what tends to become real.'
André Breton

To reiterate a key point: One could argue that all fiction is imaginative – in the way it re-creates (versions of) reality and models hypothetical situations – but in Fantasy the imaginary aspect is emphasized.

The critical word here is 'imagining'. This is where the real work of Fantasy takes place – not in simply re-arranging the furniture of genre convention. The quality of Fantasy fiction stands or falls on the amount of imaginative groundwork done beforehand – what is often called 'world-building' – as well as the skill of its execution: imagining not only the ecosystem of the world, its geopolitics, its technologies and belief systems; but also the interior worlds of the main characters, relationship dynamics, and character arcs. If you want your readers to care about your characters, then you have to make them as believable as possible – however exotic they might appear on the surface. Novelist Lindsay Clarke once offered this advice:[64] if you want to describe the fantastical, you have to make it as believable as possible. He warned that it is *harder work* to write imaginative fiction – because the author has to do far more to convince the reader than if it is set in the 'here and now'. You can only rely upon the 'goodwill' of the Fantasy fan for so long. They want to be dazzled and disturbed by fantastic realms and grotesque beasts, but as soon as they sense the shoddy or the bogus, they'll be off like a shot. Do not proffer the equivalent of poor Special FX (as in old-fashioned low budget SF movie), by having substandard world-building; or the equivalent of a mega-budget Hollywood turkey, with dismal dialogue, flaccid characterisation, and 'Frankenstein' plots-by-committee.

Part of the allure of 'magic and adventure' is that they don't (generally) happen in 'real life', but *we want them to*. So in Fantasy, there's a large element of wish-fulfilment, but also a loyalty to that which is not: the improbable, the incredible, the fantastic. Roman poet Sallustius said: 'These things never happened but are always,'[65] and a Latin expression of faith echoes this: *Credo Quia Impossibile* – roughly translated as 'I believe because it is impossible.' The very appeal of Fantasy is in depicting things have not been (completely) mapped, catalogued and controlled. As a genre, it has been studied, critiqued and anthologised ad nauseam, but there are always something overlooked and more being created. Not even the sky is the limit – the glass ceiling has been taken off completely, and if we can convince ourselves it isn't there, our minds and souls can soar unshackled across the universe and through other dimensions.

With such permeable boundaries it is no wonder Fantasy keeps escaping the parameters of its definition. The presence of dragons, elves, magic swords, or princesses is not enough to guarantee its genre. Five criteria which I venture may help to identify such works are:

1. **An archetypal quality** – dream-like, disturbing, with characters of an iconic nature: the Mother, the Father, the Shadow, the Lover, the Fool, the Warrior, the Trickster.
2. **A Romantic quality** – in the sense of the original Romantic movement. A profound connection to the natural world; grand themes; the validity of the personal, subjective 'interior' life against a backdrop of geopolitical turmoil and apocalyptic anxieties; a deep and lyrical questioning.
3. **The sense that anything is possible** – within the laws of the context created (see The Law of the Green Sun, below).

4. **An aesthetic which perhaps favours the historical** – most frequently pseudo-medieval — over the modern or futuristic. This, of course, is being challenged continually in works of daring innovation (e.g. Future Primitive novels, where Science Fiction and Fantasy might blend in unexpected ways).
5. **A magical explanation of the universe** (as opposed to a strictly scientific one) – one that acknowledges the possibility of spirits, deities, and other supernatural forces. This is often conveyed by tonal choices as much as the 'hardware' – the language the world is painted in.

These five principles will no doubt be porous; with countless exceptions that prove the rule – but perhaps they will serve as a starting point: co-ordinates to establish a search-pattern in the vast ocean of possibility.

One of the key principles, is what could be called 'The Law of the Green Sun'. This relates to Clute's attempt at a definition of Fantasy text as a 'self-coherent narrative:'[66] 'When set in this world, it tells a story which is impossible in the world as we perceive it; when set in the otherworld, that otherworld will be impossible, though stories set there *may be possible in its terms*.' (my italics)

This is the critical caveat. Fantasy, as Clute, neatly sums up, is 'a way to tell stories about the fantastic.'[67] The genre provides the container; as though in itself it is a kind of Secondary World, in which the lives of the protagonists – indigenous or otherwise – unfold. What sets Fantasy apart from other 'narrative presentation of the unreal' (Clute) is this notion of 'self-coherence', which implies both internal consistence and narrative consistency, separating it from the works of Surrealism and Post-Modernism meta-narratives. The spell remains unbroken, as a general rule of thumb, and one of the greatest magicians of the art is Tolkien.

Tolkien never thought of himself as a 'Fantasy author'. He liked to describe his stories as Fairy Stories in the truest sense, that is, set in an Otherworld: 'most good fairy tales are about *aventures* of men in the Perilous Realm'. He argues that the successful writer of 'fairy stories' is one who: 'makes a Secondary World which your mind can enter. Inside, what he relates is 'true': it accords with the laws of that world.'[68] It has an internal logic – consistency, causality and ecology of its own (often sharing some laws with our own world, e.g. gravity, night and day, hunger, sleep). This Secondary World may have, for example, a green sun, but that is not enough: 'To make a Secondary World inside which the green sun will be credible, commanding Secondary Belief, will probably require labour and thought, and will certainly demand a special skill, a kind of elvish craft.'[69] We will look at this 'elvish craft' in more detail in the next chapter, but for now, let us emphasize this notion — that the forging of successful Fantasy involves the creation of 'an internally coherent impossible world in which that tale *is* possible.'[70] Each variation from the 'world we know,' however great or small is tracked with infinitesimal attention to detail – the ultimate trainset or doll's house, built with painstaking care.

Tolkien, meanwhile, goes onto argue that Fantasy is a 'natural human activity', and it does not deny or negate a rational mind. Thus, his dictum: 'The keener and clearer the reason, the better Fantasy will it make.'[71] This is a fundamental notion to bear in mind during the writing of Fantasy. Fantasy may be a 'fuzzy set', but the best Fantasy is not written in a fuzzy-headed way. The ideas may emerge mysteriously; the impulse to write it; the subject matter too, may be full of mysterious things – but the logistics of the story-world, the mechanics of characters, and the construction of text should be done with a certain level-headedness if it is to move beyond mere indulgent day-dreaming, a solo role-playing game, the sound of one hand clicking.

A Fantasy story could be seen as a roller-coaster ride – at its best, offering white-knuckle thrills and spills – but you can only expect it to be enjoyed (by others) if it is soundly made, holding together at the points of greatest pressure (the greater the peaks and troughs, the hairier the bends, the stronger the structure needs to be to cope).

In their exploration of several famous Secondary Worlds, *Realms of Fantasy*, Edwards and Holdstock say: 'The writer must not cheat: the laws governing the invented world may be different from our own, but they must be applied consistently.'[72] Essential qualities are Realism and Conviction – the author has to totally believe in their world, and if they do so thoroughly and skilfully enough, they may make the reader forget that it is invented, or at least willingly suspend their disbelief without having to throttle it.

Not all Fantasy is set in a Secondary World, but it is by far the most common trope. It is almost given that it will be, to the point it has become a lazy convention of the genre, a hand-me-down idea, worn out and ill-fitting (rough-hewn barbarians sporting Tolkien's elbow patches).

A Secondary World Fantasy: 'takes place in an invented world, which may or may not have some doorway into our own.'[73] A general survey of different kinds of Secondary Worlds by Edwards and Holdstock include: Stories set in the ancient past; Stories set in present-day lost worlds; Stories set on other planets; Stories set in the distant future; Stories set on Fantasy Earths quite separate from our own but with affinities to it. Notice that many of them tread in Science Fiction territory, but it all depends on the 'explanation' behind the Way Things Work, as well as language, or tone, e.g. there is a world of difference between *The Worm Ouroboros* (1922) by ER Eddison; and *The Dispossessed* (1974) by Ursula K Le Guin (both set on other planets: Mercury and the twin worlds of Tau Ceti).

As in all genres, there is undoubtedly good and bad Fantasy.

The mainstream notion of Fantasy today – Sword and Sorcery – is the degenerate child of what has in fact a fine pedigree. Its roots go back to the origins not only of literature, but of story itself. The world's Creation Myths, and even religious myths, are, on one level, great Fantasy stories. What is cited as the world's first written story, Gilgamesh, is epic Fantasy of the highest calibre. The Homeric epics of gods and heroes, *The Iliad* and *The Odyssey;* plus *The Voyage of the Argo* and *The Aeneid* are also great Fantasy stories. *Beowulf,* although written in tongue-twisting Anglo-Saxon verse, is a classic dragon-slaying saga. *Gawain and the Green Knight* and all the stories of Arthur – rightly called the Matter of Britain – are the bedrock of British fiction. Spenser's *Faerie Queen;* Marlowe's *Dr Faustus;* Shakespeare's *A Midsummer Night's Dream;* and *The Tempest*...all fit the bill, whatever form they are in. Fantasy is the mother-genre which gave birth to the subgenres of Science Fiction and Horror — wondrous prodigies which first saw the light of day in the 18th Century: Mary Shelley's *Frankenstein;* William Beckford's *Vathek;* Walpole's *The Monk; and Melmoth the Wanderer...* Gothic – literature's equivalent of the apocalyptic sublime – spawned many monsters in the minds of such writers of the night as Edgar Allen Poe, Bram Stoker, H.P. Lovecraft, Clark Ashton Smith, and Robert Louis Stevenson with his schizophrenic icons of Victorian hypocrisy, Jekyll and Hyde. In the 'rational' light of day early science fiction writers Jules Verne and HG Wells echoed people's anxieties about progress born from the runaway steam train of the Industrial Revolution. Meanwhile Conan Doyle, H. Rider Haggard, Wilkie Collins, and Kipling were eulogising the embers of an Empire with adventure stories spiced with the fantastic. Simultaneously, William Morris and George Macdonald, were hearkening back to the Medieval, to Norse Myths and to the timeless world of Fairy. Standing in singular fashion, was mathematician Charles Lutwidge Dodgson, aka Lewis Carroll, contributing the world of dreams and psychological subtext to his children's stories. Then there were the Edwardians and the Lost Generation: JM Barrie, Lord Dunsany, Arthur Machen, MR James, Algernon Blackwood, Hope Mirrlees, Walter De La Mare, Charles Causley, ER Eddison, David Lindsay… All this before the Fantasy writers we think of today, the greats of the Twentieth Century, vanguarded first and foremost by the Inklings of Oxford (Tolkien, Lewis, Charles Williams). Outside of this canon are important 'black swans', including Russian fantasist Mikhail Bulgakov (*The Master and Margarita, 1967*); Alfred Jarry (*Ubu Roi, 1896*); Jonathan Swift (*Gulliver's Travels, 1726*); Samuel Butler (*Erewhon, 1872*); Edwin Abbot Abbot (*Flatland*, 1884); and Antoine de St-Exupéry (*The Little Prince*).

There is an element of it in all *fiction* (as the very word suggests). However, there is a kind of swing-o-meter ranging from realism to extreme Fantasy which varies with each book. In contemporary literature the blurring of fact and fiction is even more prevalent with such chimeras as autobiographical fiction, where people share their most personal and prosaic details in a novelistic confessional – often obfuscating the plain truth with unreliable narrators; and fictional biographies, of which Peter Ackroyd has carved himself something of a niche with works such as *Hawksmoor* (1985), *Chatterton* (1987), *Blake* (1995) and *Dickens* (1990) – in the latter, the author famously has a conversation with the great Victorian writer.

From the heady heights of Creation Myths, it seems Fantasy (and thus fiction) has come to Earth with a jarring bump, where it struggles to take off again – weighed down with heavy reality. Yet Fantasy can still take wing – it seems to exist in a literary universe independent of the prevailing literary fad. As Michael Moorcock says in his introduction to *Wizardry and Wild Romance*, 'fashion is our enemy'. Plenty of wannabes and cynical commercialists attempt to jump on the gravy train which occasionally hoots by – most loudly the Harry Potter express, which has become the most successful book phenomenon, let alone Fantasy book series, ever (derivative, perhaps, but fizzing with enough imaginative wit, colourful characters and verbal inventiveness to transcend its influences) – but as soon as a band wagon is there to be jumped on, you can guarantee the box car is already chock-a-block of literary hoboes.

The latest of these fictional freight cars is Steampunk – which on the page already feels like a tired formula (a hackneyed carriage), even as it mutates in interesting ways on the stage, in digital media, and in other art-forms (notably music and comic-books). It is the *methodology* of Steampunk which lends itself to innovation – a kind of anarchic scavenging resulting in fabulous hybrids – rather than a shopping list of predictable ingredients (e.g. airships, Imperialism, Victorian bombast).

In good fiction, one cannot second guess the market place and write with an eye on the cash-till – because such shallow endeavours shine through in every word. With no guarantee of publication, all a writer can do is write from the heart and enjoy the journey. If we cannot follow our dreams in Fantasy, where can we follow them?

Ursula K Le Guin, in *From Elfland to Poughkeepsie* (1973), writes: 'Its affinity is not with daydream, but with dream. It is a different approach to reality, an alternative technique for apprehending and coping with existence... It employs archetypes, which, as Jung warned us, are dangerous things... Fantasy is nearer to poetry, to mysticism, and to insanity than naturalistic fiction is. It is a real wilderness, and those who go there should not feel too safe. And their guides, the writers of Fantasy, should take their responsibility seriously.'

This notion of ethics is a tricky one, and is rarely tackled in discussions on Fantasy, even though it is a potential mine-field (as the questionable Secondary World of *Gor* and its cult-following illustrates) but is tackled head-on in *An Ecobardic Manifesto,* by Fire Springs (Awen 2008), a group of Bath-and-

Stroud based storytellers (of whom the author is a founding member) who proposed the following principles for work of an 'ecobardic' nature, in any art-form:

- connecting with our own roots in time and place while celebrating the diversity of other cultures and traditions.
- daring to discern, discriminate, and critique in order to provide cultural leadership.
- respecting and dynamically engaging with one's audience as a creative partner.
- cultivating the appreciation of beauty and excellence through well-wrought craft
- re-enchanting nature and existence as filled with significance.

(*An Ecobardic Manifesto*, Fire Springs, 2008)

What we choose to 'bring through' is of deepest importance. Not that we should focus on the anodyne – spare the insipid New Ageisms, please – by any means. The best works tackle the darkest subjects, but with a sharp intelligence and compassion for all protagonists and antagonists. Fantasy is a safe forum for our collective Shadow to dance in – be it in the amorphous form of Sauron, or something more tangible: villains closer to home.

Fantasy allows our deepest desires to emerge into the healthy light of day, breathe the fresh air rather than fester in the dungeon of the Id – they provide a safety valve. We play and we forget our woes for a while – but also acknowledge different aspects of our personality repressed by daily pressures, e.g. the Fool, King, Hero, Warrior, Lover. As Bowie said: 'we can be heroes, just for one day'.

Unfortunately a lot of Fantasy fiction has been dumbed down by hack writings fuelling teenagers' power fantasies (or their own) – resulting in (during the 70s and 80s) muscle-bound Neanderthal-browed heroes with scantily clad women with oversized breasts draped against them: Conan and his fellow Alpha males, purported by Robert Howard, who at least created the prototype. Michael Moorcock did much to give such knuckle-headed stereotypes an overhaul with his psychedelic Sword and Sorcery, especially in his notion of the Eternal Champion and the Multiverse. Moorcock, in *Wizardry and Wild Romance* is highly critical of Tolkien's reactionary paradigm, calling it 'Epic Pooh', as one would expect of a Sixties' Counter Culture rebel. By the Nineties the genre was in need of another much-needed shake-down, and the eclectic genius of Terry Pratchett was fit for purpose, but his imitators have satirised these clichés into meaningless oblivion.

Some have carried on regardless with unapologetic 'old school' Fantasy, e.g. the late David Gemmings and Robert Jordan. George RR Martin has brought a screenwriter's genius for structure and sparkling dialogue; combined with a modern cynicism and anti-Romanticism to the genre – resulting a hugely successful, but chilling bloodbath (*A Song of Ice and Fire*). Many other authors continue to peddle fan-pleasing formulaic schlock (e.g. the 'man in the hooded cloak'; or the 'spunky girl who discovers hidden powers, rises to greatness, and gets her man' slew of novels). Yet it feels as though they are running on empty.

These Secondary Worlds, recycling their own clichés, risk being closed systems, and in the Second Law of Thermo-dynamics, such results in entropy.

Only by widening the genre pool can you innovate – by cross-fertilisation with unusual and original elements – otherwise it is the law of diminishing returns, resulting in substandard 'Nth generation' Fantasy novels, pastiches of pastiches, written by authors raised on a junkfood diet of fan-fodder fiction, TV and movies, rather than works of literary classics.

Yet there *is* good new work being produced by up-and-coming authors – some still under the radar (yet even the lack of a publisher is no longer the obstacle it once was).

The quality which sets true Fantasy apart from the 'fairy gold' which passes itself off as such, is what Tolkien would call *Enchantment*, and it is this we shall turn to next.

6

A Kind of Elvish Craft

'To the elvish craft, Enchantment, Fantasy aspires, and when it is successful of all forms of human art most nearly approaches.'
Tolkien[74]

Some novels have it (*Lud-in-the-Mist; The Stone and the Flute; Mists of Avalon; Little, Big; The Wood Wife; Riddley Walker; Lavondyss; His Dark Materials,* and *The Master and Margarita,* to name some) but many plainly do not. What is it that sets some Fantasy novels apart?

On one level it boils down to the quality of the writing and originality of ideas, not by a mindless rehashing of sword and sorcery clichés – which Diana Wynne Jones mercilessly lists in her *Tough Guide to Fantasy Land* (2004). To list a random selection:

- Towers (brooding; dark)
- Virgins (in demand for various reasons)
- Inn Signs (always crudely painted; purveyors of foaming ale by buxom wenches)
- Mindspeech
- Reek of Wrongness
- Gnomic Utterances
- Apostrophes
- Anglo-Saxon Cossacks
- PanCeltic Tours

And so Wynne-Jones' hilarious (and painfully true) list goes on. All such 'bogs of doom' are to be avoided (or innovated) by the original Fantasy writer – triangulating across the moors of the imagination between originality, authenticity and craft.

Yet I would argue that good Fantasy goes beyond merely steering clear of cliché and 'doing something new'. It is do with a more elusive quality: enchantment. The dictionary definition of this describes it as Enchant (v) 1. Delight, charm; 2. Put under a spell. 'Enchantment' is a noun deriving from this, and stems from Middle English, from the French *enchanter,* and from the Latin *incantare,* 'sing'. A related ballet phrase seems to sum it up even better: 'enchainement' (n) a linked sequence of steps or movements constituting a phrase. It might be useful to see our writing in this way – a graceful sequence of ballet steps creating a spell-binding effect. Too often it feels like the writer has worn steel-toe caps, and clomped through the fairy garden – so intent on getting from A to Z that they haven't spent time crafting their sentences, delighting in the sheer magic of words.

And, at the heart of the enchanting power of Fantasy is the magic of language.

Writers create this enchantment through deft skill in the use of words, akin to that of the poet. There is an old English word for this word-magic, *gramarye* – the pointy-hatted ancestor of tweedy grammar. Kipling memorably uses this in his titular poem from *Puck of Pook's Hill,* which, in a kind of literary *enchainement,* is quoted as an epigraph at the beginning of T.H. White's *The Once and Future King* :

> She is not of any common Earth
> Wood, water or air,
> But Merlin's Isle of Gramarye
> Where you and I shall fare.

Through our imagination we can all enter this Isle of Gramarye, and with our words, as writers of Fantasy, we can create it anew. By doing so, there is the possibility that we can reinvigorate our own world. When Fantasy is at its best a transfusion can occur – in the reader, in their community, even in their world.

For there to be enchantment, there has to be its opposite. In *Words of Re-enchantment: writings on storytelling, myth, and ecological desire* (2011) storyteller scholar Anthony Nanson posits the notion that the arts – at their best – can redeem a disenchanted world. He cites Max Weber's term for the condition of 'Entzauberung' (disenchantment), in 'which our sense of the significance and agency of ourselves and what's around us is diminished.'[75] Enchantment has the opposite effect – it can 'enlarge' the world, that is amplify its significance, creating a sense of numinosity. Nanson argues that art can re-enchant the world: 'For many people today who stand outside any spiritual tradition, the arts are the main connection to spiritual territory. They have incantatory, visionary and ritual power to re-enchant the world, its creatures, and our lives with significance beyond the material utility that science and economics acknowledge. Such enchantment has intrinsic value; it helps us live with joy in the face of a deepening crisis ... But it also shifts our perceptions in ways that may influence our values and choices.'[76]

I suspect that this is way Fantasy films have such massive appeal – why hordes flock to the multiplexes to the see the latest blockbuster – because there is a sense in which cinemas are the cathedrals of the modern age, where we can still receive an intimation of the sublime. Their vast screens, glowing with colour and light, are the modern equivalent of stained glass windows – the popcorn pilgrims step into the Chartres of the Cineplex, depicting scenes of wonder and awe. There is a sense of ritual in the experience of a cinema visit – the pilgrimage to the cinema; the queues; the communion substances of popcorn and cola; the procession along the corridor into the darkened 'magic space'; the hushed reverence as the film begins; the visceral reactions; the shared catharsis. It is a rite-of-passage that could be a descendant of those enacted in the painted caves of Lascaux. There, the flickering light of fires seemed to bring alive the scenes depicted on the cave wall – daubed in ochre, charcoal and lime. In the cinema, it is the projector's beam and the screen which serves the same purpose – and to the Platonic 'shadows on the cave wall' we still are enamoured, choosing to leave reality at the door.

Tolkien responded lyrically to a critic who called fairy-story making 'Breathing a lie through Silver'.[77] The creator of Middle Earth took this rather beautiful phrase as a compliment and wove it into his response, his *modus operandi* poem, 'Mythopoeia', in which he elucidated upon what he calls Sub-Creation, the creative act of Fantasy, with a rather cinematic allegory (to my eyes):

> 'Man, Sub-creator, the refracted Light
> through whom is splintered from a single White
> to many hues, and endlessly combined
> in living shapes that move from mind to mind...
> Though all the crannies of the world we filled
> With Elves and Goblins, though we dared to build
> Gods and their houses out of dark and light,
> and sowed the seed of dragons – 'twas our right
> (used or misused). That right has not decayed:
> we make still be the law in which we're made.'

Thus Tolkien suggests through the creative act of Fantasy we participate in Creation – we become a conscious part of the Universe dreaming itself into being.

It seems that there could be no better evocation of enchantment. It is a substance which cannot be added like a dollop of mayonnaise or a dash of tabasco – it needs to be carefully blended into the very substance of the prose and the story.

If we accept that enchantment is the 'Ingredient X' of good Fantasy, how can it be achieved? Beyond that already discussed, a speculative list might be the following – a **Spell for Literary**

Enchantment, if you will – although it is by no means definitive or exhaustive:

- **Well-chosen names:** the names of the characters, settings and concepts in a Fantasy novel can make or break it. Too often has a potentially workable story been ruined by grating, incongruous, or just plain ridiculous appellations. The names of a Fantasy narrative are a kind of linguistic ecosystem which should all inter-relate and have their place. Names associated with the 'word-cloud' of a particular culture (say one based upon Medieval Japan) should have an affinity and congruence. Apostrophes should be avoided at all cost. Tolkien emphasised the importance of names ('To me a name comes first and the story follows'[78]).
- **Consistency:** A Secondary World should have an internal consistency: geographical, political, cultural, technological, supernatural, ecological, and so on. Fantasy worlds have been ruined by the sudden appearance of an incongruous element, e.g. Santa Claus in Narnia.
- **Euphony:** the quality of being pleasing to the ear in this context relates to not only the aurality and orality of the story (although that is often an important part of a good tale – one passed down from generation to generation); and the musicality of the words (avoiding the discordant notes of inconsistent elements and slippages of tone); but also the overall 'harmony' of the various elements together: an aesthetic synchrony of mythology, themes, motifs, and soundscape.
- **Quality of production:** a well-made book can be a thing of beauty, with an almost talismanic quality – the cover design, binding, font, typesetting, artwork, paper, prelims and end-matter all help to make the act of reading a pleasurable experience ... one which it is hard to conceive

e-readers such as Kindle and Kobo ever replacing. Let us be frank – there is not much enchantment in holding an e-reader; while as well-loved books last a lifetime and are passed down through the family. Conversely, a poorly-made book can break the spell before even the first line is read. Such poor magic does not engender trust in the writer-reader contract. Unfortunately, we do judge books by their covers. It is a crowded marketplace – and many things compete for our consumer choices. Why should we choose shoddy goods?

- **Titles, epigraphs and other furniture:** These elements all enhance the readers' experience, and can increase or scupper the enchantment factor. The right title can act as a tuning fork, making the whole story resonate. Chapter titles can do the same. Other 'furniture', like section-breaks, footnotes, appendices, and illustrations can also help a story weave its spell – or break it completely if handled clumsily.
- **Storytelling:** Beyond all these 'whistles and bells', if a story is not well-written then no amount of packaging will make the difference. A lot of the success of a story comes down to 'how it is told', which includes choices about voice, point of view, suspense and pace – all adding to the narrative traction, which pulls the reader through the story and gives it that page-turning quality.

When all or a varying combination of these elements fall into place, something magical can happen. We all know it when it does, although we might not be able to identify what exactly happens or why. We are caught in the spell, like a character in a fairy tale. Enchantment, or Glamour, is a defining quality of Faerie, of the Otherworld. Tolkien says: 'Enchantment produces a Secondary World, into which both designer and spectator can enter to the satisfaction of their senses while they are inside.'[79]

This idea is brilliantly illustrated in Tolkien's short story 'Leaf by Niggle', where the frustrated artist, Niggle, eventually ends up in a world rendered originally in his imagination – but incomplete in reality. All he could manifest in life, through his limited skill, was one leaf, painted convincing and vivid, but that provide enough of a key to allow him to enter, after he had been judged and allowed to pass on into his personal paradise (although Tolkien and AE[80] suggest this land is already there, and its denizens are autonomous, we but catch glimpses of it). This enticing idea is beautifully brought to life in a visual way in Vincent Ward's film *What Dreams May Come* (1998), a posthumous Fantasy in which Robin William's recently deceased character literally walks into one of his wife's paintings. The important thing here, illustrated by the leaf example and the line 'to the satisfaction of one's senses', is that the writer/painter/imaginer has to make his or her Secondary World as vivid and believable as possible – firstly, by imagining it as clearly as they can, then evoking the senses so the reader can as well. This links to the other fundamental criteria for Secondary Worlds – they must have an inner consistency, an internal logic, often with overlaps with the world we know, i.e. the sun rises, gravity holds us down, folk get hungry, need to sleep, they get ill, grow old, etc. Such fundamental laws (e.g. the laws of physics, biology, and psychology) hold the fabric of its reality together. If any of these 'givens' are altered or subverted then the writer needs to track the consequences thoroughly and be consistent in the changes wrought (i.e. a world with no daylight). Many stories are based around just one or two of this Universals changing, i.e. a land where no one gets old – just imagining the consequences of that is enough for one book. It is best not to mix motifs, but to choose one (or one *novum*[81]) and pursue it relentlessly.

Tolkien added this important caveat to his Secondary World hypothesis, that enchantment produces this effect: 'in its purity it is artistic in desire and purpose'. Tolkien decreed that enchantment: 'Uncorrupted, it does not seek delusion, nor bewitchment and domination; it seeks shared enrichment, partners in making and delight, not slaves.'[82]

Visionary artist and poet William Blake would agree with this. He detested the 'mind forg'd manacles of man'. The visionary poet and artist could be called one of Britain's greatest Fantasists, but to Blake, his personal pantheon and cosmology was real. It sustained through a lifetime of struggle and neglect, as evoked in his poem 'Another Sun', contained in a letter to a Thomas Butts[83]:

My hands are labour'd day & night,
And Ease comes never in my sight.
My Wife has no indulgence given
Except what comes to her from heaven.
We eat little, we drink less;
This Earth breeds not our happiness.
Another Sun feeds our life's streams.
We are not warmed with thy beams;
Thou measurest not the Time to me,
Nor yet the Space that I do not see;
My mind is not with thy light array'd.
Thy terrors shall not make me afraid.

This moving poem illustrates the critical notion that such 'other-worlds' sustain the writer as well as the reader. They can provide a lifetime's sustenance and consolation. They can seem like the chinks in the bars of reality – through which a sweeter air, a brighter light, can sometimes by savoured.

For Blake, imagination (as personified by his Promethean figure of Los) facilitated spiritual emancipation. Through his Art Blake *was* free – he soared beyond the confines of his age.

A story does not hand you the book of truth – it lets you come to it yourself, and thus is far more powerful and empowering. The stories which resonate with us most tell us what we already know, deep down, but may have forgotten. It provides not a mirror of the world's ugliness and brutality, but a doorway. Great Fantasy does seek to bind us with its spells, it allows our imaginations to roam unhindered across new lands, new worlds.

Perhaps the acid test with Fantasy is: with great Fantasy the enchantment *lingers,* it stays with you for days, weeks, months, years – through the visceral experience of reading it, the adrenalin rush of the plot-twist, the catharsis of emotions, it has become an embodied experience – whereas in the fairy-gold which so often passes for it the story is all but forgotten as soon as you walk out of the cinema or put the book down. It doesn't inhabit you in the same way, nor does it take on an inner life which continues independent of its source: an ongoing internal narrative. When one comes across such works they grip you and don't let go – because here in your hands, or before your eyes, is something which illustrates the colour of your soul.

A good novel provides continuity and reassurance (and also challenge and transformation) through the vicissitudes of life, a baseline that helps us keep our centre, a private Dreamtime which we can walk side-by-side with our everyday lives.

7

Consoling Fictions

'universal, ageless, therapeutic, miraculous, and beautiful'
Jack Zipes, citing the merits of fairy tales[84]

Fantasy, as with all genre-based comfort reading, has a large element of the 'consoling fiction' about it. Before we look at the concept of 'Consolation' in more detail it is worth looking at this notion in a wider sense.

We all have consoling fictions – myths that we tell ourselves – that 'one day my prince will come'; that 'justice will prevail'; that 'I will get the job I deserve'; that 'with the right car/haircut/shoes/mobile phone/trainers I will get the respect I am due'; that 'I am loved unconditionally by my partner'; that 'somehow things will work out'; and that 'everything's going to be all right'; or 'the planet is going to pot anyway, so what difference does it make if I continue my unsustainable lifestyle?'. These are the little myths we live by, the white lies we tell ourselves – all part of a necessary coping strategy which, if ripped away, can sometimes lead to anger, depression or worse.

Freud was disparaging of these, stating that we should 'learn to live without consoling fictions, for in the death of such numbing and dangerous fantasies is our only hope.'[85] Yet for many such 'dangerous fantasies' offer a powerful, and often harmless (unless you are a neurotic psychoanalyst obsessed with sex) allure.

The larger myths are far more insidious – the grand narratives which we either buy into or are forced to live under anyway, the Big Stories of spiritual or authoritarian hierarchy, the worst manifestations of the major religions; Capitalism; Globalisation; Jihad; and the so-called 'Infinite Justice' of a War on Terror. The important difference is in the term 'myth' – its use and abuse – often used to denote something that is false, i.e. urban myths (the modern replacement of the mysognistic notion of 'old wives' tales'). The fictions that spin doctors tout are lies of the Machiavellian variety – these, and the reprehensible and tawdry 'gossip' touted by the tabloid press and popular media should be quarantined from the mythic corpus. While as the myths inherited from our ancestors, if they are not to be taken literally, are 'lies that tell a greater truth' (echoing Tolkien's 'lies breathed through silver'). This is a crucial distinction. One serves a higher truth; the other serves only itself.

Karen Armstrong, in her lucid overview of the subject, *A Short History of Myth* (2006), suggests the context is all important: 'A myth is not a story that can be recited in a profane or trivial setting. Because it imparts sacred knowledge, it is always recounted in a ritualised setting that sets it apart from ordinary profane experience, and can only be understood in the solemn context of spiritual and psychological transformation.'[86] She argues about the perceived falsity of these myths: 'We must disabuse ourselves of the nineteenth century fallacy that myth is false or that it represents an inferior mode of thought... We can acquire a more educated attitude to mythology.' This is what I would call Mythic Literacy (see **The Dragon's Hoard – Other Essays**).

Myths, religious or cultural can be mis-used, as Hitler's Third Reich exemplified, exploiting the core values that national myths embody and corrupting them. Yet *myth* is not just something inflicted on us. We all need myths to live by. Karen Armstrong suggests we are all 'myth-making creatures' but: 'during the twentieth century, we saw some very destructive modern myths, which have ended in massacre and genocide.'[87] Armstrong suggests these myths have failed because: 'They have not been infused with the spirit of compassion, respect for the sacredness of all life...' She says we need myths that 'help us to identify with all our fellow-beings, not simply with those who belong to our ethnic, national or ideological tribe'; that 'help us to create a spiritual attitude'; to 'see beyond our immediate requirements'; 'experience transcendent value that challenges our solipsistic selfishness'; myths that 'help us to venerate the earth as sacred once again' – all worthy 'consoling fictions'[88], all worth aspiring to, in fact essential, I humbly suggest, for humanity to survive with the planet intact.

Stories are powerful things, indeed they can be powerful enough to change the world – or at least the way we see the world, treat it and each other – but in themselves, like religions and myths, they are neither good nor evil. They are a tool, and in the right hands – a bardic-surgeon's, rather than say a story-soldier's – they can be incredibly healing and empowering. They have been used for consolation and guidance for centuries in cultures across the world. Cut open a story and you see the heart of a people, their folk-soul. Stories are the oldest human-made medicine, the simplest but most powerful of magic, as the Sufi poet Rumi suggests: 'Stories are like the water that you heat for a bath. It takes messages between the fire and the water, it lets them meet, and it cleans you.'[89]

In a world of seemingly endless bad news it is no wonder that consoling fictions (in whatever form they come) are as popular as ever – mainly in the easy-to-consume format of the movie, which with advances in technology can be downloaded onto a home computer, or watched on a tablet while on a journey – it is fast food for the imagination, the new opium of the masses, the poppy crop of pop culture.

Why this 'hunger'? Most people wouldn't be aware of any conscious reason, except perhaps some trivial trigger (e.g. a favourite movie star). More often than not it is the subconscious effect of the saturation advertising which creates a perceived need – we are sold on the false promise of a 'lost island', a golden ticket to Wonkaland, where somehow all our woes will be forgotten, all our desires met. Yet at the heart of this there is something profound and beautiful – though we often only duped into buying the superficial glamour rather than the real McCoy – and this is what Tolkien wittily demarcates: '...fairy-stories offer...in a peculiar degree or mode, these things: Fantasy, Recovery, Escape, Consolation, all things of which children have, as a rule, less need than older people.'[90]

It will be useful for our purposes to have a brief explanation of each one of these qualities:

i. Fantasy

For Tolkien, imagination was not an end unto itself. For him, this sub-creative act was called Fantasy: 'In ... Fantasy new form is made; Faerie begins; Man becomes a sub-creator.'[91] If we accept this notion, then Fantasy, in its most sublime form, is the process whereby we can engage as readers and writers with the wider Act of Creation – to play in the orchestra in the symphony of the Universe, to use a Tolkienean metaphor. Yet it is not the Music of the Spheres we play, but our own – which is often a dim echo of the original, but no less meaningful for that. Often the clarity of the vision is muted or sharpened by the sub-creator's level of skill, by their art: 'Art, the operative link between Imagination and the final result, Subcreation.'[92] Subcreation is Promethean-like in its potential. Through it the bold artist can dare 'storming Heaven'. The creative rules of the universe can be tapped into and engaged. Promethean 'foresight' can be gleaned by reaching into these Platonic realms and being the first to seize their fire. 'That the images are of things not in the primary world (if that indeed is possible) is a virtue not a vice. Fantasy (in this sense) is, I think, not a lower but a higher form of Art, indeed the most nearly pure form, and so (when achieved) the most potent.'[93]

This can be intoxicating and even dangerous. Such dabbling is not to be done lightly. On a more mundane level, this 'Sub-creation' is something all can partake in – by being the viewer of a painting or sculpture, the reader of a book, the listener of storytelling or music: art is a co-creative act between artist, audience and artefact. We bring the words, sounds, symbols, and themes, alive in our hearts and minds. We clothe them with the fabric of our life experience – and imbue them with our own personal relevance. A book is just ink and paper until it is brought alive by the imagination of the reader.

ii. Recovery

JRR Tolkien describes recovery '(which includes return and renewal of health) [as] a regaining – regaining of a clear view.'[94] This relates right back to the shamanic roots of storytelling – the shaman enacts a magical healing journey, and the soul is sung back home. The shaman externalizes the patient's 'sickness', gives it voice, and banishes it. Their ritualistic song and dance routine, costume and mask, smoke and mirrors, help to reveal the truth. The reader or listener is not glamoured by the 'illusion' of the tale, but empowered to see to the heart of the matter, the quintessence of things. A story can give us a perspective on our own. We can see our place within our own narrative – and glimpse a way through the woods. The monsters, the adversities – physical, emotional, spiritual – will be overcome and you will win through in the end. And so stories grant us the powers of Epimetheus, of 'hindsight'.

iii. Escape

Here Tolkien means escape from death, disease, the ugliness of the modern world and the brutality of Man. By it another 'more real' reality is implied to escape to (what DH Lawrence called 'the real reality'). Consensus Reality is the cage from which all awakened souls seek to transcend. And so it follows: 'in what the misuses of Escape are fond of calling Real Life, Escape is evidently as a rule very practical, and may even be heroic.' Mythic reality is actual *more substantial*, the opposite of what some might expect. For many the Divine Sphere is 'truer' than this world. This notion echoes the Platonic notion that reality as we perceive it is merely shadows on the walls of a cave, rather than what lies beyond in the light, Tolkien argues: 'Why should a man be scorned if, finding himself in prison, he tries to get out and go home? Or if, when he cannot do so, he thinks and talks about other topics than jailers and prison-walls. The world outside has not become less real because the prisoner cannot see it.' The Buddhists believe we are veiled by Maya or Samsara, and should heighten one's consciousness to see beyond the illusion and by coming to terms with one's karma escape from the Wheel of Life. Escape then, is perhaps something to aspire to – it is a turning to the Source, to a truer Reality, rather than a denying of what we think of as 'the real world'. As Mike Scott of The Waterboys sang in 'Let it Happen':

> He said "This is the real world, Buddy
> Toughen up your ass or it'll break"
> I said "I'm not your buddy, Buddy
> and your real world is a fake"[95]

However, like the Steve McQueen character in *The Great Escape* (Sturges, 1963), it is perhaps not actually escaping that counts, but the manner in which we attempt it – and in that struggle we are most fully alive and heroic.

iv. Consolation

And finally, there is consolation. In relation to fairy-stories, Tolkien saw this as 'the Consolation of the Happy Ending'. He describes this feeling as 'the sudden joyous turn', a notion he termed 'eucatastrophe', in essence, a tragedy with a happy ending (a quality increasingly prevalent in post 9/11, especially North American, narratives). The dark, bittersweet quality of life needs to be acknowledged, the shadow of life given full airing, but then redeemed. Tolkien says: 'The peculiar quality of the 'joy' in successful Fantasy can thus be explained as a sudden glimpse of the underlying reality or truth.'[96] Notice the idea of 'seeing things as they really are', as Blake and then Huxley suggested,[97] rather than a conscious self-deception. In fact, the opposite seems to be true, that is in this cleansed perception the deeper truth is revealed: 'In such stories, when the sudden 'turn' comes we get a piercing glimpse of joy, and heart's desire, that for a moment passes outside the frame, rends indeed the very web of story, and lets a gleam through.'[98] The Arthurian fool-knight Parsifal, or Perceval, who lived in innocent isolation away from the wiles of the court, the stratagems and self-aggrandisement, 'pierces the veil' as his name-destiny prophesises, and achieves the Grail, when more sophisticated worldly knights failed. The Romantic visionary poet Coleridge believed in joy as 'shaping spirit of the imagination': 'For him that creating synthesising imagination is called 'joy' – he saw it as emanating from the 'pure' in mankind; those who can sustain the imaginative transaction with nature long enough to cross the boundary between the creative mind and the phenomenal universe.'[99] This imaginative transaction Bruno Bettelheim calls 'spinning out daydreams' in *The Uses of Enchantment*. He believes in the benefit of: 'ruminating, rearranging, and fantasizing about suitable story elements in response to unconscious pressures. By doing this, the child fits unconscious content into conscious fantasies, which then enable him to deal with that content.'[100] Bettelheim says the very form and structure of fairy tales provides the child with imagistic and imaginative tools with which he can 'structure his daydreams and give better direction to his life.'[101]

A story offers the child alternative narratives, other lives, and solutions to the myriad problems of life. Difficult situations are overcome, wrongs are righted, good overcomes evil, unfairness is dealt with by justice, and the characters are recognised for their true worth. Bettelheim argues that: 'Without such encouraging conclusions, the child, after listening to the story, would feel that there is no hope of extricating himself from the despairs of life.'[102] Narrative, at its best, can offer a potentially transformative energy. WB Yeats, in his preface to Lady Gregory's *Gods and Fighting Men* (1904) epitomizes this: '...the expression of the individual soul turning itself into a pure fire and imposing its own pattern, its own music, upon the heaviness and the dumbness and in itself.'

Bettelheim suggests the key things achieved by fairy tales are: Union and Moral Unity. Union in the sense that the fragmented Self is made whole; the dysfunctional 'family' is made functional again; the male and female are united in a kind of Chymical Wedding, and consequently: 'separation anxiety (is) assuaged' – what he and many psychologists believe to be a key terror, hardwired into us from infancy. Fairy stories offer the reassuring message: 'know that you are never deserted'. Since the dream-like terrors dramatized in fairy tales seem to be fuelled by, among other things, what therapists loosely term 'abandonment issues', this is a reassuring Pay Off. Fairy Stories both wake up our night-terrors, and put them to bed. As invocation and exorcism, imaginative narrative can 'draw the poison of the wound' to the surface and release it – by giving it voice, giving it shape. It is only if these inchoate forces are not acknowledged, that the trouble begins.

The journey of the story can be seen, in Jungian terms, as a process of individuation – of integration, a kind of mandala of narrative. The fragmented self undertakes a journey to wholeness. Bettelheim says: 'Consolation requires that the right order of the world has been restored.'[103] That is why their simplicity and their happy endings are so satisfying. They offer the original 'story medicine'.

The Consolations of Fantasy

Here is a list of possible 'consolations' of the genre.

- a sense of tribe, as often manifest in 'fandom', e.g. fans of *Game of Thrones*, who meet up in costume. Some go further, into re-enactment, which can convey reassuring values of honour, romance, chivalry, an old-fashioned social order (alleviating so-called 'status anxiety') and a place within it, a role to play.
- a coherent grand narrative, with structure and meaning. This shared mythos becomes a common frame of reference between fans.
- the use of slang, jargon, 'insider' knowledge, fashion, trivia, which asserts the group identity as distinct from the 'uninitiated'.
- an ironic response to the modern world – this might not apply to all examples of the genre, but it is certainly the case for Terry Pratchett's *Discworld*, and also for Steampunk, which offers a reassuringly low-tech alternative future with mechanistic gizmos (a joyously quaint analogue aesthetic in a digital world).
- an immersive, extensive universe (e.g. Star Wars; Star Trek; Dr Who; Pottermore; Marvel).
- a sense of magic and wonder.
- a way of imbibing some of the nutrients of myth and legend.
- articulates something of our inner world. Fantasy often has the quality of dream or nightmare, populated by the disturbing imagery of the subconscious.
- thus, it could be said Fantasy offers us a glimmer of 'soulfulness'.

Thomas Moore suggests that the power of art can stir the soul: 'The arts also have the power to waken a dormant soul, and there can be no doubt that chief malady of our time is "sleeping soul sickness." Ficino put it poetically, saying that Mercury, the foremost patron of the arts, can either waken souls or put them to sleep. When you sit and listen to music or watch a play or follow a dance, your active life goes into eclipse and your soul life takes wing.'[104]

At its best, great Fantasy can help us awaken to our true potential, to remember what was lost or long dormant, a forgotten glory, an ancient and eternal soul-life that breaks free the shackles of the mundane, apparent reality. Like Neo in *The Matrix*; or Paul Atreides in *Dune*, 'the sleeper has awakened.' and we ride forth like King Arthur from the cave into the light.

A nice story ... and perhaps one with a grain of truth – like the wheat-germ found in the Pharaoh's tomb, still able to grow and create bread after millennia.

Without consoling fictions, in whatever form they come, we risk despair, existential angst, even madness. Whatever one thinks of them, they give us something extremely valuable – they give us hope.

8

The Birds in the Mind

> *'Fantasy is a necessary ingredient in living, It's a way of looking at life through the wrong end of a telescope.'*
> Dr Seuss

In his haunting Fantasy classic *Lavondyss (1990)*, the late Robert Holdstock terms the Otherworld, 'Bird Spirit Land'. Conjured out of an instinctual magical act by the young female protagonist, Tallis, it is a deep metaphor for the mysterious nature of the creative process itself. On writing *Lavondyss*, Holdstock said: 'out of allowing these birds to fly through my mind, and create images and links with the characters, I felt that I was touching something quite primitive. I enjoyed that sensation.'[105] Nevertheless, Holdstock struggled with 'that sensation' at times, experiencing a breakdown during the period of its creation. Whether the process of writing *Lavondyss* actually helped or exacerbated his condition, his sudden death from an E coli infection in 2009 prevents a full answer. However, the history of literature attests that he was not alone in experiencing a convergence of creativity and mental illness. The two seem to go hand-in-hand. The cliché is that 'genius' and 'madness' are common bedfellows – whether that is true or not, between these extremes there is a spectrum of more subtle shades experienced by the majority: whether it be a migraine before a breakthrough; mild depression after finishing a project; insomnia during its creation; mood swings, or anxiety attacks before its premiere.

One could argue that the very act of writing – spending years of one's life and vast amounts of efforts for little or no guarantee of success – is crazy in itself. To embark upon writing a novel is a huge act of faith (unless you have a good advance).

So, why do we do it?

What drives writers to write Fantasy? For many it is an undeniable creative urge. One is forced to scratch that creative itch: to do otherwise is to risk irritability, frustration, and depression. It is what WB Yeats' memorably termed the 'fire in the head':

> I went for a walk in a hazel wood
> because a fire was in my head,
> I cut and peel a hazel wand
> and hooked a berry to a thread.

This feeling, the fire in the head, is familiar to all creative types. It is when one is inspired – literally 'in-spirited', filled with spirit; or filled with enthusiasm (*en theos* – the god within). All artists know what this feels like, and also what the absence of it feels like too. It can be the best buzz in the world; and it can create the lowest low.

Gene Fuller famously said: 'Writing is easy. All you do is stare at a blank sheet of paper until drops of blood form on your forehead.' Although this might sound extreme, and a rather macho approach (the antithesis of the 'Freefall Writing' suggested by creative writing teacher Barbara Turner-Vesselago[106]) there is perhaps an element of truth in Fuller's claim. It certainly can feel like that at times. We might be writing to reach a place beyond the fire, a place of peace, as Jean Starobinski describes of Rousseau, who strove: 'to hasten the moment when the pen would fall from his hand and the essential things would be said in the *silent* embrace of reconciliation and return.'[107]

Alice W. Flaherty suggests such push/pull factors – the blood and silence, if you will – are intrinsic to the writer's *modus vivendi*: 'The pleasure of writing and the pain of its absence tells something crucial about the motivation to write and the way it springs from our instinct to communicate. It is a feeling that is essential both for our ability as writers and for our potential to interact as human beings.'[108]

Writing can nourish the writer. It provides a personal dreamtime into which they can escape. The discipline and routine of writing provides a constancy in a world of uncertainty: a baseline. One thing that can be controlled, to a certain extent, in an unpredictable and disturbing world. And it is also one of those rare things which seems to reciprocate the effort one puts into it (at least in terms of the honing of one's art, if not in terms of commercial 'success').

Tolkien listed 'consolation' as one of the criteria for true fairy stories, but the act of writing itself can provide it. Tolkien's *magnum opus* kept him going all of his life, so much so that he found it difficult to let it go, to publish it and share his private world. He started off by writing a fairy story for his son, Christopher, and ended up writing for himself.

Writing has been the consolation of life for many writers. It can keep you sane, and help you survive unsatisfying jobs, marriages, families and so on... There are many examples of writers with dysfunctional lives who really shine on the page. Often it is the best of them. They write well, but live life badly. Henry Miller is perhaps an example of a writer redeemed his transgressions by writing about them in such controversial classics as *Tropic of Cancer* (1934) – by plumbing his own depths, and using his books as a kind of confessional. Writing can forgive a multitude of sins, and redeem the worst experiences.

One wonders if many of the dark fantasies weren't enacted out through the virtual reality of the page they would manifest in real life. There seem to be so many crime writers who can inhabit the mind of a criminal so convincingly, (frequently that of a serial killer), one wonders whether they are tapping into their own shadow and finding some illicit thrill in vicarious villainy – being able to get away with things they would never dare do in the light of day. And the reader of these dark fictions probably act out their own fantasies too – and both are probably healthy. Fiction is the safety valve for the Id, for the unreconciled, unrecognised and inhibited parts of our selves. Every reader can become for a while Mr Hyde to his own Dr Jekyll.

This creative territory is where these two sides of ourselves, two worlds meet. In writing, we (in a nutshell) draw from the right side of our brain, which deals in dreams, images, the lateral; and translate it with the left – whose forté is the word, the literal, the logical. When a writer is 'on fire' with ideas, a kind of synaptic cross-fire occurs – between synapses, but also across hemispheres. Certain ambiences, i.e. the sound of waves crashing on a beach, allow brain waves to lengthen – from the shorter alpha waves of every day consciousness to the longer theta waves of liminal states (i.e. the hypnagogic state between waking and sleeping) – the longer the waves, the greater the connections made: literally joined-up thinking. Yet it is a mysterious process which works best when approached tangentially. Like meditation, the harder you try the less likely you are to succeed. Every writer has his or her own methodology: creative processes as distinct as the writing itself. Often we are not in control of the process, of what is 'coming through' – not all the time anyway. Yet the amorphous muse is manifested with skill, the left brain anchors the right, pins it down, forces it to be precise. It is a dance between the conscious and sub- or unconscious – a walking between the worlds. Author Moyra Caldecott explains something akin to this in her literary memoir, *Multidimensional Life: a writer on writing* (2007): 'My experience in writing the book is something like the game of 'leap frog'. I jump over an experience I have in everyday life to reach an imaginative transformation of it. Then I 'leapfrog' over an imaginative event to reach an understanding of an event I had in everyday life. Backwards and forwards I go between 'everyday' and 'Fantasy', each illuminating the other, having a marvellous adventure while I learn about myself and about life. The story grows all the time exponentially.'[109] She adds that the medium of story is the one most suitable for exploring the nebulous texture of reality: 'Why I prefer to express myself in story rather than in 'straight' prose is that I feel the realities of life are so intangible, so esoteric and mysterious, so delicate and subtle, that there is no way of conveying them directly.'[110]

These fleeting impressions are entwined with consciousness itself, and as David Lodge examines in his book on writing and consciousness[111] fiction itself seems best able to express these birds in the mind: 'In a world where nothing is certain, in which transcendental belief has been undermined by scientific materialism, and even the objectivity of science is qualified by relativity and uncertainty, the single human voice, telling its own story, can seem the only authentic way of rendering consciousness.' Citing Noam Chomsky in an extract of his book,[112] Lodge quotes: 'It is quite possible... that we will always learn more about human life and personality from novels than from scientific psychology.' This echoes Sigmund Freud's startling defence of writers: 'Creative writers are valuable allies and their evidence is to be prized highly, for they are apt to know a whole host of things between heaven and earth if which our philosophy has not yet let us dream. In their knowledge of the mind, they are far in advance of us everyday people, for they draw on sources which we have not yet opened up to science.'[113]

There is thought to be a therapeutic benefit to the act of writing – an unspoken by-product through the centuries, therapeutic writing (and its teaching) is becoming a discipline in its own right. Actor and director James Roose-Evans, in his memoir *Inner Journey, Outer Journey* (1998), articulates these benefits: 'The creative process enables us to absorb experience with our whole being, to give it form and shape, thereby enhancing our capacity to live... By gaining conscious control of unconscious imagery we bring into order our own chaotic psyches. It is a process of self healing.'

Writing, specifically the lens of fiction, can afford a perspective on one's own 'story'. Caldecott says: 'In writing a novel one can play with ideas and concepts that hover on the edge of one's belief and, while doing so, consider seriously one's attitude to them.'[114]

The counter-argument to this is writing is actually detrimental in some way. Rick Gekoski, in his article 'Writing is bad for you' (*Guardian*, July 2011), argues against the received wisdom of the 'improving qualities of our baptismal dips into the waters of literature', describing his own experience: '...the more I write the worse I become. More self-absorbed, less sensitive to the needs of others, less flexible, more determined to say what I have to say, when I want and how I want, if I could only be left alone to figure it out.'

Yet the need for space, peace and solitude does not have 'negative values', as both Anthony Storr articulates in *Solitude* (1997); and Sara Maitland in *The Book of Silence* (2009), who moved to a 'house on a moor high above Weardale' to 'dig deeper into my own writing': She explains her MO: 'I needed as a writer to escape the pressure to conform, to sing the harmony with what is going on rather than seek out whatever may be beyond that.'[115]

Maitland argues she is not alone in this urge: 'This journey into silence in extreme terrains has been important for a number of creative thinkers while they prepare themselves for radical new work'.[116]

Many writers have to isolate themselves, often for long periods of time, to accomplish a project. One needs the goodwill of tolerant partners, offspring and pets; a room of one's own; and a strong dose of self-discipline – to not allow yourself to be disturbed by mundane demands. The act has 'selfishness' written all over it, and perhaps something more.

The sheer drive that is needed to accomplish a long-term

project bears close resemblance to monomania. The repetitive, ritualistic element of one's writing practice – writing every day, at a set time, a set number of words, with a particular pen, or with one's desk just so – can appear on the outside to be uncannily like an Obsessive Compulsive Disorder. There is even an acknowledged condition: hypergraphia – the overwhelming urge to write, which neurologist Alice Flaherty's book, *The Midnight Disease: The Drive to Write, Writer's Block, and the Creative Brain*, brought to public attention. Its opposite – Writer's Block – has a string of associated symptoms: depression, anxiety, and related mood disorders. Some writers can swing from one to the other – an unbearable seesaw – which might be signs of a Bipolar disorder: manic depression. In aboriginal cultures this behaviour might be perceived as a 'crazy sacredness', which makes for ideal shaman material. A debilitating sickness at the onset of puberty is often seen as sign of the Underworld Initiation which will make or break the sufferer (a near-death experience, where the fledgling soul is tested and, if it survives replaced by a 'diamond body') and may lead to their becoming a shaman.

Rather than avoid, prevent or deny such problems, we can choose to see them as part of who we are; and what makes us human. Rumi wrote: 'The wound is the place where the Light enters you.' And centuries later Leonard Cohen in his 'Anthem' sang: 'There is a crack in everything/That's how the light gets in.'

The Druids studied the formations of birds in flight – from them (specifically the shapes of cranes' legs) they were said to have devised the sacred Celtic Ogham alphabet. Poets, in the Celtic tradition, were said to be able to know and speak 'the Language of Birds'. They were the messenger of the Gods, like the gold-crested Hoopoe in *The Conference of the Birds*, a 12th Century poem by Farid ud-Din Attar. The story begins when the birds of the world assembled together to choose a king:

The Hoopoe, excited and full of hope, came forward and placed herself in the middle of the assembled birds. On her breast was the ornament which symbolized that she had entered the way of spiritual knowledge; the crest on her head was the crown of truth, and she had knowledge of both good and evil.

'Dear Birds,' she began, 'I am one who is engaged in divine warfare, and I am messenger of the world invisible. I have knowledge of God and of the secrets of creation.'[117]

The conscious writer, speaking the 'Language of Birds' becomes an ambassador of them all. At times, it might seem like his or her mind is like a crowded menagerie, full of squawking birds demanding attention. The writer must become 'king' of them all. This might seem like an insurmountable task, but if we follow the parable of Attar's Parliament, we discover that of the thousands of birds who had set out on their quest to find a king, only thirty stayed the distance. Could we see in this a metaphor of the creative process? From a hyper-abundance of ideas, of narrative possibilities, we must cut back. The final thirty pilgrim-birds are pared down to their essence: '...bewildered, weary and dejected, with neither feathers nor wings.' And yet, despite their state, they had reached the door of their Majesty. Here, they received enlightenment: 'Then flash the lightning of fulfilment and a hundred worlds were consumed in a moment.'[118] The birds, absorbed by the Godhead, are 'annihilated' in bliss. Perfection is achieved in this Sufi myth. The creative process is seldom so consummated, although we can aspire towards this.

And in the striving, the art of humanity is forged.

Writing may not be able to quieten all the birds in the mind, but it let's them out of the cage – providing a release of pressure. It may not be a flawless method, but hell, it beats trepanning!

Yet, perhaps there is another, less extreme way to create a portal – one that we'll look at in the next chapter.

9

The Door in the Hedge

'The Locked Door stands as an eternal Temptation.'
JRR Tolkien[119]

'Let us...suppose a violation of frontier,' wrote CS Lewis, defending Fantasy in 1949, the year he completed *The Lion, the Witch and the Wardrobe*. In many classic Fantasy stories there is a portal on a threshold which the characters have to pass through to go from the 'Ordinary World' to the 'Special World' (to use the terminology of The Hero's Journey). CS Lewis's device of the fur-coat lined wardrobe in the Narnia books is only one of many, e.g. the purple tollbooth in *The Phantom Tollbooth* (1961); the tree in *The Magic Faraway Tree* (1943); *Alice in Wonderland* (1865) and the famous rabbit hole – which has become to symbolise, post-Matrix, any 'bottomless pit' of information and experience. All of these are magical doorways into otherworlds. Yet one of the most re-occurring motifs is the 'door in the hedge', which rose to prominence in Frances Hodgson Burnett's *The Secret Garden* – first published in serial format in 1910. In Hodson Burnett's story, the secret garden is a place of healing: of lost wonder, friendship, and natural regeneration. Associated with his late wife's memory, the widower Mr Craven keeps it locked and out of bounds – and this could be seen, in a wider sense, as a possible metaphor for the buttoned-up Victorian era, where the feminine was hidden beneath bodices and bustles, long skirts and prim lace. The stifled and smothered feminine is evoked more explicitly in the ghost stories *The Yellow Wallpaper* (1892) and *The Turn of the Screw* (1898). Freudians would argue that the 'door in the hedge' has sexual connotations – a visual euphemism for a woman's vagina, the doorway of life. Yet the symbol persisted late into the

Twentieth Century and seems to represent more than this reductionist interpretation. It refuses to become smaller – as one would expect in the transition from the known to the unknown: an oceanic quality of fathomless lingers at the threshold. In the first Narnia book, *The Magician's Nephew* (1955), this portal is the place of pools – where many worlds can be accessed. In Neil Gaiman's consciously old-fashioned fairy tale, *Stardust* (1999), it is the gap in the Wall (a village on the border of Faerie); a nod and a wink to that neglected classic of English Fantasy written by Russian translator Hope Mirrlees, *Lud-in-the Mist* (1926), a strait-laced village on the border-country of reality where the smuggling of contraband fairy-fruit is becoming a problem; to the Hedge, demarcating the edge of the Shire where Sam Gamgee falters at the edge of his world. In *Little, Big* (1981), an epic American fairy tale spanning generations by John Cowley it is the extensive house itself. In *Mythago Wood*, (1984) it is Ryhope Wood – a remnant of ancient woodland left over from the last Ice Age, an islandised polder withstanding the tides of time and technology, providing a wildlife corridor to the Otherworld, at a terrible cost.

Tolkien warns: 'The boundaries of the Little Kingdom, either in time or space, are not easy to determine from the scarcity of evidence.'[120] As nebulous as Faerie is, the way to it are even chancier. Such 'doorways' are often moveable feasts – elusive as the questing beast. In *Doctor Who*, the portal is the ship of the timelord protagonist, the TARDIS (Time-and-Relative-Dimensions in Space), stuck in the homely and eternally anachronistic form of a 1950's police box.

There is often a transaction that occurs in the crossing of such borders. In Greek mythology, it is the paying of Charon, the ferryman of the dead (hence the tradition of placing two coins on the eyes of the deceased). In Philip Pullman's late Twentieth Century crossover epic, *His Dark Materials*, the passage is created by either the traumatic severance of a child from its daemon; or by the use of a 'subtle knife' – which can cut doorways between the worlds: both processes creating their toxic side-effects, as wraith-like creatures bleed from the world of the dead into the living.

Sometimes, the transaction is an amorous one, although no less deadly. The borderlands of the heart are a treacherous terrain. Scottish folk tradition provides three examples of 'soul-reaving'. For Thomas of Ercildoune the Eildon Hills would be his liminal zone, as captured in 'Thomas the Rhymer'; for Janet, in the sister ballad 'Tam Lin', it was Carterhaugh; for 'Tam o' Shanter' it was the Brig o' Doon. Fords, streams, springs, bridges, shorelines, crossroads, caves, dark woods, lonely moors ... all places to avoid if you don't want to be 'faeried off' to Faerie, or places to frequent if you *do* – as was the case with the eccentric Reverend Robert Kirk, a 17th Century Presbyterian minister and author of *The Secret Commonwealth of Elves, Fauns and Fairies*[121], who was said to have been transported to Faerie after stepping into a fairy-ring on the hills near Aberfoyle, his Lowlands home in Scotland. He was believed to have been replaced by a Changeling, and according to legend is a prisoner or guest in 'Elfhame' still.

Such stories and ballads provide gateways, as Tolkien says: 'they open a door or Other Time, and if we pass through, though only for a moment, we stand outside our own time, outside Time itself, maybe.' Step through, by all means, but there's no guarantee that you or the world you knew will be the same when you return, as Tolkien warns: 'Creative Fantasy, because it is mainly trying to do something else (make something new), may open your hoard and let all the locked things fly away like caged birds. The gems all turn into flowers or flames, and you will be warned that all you had (or knew) was not really effectively chained, free and wild; no more yours than they were you.'

These 'doors in the hedge' are, on a Jungian level, openings into our subconscious or Collective Unconscious, to Freudians, the trapdoor of the Id. We project our fears and fantasies into these negative spaces – and if we pass through, often find what we have taken in with us. In George Macdonald's remarkably deep and disturbing novels *Phantastes* (1858) and *Lilith* (1895) it is death itself whose realm we enter.

Alice W. Flaherty describes how wonder can transmogrify to horror as we venture into the littoral spaces of consciousness and creativity, at once alluring and edgy: 'On good days, ideas would wake me at four in the morning, tendrils of words coiling around me like heady perfume. It was as if a door had opened onto a hot wind from the tropics, the sort of wind that propels ships carrying peacock feathers and rubies and apes and incense. On bad days, the words were like a charnel house through which I had to search for the bodies of the people I loved.' [122]

Fantasy opens up the Pandora's Box of the Id, but leaves us with Hope: that if Man can imagine the worst of evils, he can also create the best of goods. Every wicked witch is balanced out by a fairy godmother. Bettelheim says: '...when unconscious material is to some degree permitted to come to awareness and worked through in imagination, its potential for causing harm – to ourselves and others – is much reduced; some of its forces can then be made to serve positive purposes.'[123]

There is a sense in which heightened language *itself* can act as a 'door in the hedge' – both in its incantatory quality and in its use of imagery. Some writers have used such imagery consciously – as a form of initiation into deeper realms. William Sharp, AKA Fiona MacLeod, wrote haunting Celtic fantasies populated by: 'images and songs which open the doors of psychic consciousness that lead into (what Sharp called) 'the Green Life'.'[124] The works of George Macdonald and MacLeod have a timeless quality. In the foreword Sutherland describes them as: 'mythopoetists whose tales do no date, but like copper coins drop into the deep well of the mind to stir the imagination and inspire the soul.'[125] The heightened register of such fantasists (joined by an elite fellowship comprising William Morris, Sylvia Townsend Warner, Lord Dunsany, JRR Tolkien, David Lindsay and Charles Williams) may seem overly lyrical to modern palates but provides a linguistic gateway to other realms, in the way that the best storytellers do with their voice. And in this respect, it is the oldest of magics.

10

Imagination as a Gateway

> *'Without this playing with Fantasy no creative work has ever yet come to birth. The debt we owe to the play of the imagination is incalculable.'*
> Carl Jung

There is a sense in which imagination itself is a gateway. It can be far more than mere make-believe. Albert Einstein said 'Imagination is more important than knowledge', (*On Science*). I believe it is not simply the 'making of pictures', (to use its etymology: '*imaginari*' picture to oneself) but seeing beyond the walls of reality. As William Blake, that ambassador of the imagination, once engraved: 'when the doors of perception are cleansed man will see things as they truly are, infinite'. I would argue that imagination, in its purest form, is a visionary faculty (one that is attested to in many world cultures, e.g. the Druidic seer, the ovate; and the Irish seer-poet, the *filidh*), a faculty which enables to glimpse other worlds, other realities. This proffers the tantalising notion that the Secondary Worlds imagined by Fantasy writers exist in some way. Irish visionary poet AE (George William Russell) suggested this hypothesis in his seminal work, *The Candle of Vision* (1918), in which he describes wondrous scenes and beings that seem to have an autonomous existence. For him, the limited circle of light cast by the 'candle of vision' could not create such shining visions, beings and worlds so instantaneously. They seem to come and go with their own volition. And those with the seer's eye catch glimpses of them.

In *The Gist: a celebration of the imagination* (2012), several authors discuss the importance of the imagination – inspired by

Arvon co-founder John Moat's eponymous essay, where he advocates its primacy: '...whatever mystery the Imagination amounts to, the field of its operation reaches beyond the individual creativity we usually connect it with. Reaches beyond it, and is wholly concerned with it. It has the capacity to relate the individual to the universal, and would seem intent on enabling the individual by expressing him or herself to realise that the unique story they have to tell is essential to the completion of the all-inclusive story of the universe.'[126]

Bold claims, but Moat is not alone in believing this. In his essay on 'Mythic Imagination', included in *The Gist*, Jules Cashford cites psychologists alongside poets in his defence of its quintessential value: 'Jung and James Hillman, like Blake, Coleridge and Yeats, also reinstate Imagination as the origin and ground of life. When Jung writes that 'Psyche is image' and Hillman says that 'All existence is structured by imagination' they are calling for a 'poetic basis of mind'.

Lindsay Clarke talks of the *vesica pisces* as a symbol of the imagination[127]. In its sacred geometry, found within the ground plans of temples (see John Michel, *The View Over Atlantis, 1969*), Clarke sees one circle as representing consciousness; the other, unconsciousness, and where they overlap, an almond shape is create called a 'mandorla' – which to Clarke represents a gateway for the imagination, an opening to the subconscious and to all that is unknown and potentiate: 'This is a very ancient symbol for the mysterious reconciliation of opposing principles through which something new enters into life.'[128]

For Clarke, the imagination is a visionary tool of transformation: 'I regard the imagination as the means by which ... we shape our vision of the world and our place within it, and also as the primary means by which we can transform it.' (Clarke, ibid) This he sums up in his novel *The Water Theatr*e (2011) in the 'mission statement' of a mysterious organisation called Heartsease:

1. Our lives are as we imagine them to be.
2. Imagination is the agency of change.
3. Change in the collective begins with change in the individual.
4. Compassion is an act of the imagination.
5. Let us re-imagine the world.[129]

There is a long established English visionary tradition, as explored in *Albion and the English Imagination* (2004) by Peter Ackroyd; and *The Green Fuse: pastoral vision in English Art 1820-2000* (Jerrold Northrop Moore, 2006). Clarke adds: 'This tradition is best articulated in English by the poet S. T. Coleridge who regarded the imagination as 'the prime agent of human perception', and by William Blake who said that 'to me this whole world is but one continuous vision of fancy and imagination.'[130]

Blake believed in the emancipation of the imagination. 'For Blake the imagination is the source of mankind's redemption, his access to the New Jerusalem, or Paradise on earth.'[131] But Clarke argues: 'this tradition is much older than the romantic poets and philosophers. It can be traced back through the hermetic tradition of the alchemists, one of whom, Rutland the Lexicographer, beautifully declared that 'the Imagination is the star in man,' (Clarke, *ibid*).

Perhaps this 'star in man' it is the Divine Spark we are all said to possess, a star upon the brow (as in the 6th Century Welsh bard Taliesin – whose name means literally 'shining, or radiant brow') which will guide us back to the Source; or simply an awakened Third Eye of a fully developed and operational pineal gland. C.S. Lewis considered that 'reason is the organ of truth, but imagination is the organ of meaning.'[132] In the Romantic tradition Imagination is seen as a spiritual organ by the likes of Coleridge. This has been developed into the concept of 'Active Imagination': a path of cognition that uses the imagination as an organ of understanding, as advocated in particular by Carl Jung – although the tradition relates back to Blake, and to the Theosophical works of Jakob Bohme, Swedenborg and Steiner; and earlier to Islamic philosophy, where the imaginal realm is known in Islamic philosophy as *alam al-mithal*. In the Sufi tradition the imagination mediated between, and thus unified, human reason and divine being.

And so imagination seems to be a technique for accessing other realms, one that is outside time and the sphere of human history: 'The history element comes from the careful background research and the Fantasy element comes from trying to 'feel inside' the myths and religious beliefs of the ancient civilizations and so it is not Fantasy at all to me – but a kind of imaginal reality.'[133] Karen Armstrong echoes this: 'A myth...is an event that happened once, but which also happens all the time.'[134]

The great stories continue to happen outside time, and can be revisited again and again. They speak eternal truths and are never archaic or irrelevant, however obscure, because all stories, whether they be about elves, aliens, animals, the ocean or ghosts, speak about the human condition and humanities connection to the Earth, Cosmos and each other.

By accessing them, we are enriched – as both writers and readers, tellers and listeners, as Nancy Mellon emphasises: 'A treasure trove of imaginative powers lives within us all. These powers often lie stunned and dormant, yet to awaken the pictures that live in our story–imagination is to become more fully and radiantly alive.'[135] That imagination is not only an enhancement of life, but intrinsic to its full potential is something author Moyra Caldecott whole-heartedly believes: 'The process of writing fiction involves a continual exchange between the author's own experience and the reach of his or her imagination – the Imagination being a creative act of extraordinary relevance to life.'[136]

Before we can enter such a portal of potentiality, we must first run the gauntlet of a Threshold Guardian. So let us go and open the door to an unexpected guest whose loud knock has rudely shattered our reverie.

11

The Man from Porlock

The Romantic poet Samuel Taylor Coleridge was famously interrupted mid-flow while writing his classic 'Kubla Khan' by a man who knocked at an inopportune moment 'on business from Porlock'[137]. Coleridge had received, in an opium reverie, hundreds of lines of poetry – but just as he went to write it down, the catastrophic knock at the door came. When he had dealt with the unexpected visitor, all he could recall of his vision were a few tantalising lines – 'a vision in a dream', as it became subtitled.

Or so the apocryphal story goes.

Whether it truly happened, was Coleridge's excuse for Writer's Block, or a shrewd 'marketing hook' (making the surviving fragment all the more alluring), we can never know for sure – but it is a good tale with an element of truth about it (as all good stories have): a universal truth about the creative cycle.

There is always going to be a 'man from Porlock' of one kind or another. Julia Cameron in *The Artist's Way* (1995) calls them Crazymakers. Do not let them block your creativity! These Threshold Guardians – no less than everyday Cerberuses, guarding the entrance to deeper realms – exist to test our resolve, as in Tolkien's classic fairy tale of frustrated creativity: 'Leaf by Niggle', in which an amateur artist, Niggle, continually finds himself interrupted in his life's work – the painting of a masterpiece. They are the parentheses which block the flow of the sentence, the phonecall which breaks your concentration.

In truth, the most insidious 'man from Porlock' is our self. The traffic lights of the mind.

We can self-sabotage our own creativity in countless ways – by checking our emails; following our friends on Facebook; surfing the web; answering the phone; tidying our desk; clearing out an old cupboard, attending to the 'needs' of our pets. It is amazing how many long-delayed household chores get done when a budding writer is faced with actually sitting down and writing. These almost neurotic compulsions to do anything but the task at hand are called Displacement Activities. They are cousin to the Ten Thousand Things the Buddhists talk about: the Samsara, or Maya – the veil of illusion between you and the Reality of your Otherworld. Do not let them stop you rendering your Xanadu.

The early stages of the creative 'zone' – when you are on the cusp of putting pen to paper, digit to keyboard – is the most fragile of spaces, so easily shattered by a comment, a door-bell, hedge-strimmer, or other noise pollution. One needs to jealously guard this space, as fiercely as any dragon does its hoard. Make it clear to a partner, to children, or housemates, that this is your writing time – ideally a regular slot, so they get used to leaving you in peace at this time. Dorothea Brande, in *Becoming a Writer* (1934) suggests the Morning Pages – writing three pages of uninterrupted stream-of-consciousness writing every morning at the same time. This 'downloads' all the thoughts cluttering your mind, gets your writing regularly without expectation of 'product', and warms you up so you are ready for writing. This is a good habit to cultivate, as Julia Cameron advocates – by doing the Morning Pages first thing, even before breakfast, we can catch the coat-tails of dreams before they slip away, and invest our writing is some of dream-life's vivid, disturbing, and original quality.

As Coleridge found, retrieval is always a problem ('Could I revive within me/ Her symphony and song...'). Some can recall their dreams clearly, but others claim not to dream at all, even though it's an essential process of our mental health to be able to do so (it is not sleep-deprivation that drives one mad, but dream-deprivation – being unable to 'download' and process, pause and put the conscious mind on 'standby'). Tolkien said of fairy-story, that '...its very richness and strangeness tie the tongue of a traveller who would report them.' The creative 'zone' has its own rules. Upon returning to 'this world' (ordinary reality) too suddenly (e.g. because of an unexpected interruption) disorientation can occur, (what could be called the 'reality bends) and the violent transition can mean the inspiration is lost in translation – we are unable to relate it in everyday terms because the world of our dream-life speaks a different tongue. This makes the fragments that we do have – plucked from oblivion – all the more precious. They are like ruins of glorious palaces from a distant age, stumbled upon in waking life.

Tolkien's Tower

In his defence of Beowulf, Tolkien uses a rare allegory. It is worth citing in full as a mini-Tolkienian fairy tale, and a metaphor for the (interrupted) creative process:

> 'A man inherited a field in which was an accumulation of old stone, part of an older hall. Of the old stone some had already been used in building the house in which he actually lived, not far from the house of his fathers. Of the rest he took some and built a tower. But his friends coming perceived at once (without troubling to climb the steps) that these stones had formerly belonged to a more ancient building. So they pushed the tower over, with no little labour, in order to look for hidden carvings and inscriptions, or to discover whence the man's distant forefathers had obtained their building material. Some suspecting a deposit of coal under the soil began to dig for it, and forgot even the stones. They all said: 'This tower is most interesting!' But they also said (after pushing it over): 'What a muddle it is in!' And even the man's own descendants, who might have been expected to consider what he had been about, were heard to murmur: 'He is such an odd fellow! Imagine his using these old stones just to build a nonsensical

> tower! Why did he not restore the old house? He had no sense of proportion.' But from the top of that tower the man had been able to look out upon the sea.[138]

This charming allegory neatly sums up the desire to fashion stories from ancient materials – mythology, folklore, archetypes – and the folly in trying to 'interpret' or deconstruct them (not that there is no place for literary analysis, but the sledgehammer approach of some theories does not respect the narrative *as a narrative* – working on its own terms, for its own sake). A story is rarely written to please critics (many of the Porlock breed) and so they are the least likely to appreciate it. Coleridge seems to sum up this reaction vividly:

> And all should cry, Beware! Beware!
> His flashing eyes, his floating hair!
> Weave a circle round him thrice,
> And close your eyes with holy dread,
> For he on honey-dew hath fed,
> And drunk the milk of Paradise.

If possessed to build foolish towers from the rubble of giants, then do so – and don't let anyone stop you! If you persist in your folly, and complete your Quixotic projects, from such heights you might be afforded a fine view of the 'sea' – that is, another paradigm, beyond the limited sphere of academe, or even your fellow 'countrymen' (physical or intentional; writers or neighbours).

Do not allow these 'measurers', as Julia Cameron calls them, from blocking your creativity. Believe in your vision, and make it happen.

12

Explorers of an Unknown Region

'Strider sitting in the corner at the Inn was a shock, and I had no more idea who he was than had Frodo.'
JRR Tolkien[139]

Being a writer of the imagination is like being an explorer discovering and surveying a new land – a Marco Polo of the mind's distant shores. There is a distinctive thrill to being the first to step foot in this undiscovered country. Although the writer eventually wants to share this world with as many people as possible, to begin with there is wisdom in being jealously protective of your discovery as you venture out into virgin territory. The further you walk, the more there is to see. Every time a writer creates a new world they become a Columbus, a Cortés. All too soon, you will have to let the world in; but for a while it is all yours.

Tolkien worried if he revealed too much of the background story of the Ring trilogy[140]. He speculates that a good story involves: 'an attraction like that of viewing far off an unvisited island, or seeing the towers of a distant city gleaming in a sunlit mist. To go there is to destroy the magic, unless new unattainable vistas are again revealed.' In his elegiac poem, 'The Cottage of Lost Play' he seems to be describing such 'unattainable vistas' charged with a bittersweet evanescence. Let us revisit it again, exploring a little deeper:

We wandered shyly hand in hand,
small footprints in the golden sand,
and gathered pearls and shells in pails,
while all about the nightingales

were singing in the trees.
We dug for silver with our spades,
and caught the sparkles of the seas,
then ran ashore to greenlit glades,
and found the warm and winding lane
that now we cannot find again,
between all whispering trees.

Here liminal states, thresholds, and that yearning for the sea and what is over the horizon all weave together into a eulogy for a 'lost island' state of being, which Tolkien seemed to spend his whole life trying to regain – his own 'lost domain' – and we are the richer for it.

In *Le Grand Meaulnes* (1913) the narrator captures the yearning which obsesses the title character: 'Taking a cross-path I soon came to the edge of the wood. For the first time in my life I was alone in unfamiliar country, like some patrol with whom the corporal has lost touch.

And now I imagine myself on the brink of that mysterious felicity Meaulnes had one day caught a glimpse of…'[141]

Maybe Fantasy writers write Fantasy not 'because it's there' – because their Secondary Worlds do not exist until they create them – but because it is *not* there.

Tolkien talked of stories concerned with: 'Images of things that are not only 'not actually present', but which are indeed not to be found in our primary world at all, or generally believed not to be found there.'[142] The writer of the imagination senses the absence of such places – often with unbearable longing – and this helps fuel their creation. The 'known world' repels them like two magnets; while the 'unknown' becomes their magnetic north, drawing the compass of their imagination.

It is a strong pull, one which Walt Whitman evokes 'Darest Thou Now, O Soul':

> Darest thou now, O Soul,
> Walk out with me toward the Unknown Region,
> Where neither ground is for the feet, nor
> any path to follow…[143]

The writer of the imagination is driven by a similar daemon to the pioneers of the Wild West – in search of the 'Final Frontier', whether it is sought in deep space, in a Secondary World, or the inner worlds of the human mind.

Yet sometimes – unexpectedly, at the bottom of a rabbit hole, a dwarven mine, even at the far edge of the universe – the door is back into this world.

A curious character in the story of Bran and Branwen from *Y Mabinogi* opens this 'strong door' – breaking the spell of the Singing Head. The ragged company of war-traumatised warriors have spent eighty years in the carousing company of their fallen leader's dismembered 'crown' on the lost island of Gwales, off the coast of Wales. All their woes come back to the company of seven – the only survivors of a raid on the Irish to rescue Bran's sister, Branwen, from the clutches of a cruel king. They must continue and complete their quest: bury their leader's head under the White Mount (the Tower of London), where it would continue to guard the land. Yet this is transgressed also, as King Arthur comes and digs it up (one of 'The Three Unfortunate Disclosures'), in effect replacing Bran as Britain's tutelary guardian. The ravens of Bran can be found at the Tower to this day – albeit with their wings clipped, for their departure would symbolise the doom of the land. The best 'flights of fancy' often need such wings clipping, to stop them going too far. By keeping close to terra firma, a Fantasy story is often grittier and more impactful.

Ultimately, every story – whatever its prevailing aesthetic, the trappings of its genre – should be about the human heart, as George RR Martin agrees: 'Faulkner said that the only thing worth writing about is the human heart in conflict with itself, and I agree with that. But I think you can have the human heart in conflict with itself in a Fantasy, in a mystery, in a romance novel – I don't think the genre matters.' [144]

By venturing into the unknown, we can come to know ourself. Having ventured to Mordor (or any Perilous Realm) we will see our own 'Shire' (not only home, but the human condition) in a new light:

> We shall not cease from exploration
> And the end of all our exploring
> Will be to arrive where we started
> And know the place for the first time.
> T.S. Eliot[145]

We *must* step through the door in the hedge, we *must* bite that forbidden fruit, we *must* transgress, as Philip Pullman argues[146], if we are to mature, if we are to take the path of knowledge and eventually perhaps, wisdom. This is the journey of the Fool in the Tarot through the Major Arcana, of virtually all characters in fairy tales, and it is the journey we must all go on if we are to learn: '...that on callow, lumpish, and selfish youth peril, sorrow, and the shadow of death can bestow dignity, and sometimes wisdom.'[147]

The journey into the unknown transforms us. The telling absences await for their stories to be told. For writers of the imagination, it is in our nature to *adore* the vacuum. Champion of the wild, John Muir, who through his much-loved writings on wilderness, said: 'To those devoid of imagination, a blank place on a map is a useless waste; to others, the most valuable part.'[148]

Henry David Thoreau insisted that: 'We need the tonic of the wildness… At the same time that we are earnest to explore and learn all things, we require that all things be mysterious and unexplorable, that land and sea be indefinitely wild, unsurveyed and unfathomed by us because unfathomable.'[149] And yet, in an age of Google Earth and sophisticated cartography, this notion seems sadly untenable – which is perhaps what drives us to invent and explore imaginary worlds.

British nature writer and traveller, Robert Macfarlane describes this life-long hankering for the untamed: 'I could not now say when I first grew to love the wild, only that I did, and that a need for it will always remain strong in me. As a child, whenever I read the word, it conjured images of wide spaces, remote and figureless. Isolated islands off Atlantic coasts. Unbounded forests and blue snow-light falling on to drifts marked with the paw-prints of wolves. Frost-shattered summits and corries holding lochs of great depth. And this was the vision of a wild place that stayed with me: somewhere boreal, wintry, vast, isolated, elemental, demanding of the traveller in its asperities. To reach a wild place was, for me, to step outside human history.' [150]

The desire for such places, such an experience – at least vicariously – drives many a writer to delve increasingly deeper into the untracked wilds of the human mind.

In our final chapter we will consider how limitless these wildernesses can be.

13

Many Worlds

> *'If one is lucky, a solitary Fantasy can totally transform one million realities.'*
> Maya Angelou

We began this essay with three questions:

1. Where does the impulse to write Fantasy come from?
2. What takes place in the act of writing, i.e. the creative process – specifically in the creation of works of Fantasy?
3. What benefits are there, if any, for the writer, as well as the reader?

I hope we have at least started to answer them, although as with all threads of inquiry they are as long as you want them to be – keep following them and more will follow: our very act of consciousness spins them into being. Spiderwebs of the cave-mind, we can become entranced with the patterns we make – as indeed we must, for through this hypnotic delight worlds are fashioned. Simon Tolkien, grandson of JRR Tolkien, said of his grandfather: 'What separated him from other Fantasy writers was that the depth of his world was so real. He told me that he devised the languages before he wrote the stories, so he really was building new worlds from the foundations up.'[151]

We write Fantasy to nourish ourselves. The imagination can act as an actual doorway through which we pass – we journey to the Otherworld, like Thomas the Rhymer, and return with our riches, hopefully not Fairy dust... Like the protagonist in the Hero's Journey we go on a quest to find the 'elixir' and if we succeed, return with it, for the healing of others, the healing of ourselves. Writing Fantasy is a kind of vision-quest – the writer spends extended periods of time in solitude, communing with the source and receive their 'vision', but it is only when this vision (story, song, poem, play, opera, screenplay) is shared with the 'tribe', does it gain any validity. Fantasy enriches this world – it helps us to see it anew, with fresh possibilities. Reality no longer feels so definitive or dictatorial – we can change it. The playful realm of Faerie teaches us 'plasticity', that is a flexible approach to reality, brain-muscles more supple, opinions less entrenched[152]. Every time one of us ventures into that unknown realm we make the links between the worlds more established – natural lines of drift, cutting across the prim lawns of the mainstream – and we make it more possible for others to journey there also, our stories become like portable gateways, or windows of the Otherworld. By using our imaginations, anything is possible – other worlds, other ways of being – it is a defiant act of rebellion, in support of the primacy of the human spirit against all those who would crush it.

Subcomandante Marcos, of the Zapatista Army of Liberation, EZLN Mexico, said in 2000: 'We seek a world in which there is room for many worlds.'[153]

Ben Okri, in *A Way of Being Free* (1998), writes: 'There are as many worlds as there are lives. It is not those who have no imagination who are the problem, for we all possess imagination, few of us use it well. The problem is with those who are frightened of the rather limitless validity of the imagination, frightened of people who continually extend the boundaries of the possible, people who ceaselessly redream the world and reinvent existence; frontiers people of the unknown and uncharted.'[154]

Imagination is a writer's greatest resource. Ursula K Le Guin, writes: 'It is above all by the imagination that we achieve perception, compassion and hope.'[155] And perhaps this is the best reason of all to 'desire dragons' – to walk two moons in another's moccasins facilitates empathy and compassion – that most precious commodity. In a world that seems to be plagued by a dearth of the imagination we need to 'desire dragons' – that is imagine alternative narratives – as much as possible.

In this sense the writing of Fantasy is a revolutionary act – the worlds the writer conjures act as a doorway which invite us to challenge the way things are; and awaken our true potential ... as compassionate citizens of the cosmos.

Coda

The Long Earth

(Written after reading the book of the same name by Terry Pratchett and Stephen Baxter)

If all it took was just a sideways step
to break your shackle to this tired earth,
untangle the strings of quantum physics
to shimmer down the mirror parallel,
find worlds which Darwin could have barely dreamed,
would you not do it? Would you not run?

I'd be off faster than the starting gun
to seek the Long Earth flickering unreamed;
new genera; and what mutations dwell
under different suns. I'd hunt strange musics
courting river banks, mountains and the surf.
If all it took were but a sideways step.

Yet here we stay. There is no interstitial strait,
just dreams; the faith of science. All that we create.

Adam Horovitz

Part Two

The Writer's Quest

The Hero's Journey, based upon the work of Joseph Campbell, became an influential idea in late Twentieth Century cultural life – notably in the field of screenwriting, thanks to the 'industry bible', *The Writer's Journey: mythic structure for storytellers and screenwriters* (Vogler, 1999). Although the latter is an extremely useful application of Campbell's monomyth to screenwriting structure, I personally was disappointed that it didn't explore the journey the writer actually undergoes during their creative process, as the title suggested. It focused more on the product – but it is always 'the journey not the destination' that is critical, in life and certainly in writing – for if we do not savour the words, and delight in crafting them, then no good will arise from our efforts, however 'high' the concept. The devil is always in the detail. Another practical tome, sharing the same main title (*The Writer's Journey – from inspiration to publication*, a 2004 title by former commissioning editor for Harper Collins, Julia Cameron) is aimed at pitching non-fiction proposals, and as such, does a good job – but again, misses out on exploring the *actual journey* of a writer in creating their work beyond the 'concept' and the 'pitch'. What of the mysterious process of creativity itself? I felt this had not been explored directly in relation to writers of fiction, especially imaginative fiction. Eschewing the slew of books showing you 'how to write an xxxxx novel' (surely the very antithesis of imaginative writing?) – I will attempt to chart the nebulous process of creativity which most writers undergo in one form or another. I have chosen the 9th Century Anglo-Saxon poem, *Beowulf*, as my mythic template – as an iconic piece of early English literature, it contains all the essential elements of the Writer's Quest, as though they had been hiding in plain sight from the start, the bardic blueprint in embryo – although there are many such myths and legends that would have served. I have done so partly because I am familiar and deeply fond of it, having performed an oral version of it in an Iron Age roundhouse in a storm (Peat Moors Visitor Centre, Samhain Fair, Somerset 2000);

this was after creating a cyberpunk version of it called Bio*Wolf, (Bath, 1999) in response to concerns over GMOs. As well as straddling both the Science Fiction and Fantasy genres, it showed me how flexible and adaptable a narrative it is – both timeless and ancient. Classic verbatim recitals of it by actor Julian Glover; lively storytelling versions of it by Hugh Lupton; a modern translation by poet Seamus Heaney (whose serial reading of it on BBC Radio 4 thrilled me the winter I spent on a narrow boat); and the blockbusting computer-animated version (Zemekis, 2007; Gaiman/Avery) show this. It truly is a tale for all ages. By being one of the very first poems written down in the English language it showed the lasting magic of words and both the poetic and narrative art. What better example of excellence do we need to jumpstart our own immortal masterpiece?

NB I have paraphrased the text (highlighted in italics), and cited when necessary from an out-of-copyright version[156]*, although I refer the reader to more recent translations, notably Seamus Heaney's*[157]*, which for my money is the most poetically muscular. My prose summaries pale in comparison and are meant to be merely functional and efficient.*

I

The Monster in the Night

> 'Writing a book is a horrible, exhausting struggle, like a long bout of some painful illness. One would never undertake such a thing if one were not driven on by some demon whom one can neither resist nor understand.'
> George Orwell, *Why I Write*[158]

The Writer's Quest begins in uncertainty. As writers about to embark upon our journey (although we do not know it yet) we are often 'benighted' – feeling ill-at-ease with life, or maybe *outwardly* content ... except for that little niggle that won't go away (Tolkien personified this in his charming parable of displacement activity, 'Leaf by Niggle'). You might not be able to put it into words (yet), but it is the 'voice that won't go away' – even if you cannot quite make out what it is saying, or wants to say at this stage. All you know is – there is something in your life that isn't being expressed, acknowledged or celebrated. You might be suffering from low spirits, possibly depression – because a part of you is 'buried' somewhere. If we want to get shamanic about this (and the creative process shares some intriguing parallels as we'll discover) then you could be said to suffering from 'soul-loss'. An essential part of you is missing and needs to be sung back home. That long denied voice – the real you, who has been put to one side while you have got on with the business of life (education; career; family). Parts of you might be engaged in these essential things – but not all of you. And your quality of life might be being affected as a result – manifesting in a certain lingering sadness, malcontent, ennui, or even anger. Something is definitely rotten in the state of Denmark.

But all of that is about to change.

The Anglo-Saxon epic of *Beowulf* starts in a surprisingly upbeat mood. To summarise the opening section:

After Halfdane, Hrothgar stepped forward to rule the Danes. Under Hrothgar, the kingdom prospered and enjoyed great military success, and Hrothgar decided to construct a monument to his success–a mead-hall where he would distribute booty to his retainers. The hall was called Heorot, and there the men gathered with their lord to drink mead and listen to the songs of the bards.

For a time, the kingdom enjoyed peace and prosperity.

Even if things seem 'functional', even successful on the surface, all is not what it appears. There is a 'long denied voice' waiting to burst through. William Faulkner describes how: 'an artist is a creature driven by demons... He has a dream. It anguishes him so much he must get rid of it.'[159] In the saga of *Beowulf*, this is personified as the deformed and tortured figure of Grendel – the very embodiment of a strangled cry.

But, one night, Grendel, a demon descended from Cain (who, according to the Bible, slew his brother Abel), emerged from the swampy lowlands, to listen to the nightly entertainment at Heorot. The bards' songs about God's creation of the Earth angered the monster. Once the men in the mead-hall fell asleep, Grendel lumbered inside and slaughtered thirty of them. Hrothgar's warriors were powerless against him.

The very fact that the songs of the scops, the Danish bards, seemed to enrage Grendel is telling – their eloquence mocks the lack of his own. It rubs salt into the wound of his broken tongue. The voice of the dispossessed (as Grendel possibly is – was he an original inhabitant of the land Hrothgar's ancestors claimed?); of the marginalised, the disenfranchised, can be fierce. Who likes to be ignored? Or worse – ridiculed, loathed, demonised? You have been so busy with your life you haven't allowed yourself to listen to this voice. But now it is making itself heard. The monster in the night has come calling, and will not leave you alone.

The following night, Grendel struck again, and continued to wreak havoc on the Danes for twelve years. He took over Heorot, and Hrothgar and his men remain unable to challenge him.

The voice in the shadows has made itself known – terrifying at first, as inevitably it is when the lid is taken off the Id. The subconscious has burst through into waking consciousness – symbolised by golden-gabled Heorot. When our soul-life is repressed, the consequence is often disease, injury, unexpected trauma – our world is turned 'upside-down'. Our life becomes a 'nightmare'. We find ourselves captives in a hellish prison – our home has become a charnel house (arguments; bruised silences; divorce; dysfunctional relationships; trouble at work; bills piling up...). We might be driven to drink or other vices, and find ourselves exacerbating the problem – sliding headfirst down a slippery slope. We can feel powerless to stop it – like Hrothgar's men. It is like watching a car-crash in slow motion. Don't. Look. This. Is. My. Life. Going. Down. The. Tubes. Whatever we do to attempt to 'fix it' fails: talking to friends, therapy, expensive courses, self-help books, holidays, new toys, new partners – the problem does not go away.

All of this can be expressed through the medium of the written word. There is certainly a therapeutic aspect to writing, although one has to be careful. Our catharsis does not easily become the readers unless it is well-crafted. Critical distance is essential to achieve this – otherwise it becomes the mere venting of spleen.

They make offerings at pagan shrines in hopes of harming Grendel, but their efforts are fruitless.

The monster in the night has struck – the idea that won't let you go, grabbing you with its claws and breathing its hot, foetid breath in your face until you write it down, tell its story. You have been hit by inspiration – although it might not feel it at this stage. No one knows when it will strike. That 'monster' – however apparently repugnant – is trying to tell you a message, and it will not go away until you listen. It will continue to manifest in dysfunctional ways unless you give it a voice. Unless you name your demon.

Such beasts raise their frightful heads in myths and legends across the world – often acting as a 'call to adventure' for the hero or heroine. In the Welsh collection of ancient tales, *Y Mabinogi*, a monstrous arm reaches into a stable every night and steals a new born foal until Pwyll, Lord of Dyfed, deals with it. In the Babylonian epic of *Gilgamesh*, it is the monster Humbaba – laying waste to the land, which forces the King into action. In the Greek myth of Perseus and Andromeda, it is the Kraken who was causing havoc. In George and the Dragon, a realm is threatened with a dragon which devastates the livestock and land, and is offered a regular human sacrifice to appease it – until the hero rides into town. In the tale of Theseus, it is the half-man/half-bull minotaur who is exacting its deadly tithe on the young men and women of Athens – like an austerity measure of a modern King Minos made incarnate. In other stories, the monster might be less obvious, but equally as terrible. A spell cast over a kingdom. A wicked stepmother or father. The death of one or both parents. A sickening land – The Wasteland. A cruel or ailing king. Tyrants and despots, dragons all. So is the 'boss from Hell'. Everyone of these 'dragons' make life unbearable and forces us to act.

The Danes endure constant terror, and their suffering is so extreme that the news of it travels far and wide.

In the writer's case, when the 'monster in the night' strikes, it is time to pick up the pen – and start writing. Your pen (or qwerty keyboard) is the only thing that will slay the beast. Here, the pen really is mightier than the sword – it is your Weapon of Magic. With it, you begin the Writer's Quest – plucking up your courage to face this fearsome foe (you wouldn't be the hero or heroine otherwise). It takes a certain fearlessness to be a writer. To show up to the page. Remember, fortune favours the bold! We have to be like the Fool in the Tarot and step off the cliff, even if the dog of doubt is pulling out our trouser leg. It is a leap of faith, a leap into the dark – but you have no choice.

As with all great works of art – you didn't 'choose it', it 'chose' you. It came calling, unexpectedly: trick or treating in your brain. You have gone down with what novelist Michael Chabon calls (after Coleridge) 'the midnight disease': 'The midnight disease is a kind of emotional insomnia; at every conscious moment its victim – even if he or she writes at dawn, or in the middle of the afternoon – feels like a person lying in a sweltering bedroom, with the window thrown open, looking up at a sky filled with stars and airplanes, listening to the narrative of a rattling blind, an ambulance, a fly trapped in a Coke bottle, while all around the neighbours soundly sleep.' [160]

The condition is almost incurable. The only remedy is ... to write it out of your system. This might take sometime (possibly years...). It is a daunting prospect that makes most wannabe scribblers break out into a cold sweat and stop dead in their tracks – placing their unwritten book of dreams back in the 'Might-Have-Been' Box. You are going to need some true mettle to overcome this particularly beastie – someone with strength, stamina, conviction and unwavering nerve.

Time to summon the hero.

The Monster in the Night questings:

- What long-denied part of you is not being expressed? Giving yourself permission to write anything, explore this notion – allowing the pen to take you where it will, even to uncomfortable places. Write as raw and raggedly as you like – no one has to see this. Write from the guts. Get it off your chest. Hatch the butterflies in the heart waiting to take wing.
- Look at this the next day. Read these passionate words with wonder. Does the writing have energy, muscularity, edge and spark? What subject matter or material emerged? Anything that would make a good short story, poem, play, novel or script? Follow your fire.
- Summarise this core concept/core emotion and hang it – your bloody stump – by your desk.

2

Summoning the Hero

At this time, Beowulf, nephew of the Geatish king Hygelac, is the greatest hero in the world. He lives in Geatland, a realm not far from Denmark, in what is now southern Sweden. When Beowulf hears tales of the destruction wrought by Grendel, he decides to travel to the land of the Danes and help Hrothgar defeat the demon. He voyages across the sea with fourteen of his bravest warriors until he reaches Hrothgar's kingdom.

Every creative act is an act of courage – it is 'yah-boo-sucks!' to death, to oblivion, to mediocrity, to being a passive consumer of life. We have everything against us – common sense; the pressure of earning a living; unhelpful peers; inner critics; crazymakers; noisy neighbours; that household chore that *really* needs your attention; that cold call; Climate Chaos; global financial meltdown; random asteroids and super volcanoes threatening to Destroy The World in an instant! See these as threshold guardians – they are the equivalent of the three-headed dog Cerberus that guarded the entrance to the realm of Hades. They are there to test your mettle, your tenacity. How much do you want to follow your dreams? Is your Push bigger than your Pull? Hollywood screenwriters use the useful idea of the 'Fear/Desire Axis' – which, despite its name is not some terrorist cell, or Bond-like super-baddy organisation. Basically, the actions of every character (and, possibly, every human being) is governed by the principle. Imagine it like a see-saw, with Fear at one end, Desire at the other. When a character's desire outweighs their fear, they move forward. When that mean old bully fear tips the balance, they freeze or retreat. The locus of optimum dramatic tension is the tipping point between the two – the trick is to sustain this as long as possible. Shakespeare kept Hamlet stewing in his own juices for five acts, prevaricating, unable to act. This was the Prince of Denmark's fatal flaw – he oscillated between 'to be or not to be', like some dodgy alternator. If he had killed Claudius in Act One, Scene One – end of story. Instead, Shakespeare wisely spun it out and elicited powerful drama from the psychological anguish experienced by the Dane at his tipping point, creating early Nordic noir.

`Yet, finally, the Hero must act – whatever the consequences. In *The Lord of the Rings*, Frodo and Sam reach the uninviting entrance to Shelob's Lair, reeking of carrion, plot snags and foul things. Neither of them are keen to enter – but they have a mission, to take the One Ring to Mount Doom and destroy it. This 'desire' outweighs their 'fear' and, steeling themselves (Frodo, with Sting) they step into the dark. This makes them heroes. Of course, if they had thought – 'sod this for a game of soldiers', and gone back to the Shire, they wouldn't have been (and they wouldn't have found much of a Shire to go back to). Novelist John Cowper Powys talked about how a character's behaviour is governed by a 'concatenation of imperatives'[161] – incrementally, things build up (like ounce weights on the scales) until the protagonists simply have no choice (or so it would seem to them), or if they do, it's a Hobson's Choice – a choice which is really no choice at all.

And so into the darkness the plucky hobbits step – with their magic sword in one hand, and the Light of Elendil in the other. And so must we, as writers – armed with only a pen (or keyboard) and the frail light of our inspiration. In the Welsh legend of the bard Taliesin, Gwion Bach is reborn shining with awen (inspiration), stolen from Ceridwen's cauldron – 'Behold the radiant brow!' cries the weir-ward when he is rediscovered, a helpless babe in a coracle. Consumed by our 'illumination' we venture into the Perilous Realm, like Wandering Aengus in WB Yeats' classic poem: 'I went for a walk in a hazel wood because a fire was in my head...'

Setting off on the Writer's Quest of the creative process is perhaps akin to being a knight in a medieval romance, venturing into the forest (although we are probably more like Parsifal at this stage – the Holy Fool – more than the accomplished Paladin). Be prepared to make a fool of yourself, turning up at Court on a donkey in a patchwork costume. Let yourself make mistakes – give yourself permission – because so much success comes from creative 'failure', from trial and error and happy accidents. Embark in the spirit of creative play – and you will be more likely to create something original. Start thinking that you 'know it all', that you have the answers, and you will have nothing to learn (and readers will probably be less inclined to listen). Start your quest with questions – and your journey will be a journey of discovery, fuelled by curiosity and delight, some of the essentials for a writer.

10 Essentials for a Writer

- Pen. Paper. A lack of excuses.
- Curiosity & Delight.
- A willingness to say 'yes' to life/a rebuttal of the 'no's'.
- Ability to rewrite and listen to feedback.
- Staying power (an internal composition engine).
- An appetite for adventure.
- Risk-taking.
- Boldness.
- Humour.
- A healthy book habit.

Gawain had a pentagram on his shield to remind him of the 'five Christian virtues'. In Scotland, at the Castle of the Muses, I met a South-African 'knight' called David told me of the essential chivalrous qualities as he sees them. A knight has:

- the wisdom to do what is right
- the will to make it happen
- and the strength to make it endure.

And he suggested the three traits of a warrior are: impeccability, unpredictability, and responsibility. These latter qualities could certainly apply to a writer: impeccability in terms of being conscientious of one's craft, attending to the details, keeping one's house in order; unpredictability, in terms of originality of thought, ideas and execution; and responsibility, in terms of what you write, what you choose to bring into the world. These are the qualities we need to summon in ourself as we heed the call to adventure and set off to face our foe. In essence, the Hero is our Higher Self – and writing can help us connect to it (as well as to our Lower Self, our Shadow).

I call these the Avatarian and Atavistic? Impulses.

Basically, writing can bring out the best and the worst in us – both in its execution and on the page. Writers can be beasts and saints, charismatic or tedious bores. Good to be around, or the partner/friend from Hell. Selfless, or selfish. Certainly there is an element of selfishness in writing – in indulging in one's fantasies, as well as in the single-mindedness needed to see a project through to completion; and yet one could argue that in spending precious years slaving away at a manuscript that *might* have an altruistic element (the edification of humanity!) we are being selfless to a certain extent (although in reality the act of writing is probably a blending of the -less and the -ish!). On the page, the Avatarian and Atavistic Impulses can manifest in the form of characters – we can personify them.

It could be argued that all characters are aspects of the author's personality (for where else do they come from? who else is writing it?). The Hero and Villain of a tale could be seen as the Higher and Lower Self of the author, although this is perhaps a crude analysis and things are often more nuanced than that.

Villains often 'act out' our Super-Egos (over-confident, slick, successful, sexually magnetic, etc); and Heroes can often be dysfunctional and even amoral. Martin Amis said that 'novels come from the base of the spine' – echoing Nabokov's 'tell-tale tingle down the spine'[162] – in the way that they explore powerful primal issues around security and identity. They can be an instinctual response to the world, almost beyond cognition – hence the mystery around the creative process, and where authors get their ideas from. Often, we can't say for certain – until afterwards. The first draft is often written 'in the dark' – in the process of unknowing, of seeking, or being 'driven' – and the second with the 'lights on'. The 'scary thing in the shadows' disturbs our status quo and forces us to give it voice, and then we 'wake up and smell the coffee' (or the stench of blood) and go in all guns blazing. First, Grendel; then Beowulf.

Of Beowulf, the bards sang:

'And many men stated that south or north,
Over all the world, or between the seas,
Or under the heaven, no hero was greater.'[163]

When we summon the Hero we are, in a way, evoking our better qualities – our unrealised potential – and giving them a form. There is often an element of wish-fulfilment, of power-fantasy (think of James Bond; Sherlock Holmes; Jason Bourne, etc). The Hero can carry for us all the things we wish we could do or be if only... By writing, we literally tap into these and give them dramatic form; and in the process, we inhabit these qualities. By channelling the archetype, for a while we become it. And this is part of the visceral (as well as intellectual) thrill of writing which is rarely discussed. The adrenalin rush of writing can be intoxicating and ... addictive. 'I feel gripped by something stronger than my will,' is how Alice W. Flaherty describes it.[164]

That is why, I believe, writing is the 'best of me' (as I tap into my Higher Self) and also when I often feel most fully alive (it can be exhilarating). When I am firing on all cylinders, the writer is a turbo-charged version of myself – I feel like I am stepping into my power and being most fully myself. I am living up to my own potential.

And so by becoming writers, we become in effect, the Hero of our own story. We are no longer the passive recipient of another's narrative. We have seized control of our own and writing our destiny into being.

Whether we accomplish it is another matter.

The way is littered with perils and pitfalls – not least that of Ego the Giant, who lumbers onto our path and threatens to overshadow the whole proceedings unless he is handled with care.

Next we will look at the Art of Bragging and how that feckless lunk, Ego, can be put to good use.

Summoning the Hero questings:

- Identify a writer/role model that you admire. Pin a postcard or quote from them by your desk.
- Consider what qualities do you admire in this writer. List them. How can you manifest them in your life? Create vows or affirmations to repeat daily before writing.
- A thought experiment. Picture yourself as a successful writer. Imagine what that would feel like. Visualise the life you would lead. How would you come across? What books would you have written? Now describe yourself as a successful writer in third person, as though it was a 'biog' on a book jacket. Dream big.
- Get an 'author photo' done – ask a friend and have a laugh posing in your glad rags; or have it done professionally. Design a mock book jacket of the 'book of your dreams'. Create a 'beta' website or blog to explore the hypothesis.

Fake it to make it, if necessary (many a successful writer are simply fakirs who made it). Start *believing* you are a writer and you will start *being* a writer.

3

Ego the Giant and the Art of Bragging

The arriving band of warriors are challenged on the shore by Hrothgar's thane. They bandy words in ritual exchange. The coast-guard accepts Beowulf at his word, and agrees to escort them to Heorot. He arranges for their ship to be guarded. Off to Hrothgar's hall they set, the sight of which impresses the Geats. Here, they are challenged a second time, by the royal herald. When the King is convinced of their honourable intent they are allowed in. Hrothgar fondly remembers how in his youth he had taken service with King Hrethel of Geatland. He has heard of Beowulf, who now declares his intent – to banish the curse of Grendel from the hall once and for all, without arms or armour to boot. Beowulf boasts of his prowess, but at the welcoming feast is challenged a third time – by Unferth, the King's advisor, who mocks the validity of his account of a swimming match against Breca. Beowulf soundly rebuffs this attack on his honour. He wins mead from the hand of Wealtheow the Queen. As the banquet ends and the company departs, Beowulf prepares for the intruder.

Reputation is everything in this Age of Heroes. As our hero Beowulf makes landfall on Danish shores he is confronted by no less than three threshold guardians: the watchman on the wall (who first challenges him on landing); Hrothgar's herald (who makes him follow the etiquette of the court); and Unferth (who mocks him at the feast). At each of these junctures Beowulf steps up to the mark, as *we* must – no matter how fierce the guardians we encounter.

Remember, they are there to test our tenacity. That is their very purpose.

Although these 'threshold guardians' could manifest in a

myriad of ways (they are the 'Ten Thousand Things' the Buddhists talk of – Maya – which we can be easily enamoured/ distracted by). In the context of Beowulf if we wanted to get symbolic about things, we could say these three guardians are the Inner Critic, the Outer Critic, and the Envious Friend – each of these can sabotage us.

The most insidious is perhaps the first – the Inner Critic – the voice inside our head that tells us that

we're not good enough, that it's not worth it, that it's all been done before. Some of these messages may actually be hand-me-downs from family, from school: a schoolteacher who ripped up your English essay in front of the class; the sneering sibling; the discouraging parent. We need to exorcise them. Prove them wrong. As with any of these guardian figures – see their challenge as a gauntlet thrown down before you. Pick it up, face them, defeat them.

The Outer Critic can be harder – it seems apparently objective. The bad review; the poor grade; the heckler; the low turnout; the lack of sales. Many artists make a point of not reading their reviews. Some feel, whatever their sales, gongs (or lack of them) they will do it anyway: create, because they must. Why should anyone deny you of your raison d'etre? The Outer Critics are like the mountain ranges, deserts, or wide oceans the hero must cross to achieve their goal. The tempests of fate, misfortune and the marketplace. Lash yourself to the mast, stop your ears with wax to ignore those maddening voices, and weather the storm. Do whatever you have to, and don't let the bastards grind you down. Your dream is more important than their hot air. It is oh-so easy to criticise, so much harder to create. The cynic never achieved anything. Let them polish the chip on their shoulder while you get on with forging art (that being said, it has to be acknowledged that there is a place for criticism at later stages of the creative process – indeed it is essential; and an insightful review can provide a good introduction, and sometimes enhance one's appreciation of the end product, placing it within a wider cultural context).

The final one, the Envious Friend, is the so-called buddy piqued by your tenacity, your achievement – the very fact you made it happen, or intend to – who sabotages you with a passing comment, a snide remark (their own shadow speaking). CS Lewis said to JRR Tolkien, upon hearing him read out an extract from *The Lord of the Rings* 'not another fucking elf!' There are those who, through their own insecurity, might want to shoot us down – although *sometimes* their ham-fisted asides *might* be healthy ballast, to stop us getting too inflated, we shouldn't let them stop our creative flow. Rather than think – 'that person's success overshadows my own'; instead try 'when a friend follows their star, it empowers me to do the same'. I like Julia Cameron's dictum: 'Success occurs in clusters and is born in generosity.'[165]

And yet, we need to be mindful of Ego the Giant. He can easily get out of hand. The way Beowulf is 'bigged up', first by the poet, then by the watchman, the herald, and then himself, it is no wonder it all seems to go to his head. He is depicted as some kind of super-hero, 'with the strength of thirty in the grip of each hand.' The sections dealing with Beowulf's arrival in Denmark, at Heorot, are full of boasting. There is a cultural reason for this – the art of bragging (from the Norse god of poetry, Bragi) was an intrinsic part of the warrior culture of the times. A man was as good as his word. The verbal contract was sacrosanct. To go back on your word was to lose honour. And honour was everything. Also, 'beautiful speech' (that is, ornate speechifying) was as much a part of a man's ornament as his torcs, armour and sword. Verbal bling to establish status. Finally, in battle, the hurling of insults and swaggering boastfulness was part of the ritual combat that acted as a kind of foreplay to the real thing – like fighting cocks brindling their feathers, raising their heads, puffing out their chests and making a lot of to-do before going in. This bardic posturing is simply the preening of wattles. In the poem, this takes on a formal quality when Beowulf states his intention to the hall, like a personal mission statement:

'I shall either perform deeds fitting an earl
Or meet in this mead-hall the coming of death![166]

Beowulf's boast has the gravitas and finality of a vow about it. The clock of destiny has been set ticking, as the poet lugubriously reminds us: 'Fate goes ever as fate must.'[167]

A writer can choose to do something similar – writing down their intention, and committing to it. Mature artists practise the art of containment, carefully incubating their project until it is ready to hatch. What one should avoid doing at all costs is telling an acquaintance (or passing stranger in a bar) about it. Whenever someone says: 'I am going to write a novel', the chances are they won't even start it, let alone finish it. If they were serious, they would be *doing it*, not talking about it. And two other things: you can tempt fate by doing so (if you want to make the gods laugh, tell them your plans); and you risk talking the life out of a project. Some 'writers' love talking about the book they are *going to* write and sharing the intricacies of the plot, the wonderfully quirky characters, the thrilling scenes – and you can hear the steam escaping from the boiler. It is all hot air and bluster – and their engine is left depleted. They are getting off on *the idea* of doing it, rather than *the act* of doing it. It can be buzz, when you feel fired up – but channel that into the actual writing. Write while the fire is in the head, and keep writing – you might find you manage to write half the first draft in one sitting, or even the whole thing (as Kerouac famously did with *On the Road* in a six-day amphetamine haze). This is when the ego can be your ally – it can give you the strength, the self-belief to keep going. You *need* to believe in yourself – if you don't, who will?

The ego is a vehicle you can use to deliver your message; as long as it doesn't get out of hand. Don't let your ego become a boy-racer. Let it be the 'Parker' to your 'Penelope', and your FAB1 will cruise to its destination, not end up a burnt-out shell in a ditch.

Beowulf is challenged in the mead-hall by the malcontent Unferth – about a particularly swimming-match undertaken against a childhood friend, Breca, who apparently won. For Unferth:

'His bold sea-voyaging, irked him sore;
He bore it ill that any man other
In all the earth should ever achieve
More fame under heaven than he himself.'[168]

Rather than being derailed by this (which would have disastrous consequences for Heorot) the hero rises to the challenge – dispatching Unferth's ungracious attacks on his reputation like so many monsters of the deep ('To slay with the sword-edge nine of the nicors' [169]). Beowulf's riposte casts himself in an even better light – he was delayed in completing the swimming-match because he was attacked by sea-monsters ('The grisly sea-beasts again and again/Beset me sore.' [170]). He wrestled with them to the sea-bed and slaughtered them all, making the shipping lanes safe for all. Swimming for five days in a freezing sea, wielding a sword *and* wearing chain-mail, fighting sea monsters single-handedly ... it all sounds rather far-fetched, and yet we are expected to swallow it. The inhabitants of Heorot clearly do, responding to the bragging match in good spirits – this is the equivalent of an Anglo-Saxon rap battle. Beowulf's boasts become outlandish:

'Bloody from battle; five foes I bound
Of the giant kindred, and crushed their clan.
Hard-driven in danger and darkness of night
I slew the nicors that swam the sea…' [171]

It would appear that a warrior's boastfulness is linked to his power – that strong words give a keener edge to his sword (akin to shamanic power; a medicine man singing his wares; a doctor in a mummers play stating his proficiency; a New Orleans Mardi Gras 'Indian' chief strutting his stuff):

> 'In the shades of darkness we'll spurn the sword.' [172]

What might appear to us as simply swagger and braggadocio is a way of preparing for the task ahead. Talking ourselves up (e.g. imagining ourselves as the writer we can be) might be a way of helping to make it happen – we enlarge our sense of self, and then step into that space. The opposite – being self-deprecating – can be self-defeating. Talking ourselves down can just be a cowardly 'get out clause', a petulant cop out (like saying: 'I didn't want to do it anyway'). Cynicism can be a mask for fear of our own failure. If we put everything 'down' (including ourselves) then nothing will be a disappointment. We don't have to try. We have let ourselves off the hook.

Attempting the 'impossible' – creating a work of originality and stunning skill – takes courage and a certain barnstorming attitude. The odds are stacked against you. But everyone loves an underdog. We love to root for Samson. It looks like Goliath is going to give him a pounding. Prove them wrong!

Beowulf sees off his competition – wiping the floor with Unferth, the epitome of sour grapes. What the Geatish champion says is almost irrelevant – it is the *way* he says it, with such conviction. Nothing can shake him; a quality that the King appreciates. Hrothgar values: 'the warrior's steadfastness and his word', and allows him to join the feast to 'relish the triumph of heroes to your heart's content.' He has earned a taste of the hero's portion – by stepping up to the mark (unlike the niggardly Unferth).

By not hiding his light under a bushel he wins the favour of the Lady of the Hall, Hrothgar's comely wife – who, in the role of mead-giver, is a variant of the Goddess of Sovereignty figure:

> 'Then the woman was pleased with the words he uttered,
> The Geat-lord's boast; the gold-decked queen
> went in state to sit by her lord.'[173]

In her sun-like imagery she is worth more than gold itself – for Beowulf has won the Muse. By being in his power, (potently fulfilling his potential) he has attracted her. The awen has descended and the Goddess graces him with Her presence. For a deeper exploration of 'Courting the Muses' see **The Dragon's Hoard**. But, for now, let us end this testosterone-driven section with a footnote to the god of bragging.

We get the word and notion of 'bragging' from the Norse god of poet, Bragi, who drunk of the skaldic mead stolen by Odin from a giant's daughter – thus, the 'gift of the gab' is seen as a gift of the Gods. An important caveat – as Odin flew back to Valhalla, godly stomach bloated with the mead he had guzzled down, some of it 'leaked' out and fell to Earth... Those who received this divine micturation (Odin's urine), instead of the good stuff direct from the source, have a tainted gift (politicians come to mind...). Their lips are lubricated by the bladder, not the vat (perhaps that is why the fool's symbol is the 'bladder-stick' – to flag up their seemingly foolish talk and acknowledge their mandate for 'taking the piss'). Yet Bragi's gift is a double-edged sword. Bragging can easily become 'full of sound and fury, signifying nothing' – as in the classic pub bore; a drunken tongue-lashing; a talk-show host; or Prime Minister's question time: rival primates either side of a territory-bounding stream, banging their chests and raising a din. We need to follow Beowulf's example – he decides to face his foe in single-combat, unarmed. When all the noisy revellers have gone to bed, he will be left to face his enemy alone. Stripped of the showy trappings of his personality – his ego – he is ready to confront the painful truth.

Ego the Giant and the Art of Bragging questings:

1. List your best qualities.
2. List your worst.
3. Consider both lists. What would help you in your Writer's Quest? What would hinder?
4. What messages does your Inner Critic give you?
5. What messages does your Outer Critic give you?
6. What messages does your Envious Friend give you?
7. What messages would you like to give to them? Write them out, read them out, shout them out!
8. Create a caricature of yourself, exaggerating your qualities. If you can draw, do this on a balloon. Then pop it. Or make a piñata of yourself and take a baseball bat to it. Learn to laugh at yourself at regular intervals. You are fallible and sometimes foolish. That's okay.
9. Create a scrapbook or album of your achievements. Reflect on what you can do, have done, and will do. Write a series of affirmations reminding yourself of these.
10. Find a 'believing mirror' – someone who wants to support you in your creative journey. Book your tired old ego in for a massage now and then.

4

A Night at Heorot

In the middle of the night Grendel arrived in bloody fashion, slaughtering sleeping warriors slumbering after the feast. Beowulf confronts the night-lurker and grapples with him hand-to-hand. The Geat rips off one of Grendel's arms, who flees into the night.

There comes a time when you finally have to knuckle down to it – the Great Task. You have summoned the Hero (within) and now you must step up to the mark (or to the desk, unless you are of the Hemingway persuasion, in which case you can stand). This will be your defining moment as a fledgling writer – as you really one, or was all that talk just hot air?

Virginia Woolf talked of the importance of a 'room of one's own'. Wherever or whatever it is – be it a boatshed like Dylan Thomas'; a garden office frequented by Philip Pullman; a cork-lined Parisian apartment resided in by Proust; or pottering in an Edinburgh café like JK Rowling, for the time you spend writing there, it is your Heorot. See Hrothgar's hall as a metaphor for your imagination – vast and majestic. This is your special place – the place you go inside yourself when you write – utterly unique to you: 'the famous mead-hall was finished and done./ To distant nations its name was known,/The Hall of the Hart...'[174] This 'hall of the heart' is a precious place and deserves protecting – like Beowulf, Hrothgar's retainer, guard it jealously.

And yet, be prepared to go through Hell while you're there. You will face your demons. You will gnash your teeth and tear out your hair. You will sweat, bleed, and weep.

Writing is a lonely business. No one else will write that masterpiece for you (unless you pay a ghost writer, in which case – get out of here, you're a celebrity). Doris Lessing wisely said:

'Literature comes from a man or woman sitting alone in a room with a phone off the hook, probably a cup of coffee, and in the good old days, a cigarette.' Don't make excuses, make it happen. Steinbeck wrote: 'This is the writing job, the loneliest work in the world. If I fail there is only one person in the world to blame...'

Although we should be wary of 'spontaneous house-work' (the compulsive sharpening of pencils, obsessive desk tidying, and other random displacement activities) there *is* something to be said for an orderly writing space. I love the description of Blake's room, from a letter of Samuel Palmer's (1860): 'his rooms, were clean and orderly; everything was in its place. His delightful working corner had its implements ready – tempting to the hand. The millionaire's upholsterer can furnish no enrichments like those of Blake's enchanted rooms.' Your study, if you are lucky enough to have one, is your Heorot. Yet imagination is the ultimate upholsterer – with it we can re-enchant the mundane. And so, we do not need a fancy 'garden office' with perfect views, however enticing that would be. All we need is a knee and a notepad. With our imagination, we are free – wherever we are, as Shakespeare so eloquently put: 'O God, I could be bounded in a nutshell, and count myself a king of infinite space ...'[175] The chilling caveat here is '...were it not that I have bad dreams…' but as writer's we can turn those 'bad dreams' into prose, poetry, and plays.

Like Beowulf, you are going to give Grendel – a bad dream incarnate – a run for his money. Hero and antagonist finally clash in a spectacular melee, and in that conflict (between Higher and Lower Self; between our dreams and our nightmares; our fears and desires) the most exciting, muscular writing is created – sentences with frisson fly off the page. However difficult circumstances can be (and writers over the centuries have endured the worst) from such creative tension the best work can be produced. A place of safety, of comfortable happiness, of artistic complacency, can produce bland results. Writing from our comfort zones, we have artistically 'snoozed off on the couch'. We have regurgitated TV dinners and soap operas. But if you are prepared to take risks and make yourself vulnerable – as Beowulf does, stripped down, armour-less and weaponless – then something good might result. Writing with an edge. It is terrifying, grappling with our demons in the night – but if you can hold your nerve you can produce something of true worth.

This is what I call the 'unflinching gaze'. If you can stay with that which you find most challenging, most unbearable – you will produce writing of real authenticity and power. You will find the voice in the shadows. It takes a warrior's heart to endure this:

> 'A terror fell on the Danish folk
> As they heard through the wall the horrible wailing,
> The groans of Grendel, the foe of God
> Howling his hideous hymn of pain,
> The hell-thane shrieking in sore defeat.'[176]

Withstand this and you will be a true hero. Burn the midnight oil – metaphorically, or literally. Stay with it. Wrestle this beast into submission – and when you finally come up for air, perhaps returning to it the next day with a cup of coffee, a bit wiped out, you'll be unspeakably satisfied, as was Beowulf: 'he was happy with his nightwork/ and the courage he had shown.' Somehow, against all odds, you have managed to wrench this 'dirty first draft' – like Beowulf ripping off Grendel's arm. It's not the whole beast, but it's one helluva start:

This bloody stump is your first draft, plucked from the abyss. It is raw and dripping – ugly to all except its creator – but you have rendered it with your own hands. Your night in Heorot has produced results. You have showed what you are made of. Perhaps you are a writer after all (many fail this first test of courage). As Hrothgar had said in his parting saw:

'Be mindful of glory, show forth your strength,
Keep watch against foe! No wish of your heart
Shall go unfulfilled if you live through the fight.'[177]

Writing can redeem the worst experiences and celebrate the best. It is essential we face our demons in the dark, share our hard-won wisdoms, and sing our journey's song. The personal is powerful. Go where the pain is – that's where the power is. In the next chapter we'll examine this bloody stump in more detail.

A Night at Heorot questings:

- What experiences have influenced you? Without pausing make an instant list of key moments. The first things that come to you often would have had the greatest impact.
- Imagine your memory as an attic full of old boxes. Is there something there which is long-neglected, or hidden away? Something you'd rather forgot or not face? Gently, carefully pick it up and take a good look inside. Describe it. Read back. Reflect. You're still here. You have survived all this time. Maybe now you are strong enough to face it and put it into perspective.
- What is your earliest memory? Describe as vividly as possibly. Evoke the 5 senses. Don't worry if you can't remember every detail. Acknowledging the fallibility of memory (rather than claiming total recall) will make it more authentic.
- Defining Moments. Consider 'the day you stepped up to the mark' – or failed to. Write about it.
- Consider inspiring people in your life: what was it about them? Have they become role models? In what way? Create a personal 'Roll of Honour'. In our writing we can honour the memory of such key figures, sing the unsung heroes/heroines of our life-story.

- Which challenging people have you met in your life? What buttons did they press? How do they seem now?
- Negativity can be used in a positive way. List all the things you dislike, detest, and loathe. Pick one and vent your spleen. Notice how your writing suddenly has an energy about it. Such qualities are good ingredients for a 'villain' in your story, or subjects to explore. Going beyond your comfort zone will give your writing edge.
- What moves you, what inspires you? What do you consider beautiful, sacred? List the things that you love.

5

The Bloody Limb

Grendel's bloody tracks are followed to the edge of the mere, where he seems to have been swallowed. The monster's defeat apparently confirmed, there is much rejoicing in the Hall. Hrothgar praises Beowulf and showers him with gold.

You have endured a night in Heorot and survived – returning from the abyss with proof: a dirty first draft. It 'ain't pretty', and it doesn't need to be. One of the key concepts the beginner writer needs to understand is – you don't have to get it right the first time. Writing is a process and the first draft is simply that – the start of the journey. Too often, fledgling writers in the euphoria of having produced something feel 'that's just the way it is', and it cannot be changed. The first draft should never be the finished draft – and even when it sees print it isn't set in stone (later editions can be revised as the printer's devil – the inevitable typo – is expunged). At this embryonic stage, the first draft is likely to full of those devils – like so many Grendels lurking in the pages – and need banishing. That is when the hard work begins – writing is in the rewriting. To present the first draft, riddled with typographical and grammatical errors, inaccuracies and bloopers, and expect readers to 'like it the way it is' is not being considerate to them. A good rule of thumb is to write the first draft for yourself – don't show it to anyone – then subsequent drafts with the reader in mind. Stephen King, master of the monstrous in the mundane, recommends to: 'write the first draft with the door closed, the second with it open', i.e. invite feedback after completing that first draft – it is a good idea to avoid feedback at this initial stage, otherwise it can stop you dead in your tracks. Certainly, when it comes to the redrafting it is wise to follow John Cowper Powys' advice and 'edit in cold blood', but to start with, write while the 'fire in the head' is with you ... and keep going until it flickers out. That first draft should come from a place of passion, from some intuition or inkling – a mysterious voice, which you start to pick up, perhaps falteringly at first – like some obscure radio station at the end of the dial. It can take a while to tune in, or it can just burst through one day (or one night) unexpectedly. It is hard to control, at first – it seems to come from 'another place', which might be the subconscious/unconscious, so I advise to 'write with the right brain, edit with the left.' In essence, the right side deals with the lateral, artistic side of things; the left with the logical, literal side. You need ultimately both – what John Fowles calls the 'wild man and the academic'. These relate to the Avatarian and Atavistic impulses discussed earlier.

Beowulf is justifiably proud of the outcome of this first battle with the 'monster in the night': 'He was happy with his nightwork/and the courage he had shown'. He had stepped up to the mark and proven his mettle. All we can do at this early stage is 'block it out, then hack it back' later.

In defeating this monster, the writer learns another key lesson – one Arthur Quiller-Couch advised: to 'Murder your darlings' – that is, to cut out any excessively lyrical passages (what is called 'purple prose'). A beginner writer might feel especially proud of these sections; mistakenly thinking they have to use the longest words they know, or write in dense sentences. Cutting out those pretty words may feel like drowning a litter of mewling kittens in a sack, but we have to – Grendel and his kin belong at the bottom of the lake:

'...the monster had sunk from the sight of men.
In that fenny covert the cursed fiend
Not long thereafter laid down his life,
His heathen spirit; and hell received him.'[178]

With the great deed accomplished, Beowulf seeks acclaim – perhaps too quickly. It is certainly wise to ask for feedback – a healthy cross-section of opinion is invaluable – but it is also wise to wait until the second draft.

'Beowulf's prowess was praised in song'[179]

However worthy the accomplishment is, we have to be wary of bland praise from well-meaning friends and family. There is nothing worse (or more useless) than someone saying 'that's nice, I liked it.' This is often because they haven't the skill to critique it properly, or they are being discreet – and damning by faint praise. Being mollycoddled won't get you anywhere. Tough love is far more effective in toughening up your writer self, in hide-tanning. A good writing teacher will not crush hope, nor will they pamper a student's illusion by praising poor work. It seems as though many students simply seek approval – they want an authority figure to tell them if they are 'good enough' or not. Well, if they need such messages to write, then they are writing for the wrong reasons. *Write for writing's sake – because you have to.* You shouldn't need permission or a gold star. No one should put you off – although one should listen to feedback, and when there is a consensus, act.

After the night at Heorot, when Grendel is defeated, Hrothgar returns in the day and lavishes great praise, and many prizes, on Beowulf. He is praised too much, too soon – for Grendel's mother is yet to strike. The battle has been won with the 'monsters in the night', but not the war.

Yet in this praise-giving, there are many examples of beautiful speech and a meta-narrative element of a tale within a tale. A scop, an Anglo-Saxon bard, relates a resonant tale of a dragon-slayer:

'Time and again a gleeman chanted,
A minstrel mindful of saga and lay.

He wove his words in a winsome pattern,
Hymning the burden of Beowulf's feat,
Clothing the story in skilful verse.'[180]

It is interesting to note the discipline here, exercised by this wordsmith in his craft. This is in sharp contrast to the 'bloody limb' of our writer-Beowulf – the product of a later stage of the creative process, by which time phrases are finely-honed, rehearsed and delivered with skill.

The core of the scop's tale is worth repeating here – for its dragon element, which could be seen as a metaphor of the creative process itself:

Sigmund was made famous for slaying a dragon who guarded a rich hoard. The hero had entered the barrow alone. There, he fought with the monster. His sword passed through its breast and into the stone. The dragon slain, the hoard was his – he loaded a boat with his booty. The dragon melted away.

The dragon is the 'guardian of the hoard' – earlier in the epic the poet used the phrase 'unlocked his word-hoard'. There is a sense that language, and its mastery, is the true treasure here. Dragons are sometimes depicted as extremely intelligent monsters. By mastering such a beast, the writer-hero masters their language. 'His daring had given him/total possession/of the treasure-hoard.' All the words of your native tongue should be at your disposal, as Edward Thomas implores in his poem 'Words':

Out of us all
That make rhymes,
Will you choose
Sometimes –
As the winds use
A crack in the wall

Or a drain,
Their joy or their pain
To whistle through–
Choose me, You English words?

With his or her sword-pen, the dragon-hoard is defeated – piercing its hide, and unlocking its blood-gold-words. 'The hot dragon melted', like hot lead type being hammered into place, ready for the press. Such a beast can be elusive, as Beowulf found with Grendel:

'I thought to grip him in stubborn grasp
And bind him down on the bed of death,
There to lie straining in struggle for life,
While I gripped him fast lest he vanish away.
But I might not hold him or hinder his going,
For God did not grant it, my fingers failed.'[181]

This is the elusive nature of inspiration – it can easily be lost by a moment's distraction (as Coleridge experience with his Kubla Khan, or a 'a vision of a dream' – hundreds of lines were composed in his head, but he was interrupted by a man from Porlock before he could write them all down) that slippery first draft is like a new born foal.

Yet, however messy that first outpouring, the writer has produced results – which silence those doubters, the Unferths of life:

'Then slower of speech was the son of Ecglaf,
More wary of boasting of warlike deeds,
While the nobles gazed at the grisly claw,
The fiend's hand fastened by hero's might
On the lofty roof.'[182]

With his daring deed, Beowulf has gained, rightly, the praise of the Queen:

'You have earned the undying honour of heroes
In regions reaching as far and wide
As the windy walls that the sea encircles.
May Fate show favour while life shall last!
I wish you wealth to your heart's content'[183]

This seems a bit premature for the fledgling writer – there is still an awfully long way to go before we can hope to achieve such glory, if ever. For now, we should acknowledge our first 'result' as a 'good start', and get stuck in to the rest.

Another useful metaphor is provided in the refurbishment of the semi-ruined Heorot, which during the battle had its hinges ripped off, and much of its interior damaged.

'In joyful haste was Heorot decked
And a willing host of women and men
Gaily dressed and adorned the guest-hall.
Splendid hangings with sheen of gold
shone on the walls, a glorious sight
To eyes that delight to behold such wonders.'[184]

In conjuring this tableaux with skill, the poet illustrates the power and precision of language to create such 'woven scenes'. A good story should be like a well-built house – with each scene like rooms, leading logically from one to the next. In rendering these scenes with the gold thread of detail, we weave them into vignettes that attract and hold the 'eye's attention'. The very fabric of Heorot is like the construction of a novel – structure is its architecture. We begin in creative 'chaos' and slowly bring our house to order – until the words, like Wealtheow's mead, flows.

Bloody Limb Questings:

- Review what you have written so far.
- Consider what you need to 'let go of' in this first draft, e.g. excessive description; redundant dialogue; exposition.
- What do you still need to 'get to grips with', in terms of the writing craft? Characterisation? Point of View? Structure? Editing? Seek guidance or tuition in your weakest areas (see **Further Reading**).

6

Needful Digressions

A victory feast is prepared. The scop entertains, relating analogous tales of monster-slayers. He then sings of warfare between the Danes and the Frisians in a famous digression. Wealtheow awards Beowulf further treasures.

Flushed with success (and mead), Beowulf is entertained by the scops of Hrothgar's hall. The poet allows us to eavesdrop upon this merry night, as the minstrel relates the saga of Finn and his sons:

'Then song and revelry rose in the hall;
Before Healfdene's leader the harp was struck
And hall-joy wakened; the song was sung'[185]

Although the sequence is beautifully wrought, does it serve the narrative? It seems to derail the forward momentum of the narrative. An *element* of this would have served perhaps better. Instead, we are forced to endure the endless merriment – which, if you are not partaking of it – can become rapidly tedious. The bard becomes the pub bore – 'harping on'.

In our own writing we have to resist the windbag – he easily creeps in, downloading his tedious anecdotes (so fascinating to the protagonist) if we're not careful. Unexpurgated exposition is known as 'info-dump' – to be avoided at all costs. The wise writer skilfully weaves in exposition in subtle ways – drip-feeding vital information to the reader, like trails of bread-crumbs ... leading them on.

The vital thing to remember is communicate *with* the reader, not *at* them. Once I was dismayed to hear one of writing students state that he was more interested in his ideas, than in the words. For a fiction-writer to wish to convey ideas, more than craft realistic characters, snappy dialogue, gripping plots, and so on, is a case of putting the cart before the horse. It smacks of the didactic agenda-peddling, and a disdain for the materials of one's craft. Entertain your reader and they might be willing to listen. Hector them from your soap-box and they will probably walk on by.

The constant risk when working on a longer writing project, is the interjection of other ideas – worthy in themselves, but not appropriate for the current book. This is like Hrothgar's scop – the windbag in the wings – there is a time and place for him to share his repertoire, but it might not be in the cut-and-thrust of your main narrative arc.

When these ideas arise – as inevitably they will, especially if your magnum opus is taking years – then simply put them on ice. Store them up until you are ready to use them. Make a note of them in your notebook; write an outline and place it in an 'Other Ideas' folder; create an 'Ideas Bank' space on your computer.

And don't let yourself be distracted! Stick to writing the main narrative. Do not waver from your goal – like a hero in a story, be focused on your great task. By doing so we avoid shoe-horning in other material, making the manuscript increasingly unwieldy – a portmanteau of all our ideas.

Yet even great heroes get waylaid. Odysseus spent nine years on Ogygia with Calypso – enjoying a protracted beach holiday and holiday romance, while his wife Penelope fended off suitors back home. In this instance, the hiatus is part of the narrative. Homer was employing a technique that all storytellers worth their salt use – the art of postponement. The greater the distance between Set Up and Pay Off, the greater the dramatic tension. If Odysseus made it home straight away ('beam me up, Hermes') there wouldn't have been the twenty four books of *The Odyssey* – one of the greatest epics even written. This protraction needs to occur in both the micro- and macro-structures of the narrative.

Each scene can have an element of Set Up and Pay Off (e.g. rushing to a meeting with a friend/arriving late/friend has left); as can each section or 'Act' of the tale (e.g. Act One could be the Bank Heist – its preparation and execution). The drama comes from subverting the expected outcome – the line of desire of the protagonist, who must encounter obstacles – otherwise there is no conflict, no drama, and therefore no story.

In Heorot the fact that the company of revellers are distracted by the scop's tale, by the feasting and ring-giving, actually *serves* the narrative – because it builds up a sense of the 'danger having passed'; lulling the reader/listener into a false sense of security – which can paradoxically actually increase the tension, because we know there is more to come (the book or saga has only just started); and so we watch the celebration with dramatic irony – aware that doom is just around the corner. The poet flags this up, introducing the recurring motif of fatalism:

> 'Men drank of the wine-cup, knowing not Fate,
> Nor the fearful doom that befell the earls
> When darkness gathered'[186]

The scop recites his beautiful words – frail and fleeting treasures in the night; as does the poet of Beowulf. A fragment of it was nearly lost. A sequence known as 'The Fight at Finnsburgh' appears in an obscure tract by George Hickes[187]. In one of these 'Indiana Jones' moments of English Literature, Hickes found it on a leaf bound up with a collection of homilies in Lambeth Palace library – the leaf has subsequently been lost. Fortunately, Hickes transcribed it. The fragment is connected to the scop's tale of Finn. It describes the defence of a hall, by Hnaef and his men (echoing Beowulf's defence of Heorot). It begins in media res, with a speech by a man guarding the door of the hall, who mistakes the distant sounds of battle for a fire, perhaps one caused by a dragon:

'...the horns of the house, hall-gables burning?'
'Battle-young' Hnaef breaks the silence, explaining the sound:

'It is not the eaves aflame, nor in the east yet
Does day break; no dragon flies this way.
It is the soft clashing of claymores you hear
that they carry to the house.' [188]

It is a tantalising fragment, with some vivid kennings:

'Hoar wolf's howl, hard wood-talk,
shield's answer to shaft'. [189]

The manuscript of Beowulf itself was nearly lost in a fire, and still bears the scorch marks of this near calamity – as though scorched by dragon-breath – which makes it all the more precious.

It is a miracle such rare leaves survive at all. And the very words of the poet are uttered in defiance of death, of the oblivion that awaits us all. The Anglo-Saxon poem known as 'The Ruin', written about the ruins of the Roman temple of Aquae Sulis echo this note of mortality:

Well-wrought the wall.
Wyrd broke it.
Wyrd this stronghold burst.
Snapped roof-beams, fell towers.
The work of stonesmith giants moulders.
Rime scours gatepost and mortar,
shattered the shower-shields,
the heavy eaves.

Age under-ate them.

And the wielders and wrights?

Gone, long gone:
held fast in graves grasp while fifty fathers and sons have passed.[190]

Yet like the custom of offering finely-wrought treasures to the ancestors – casting swords, shields, torcs and the like into bodies of water – the writer is continually casting his treasures into the depths. Editing is an act of sacrifice. We have to be prepared to cast our shining words into the dark waters (i.e. the 'cutting room floor'). It is often heart-breaking, but we need nerves of steel to be a writer – to hold true to our purpose, and not become bogged down in indulgent sentimentality. Be prepared to redact whole chapters – even to jettison a whole manuscript – if you find yourself going off on a tangent. If you have started in the wrong place, and 'gone off on one' then be honest enough to accept this – scrap it and start again, and your writing will be the better for it. I did this with a 10,000 word essay[191] – which I realised was taking the wrong approach. I dumped it and began again – yet, it wasn't wasted, because by writing those 10,000 words I got to my epiphany, the all important breakthrough.

Sometimes, you have to go to Finnsburgh to realise you don't need to be there.

Nothing is wasted – it is all part of the process – that doesn't mean you include it all. Anything but. Cut. Cut. Cut.

Needful Digressions Questings:

- What was it you were trying to say in the first place? Have you thrown the baby out with the bath-water? Write a summary of this and cross-reference. Check it is still there. If not, how can you weave it in?
- What 'needful digression' would enrich your creative journey, e.g. a research trip, a writing retreat, a visit to an inspiring exhibition?

- Once a day allow yourself to be 'distracted'. If something unexpected happens, go with it. Be spontaneous and follow this sudden surge of energy. See where it takes you. Often such moments of serendipity let the magic slip through.

7

A Dish Served Up Cold

Grendel's monstrous mother, grieving for her son, issues from her lair and makes for Heorot, where she slays Aeschere, the Royal adviser – catching the groggy revellers off-guard before they manage to fend her off. Snatching her son's limb, she returns to the lonely mere. Hrothgar is grief-stricken at the loss of his old friend, and offers Beowulf great reward if he was able to avenge the tragic loss and vanquish the bane of Heorot for good. Unferth offers his ancestral sword, Hrunting, for the task.

Heady with the apparent victory of Beowulf, Hrothgar's court is unprepared for a second onslaught. Bad luck seldom comes alone – haven't they heard of the law of threes? There is another monster lurking in the foul places, the deadlier of the species – Grendel's mother:

Although Grendel and his mother are cousins of all such monsters that lurk at the edge of the human imagination – the dragons; chimeras; wendigos; krakens; behemoths; gorgons; minotaurs; spectres; phantoms and ghouls – there is something 'closer' to them. They are humanoid, if not human, as Heaney suggests: 'they remain, for all their power to terrorize, creatures of the physical world.'[192]

It is telling that they are 'fatherless creatures'. Might Grendel's torment stem from being a bastard castaway: 'one seemed man,/An outcast wretch of another world,/Huger far than a human form./Grendel my countrymen called him, not knowing/What monster-brood spawned him, what sire begot'[193]. It is as though God fashioned him, and then, seeing his work was flawed, abandoned him in disgust.

In opposition to this 'absent father', Grendel's mother is the ultimate animus – the very embodiment of feminine rage, and one reading of the story (giving it a topical ecological spin) would be to see her as personifying the wounded earth itself: a Gaia driven mad by pollution, the destruction of her children and depletion of her natural resources. Since her and her son are both creatures of wild – 'they dwell apart', the genius loci of the liminal – in contrast to the men who dwell within the hall, or their wooden houses and ships, then this nature/human divide is made aesthetically clear.

> 'Wild and lonely the land they live in,
> Wind-swept ridges and wolf-retreats' [194]

Denied their right to exist, these monsters – on the verge of extinction – lash out.

The poet describes how they are the offspring of Cain: 'begetting a brood/ of grisly monsters'. Thus, 'banished and branded', they are the product of a crime against nature:

> 'The mother of Grendel, a monstrous hag,
> Brooded over her misery, doomed to dwell
> In evil waters and icy streams
> From ancient ages when Cain had killed
> His only brother, his father's son.' [195]

Grendel's mother 'rabid and raging' and 'resolved/On a dreadful revenge for the death of her son!'[196] enters from the dark wild wastes into the bright warm hall while the company sleep. Beowulf and Hrothgar are at rest, elsewhere. They are spared this slaughter, for now. It was another, who paid the blood-tithe: 'But one paid dear/For his evening rest.' [197]

Hell hath no fury like a woman scorned – or a mother in grief. This 'hell-dam' exacts a terrible toll on the sleeping revellers. Something crucial has been left out in the first draft. The 'monster in the night' is not finished with you yet. It will not let go until you have heard its cry. In exchange for her son's arm, she seizes Hrothgar's 'right hand man', his closest adviser, Aeschere. The toll of the deadly dame is high. She must be placated. If you are not prepared to offer you very best, she will take it anyway. She has no truck with lily-livered dabblers who give up after the first premature effort; who try to write a cynically commercial effort, or something ironically conceited. She wants the real deal – the very heart of you: 'He was of heroes the dearest to Hrothgar,/The best of comrades between two seas.'[198] If you are not putting your heart and soul into it, why bother? You are wasting your gift and other people's time. This terrible deed occurs while Beowulf is elsewhere, while the King is asleep. You need to summon them back, quickly. Turn up, fully, to the page. When Beowulf returns, '...the hero came tramping into the hall/With his chosen band – the boards resounded.'[199]

Hrothgar is beside himself with grief. There can be no rest until this wrong is righted: "Ask not of pleasure; pain is renewed/For the Danish people. Aeschere is dead!"[200]

A bitter taste is left after the splendid victory feast by this 'fierce ravager ... avenging her kinsman[201]'. This is the dish served up cold, as the fires of triumph cooled in the hearth and heads groggy with the sweetness of Wealtheow's mead lay down upon the benches to rest.

The writer cannot be complacent upon their quest – they must be ever vigilant. If his will, her watchfulness, wanes, even for an instant, an insidious tide can creep in that will wreak havoc and corrupt the project.

In story-terms, we see in this section the power of 'amplification', of upping the stakes. The poet has introduced an unexpected but not implausible turn of events. It feels like an inevitable progression. Everything has consequence. The tension-level surges once more, after the 'false dawn' of Grendel's death. We are in the hands of a master storyteller who will keep our pulses pounding. He knows he must remain at the head of this 'ship' – like Beowulf, he must take charge; otherwise he risks:

> 'Many a saddened thane/
> Who grieves in his heart for his treasure-giver.' [202]

A people need a wise and strong leader, like a narrative needs a writer who knows what he or she is doing. Let slip, and all Hell breaks loose. Any 'chaos' should be conscious – deliberate acts of savagery, not random malevolence. Everything in a story needs to have a purpose – to build up to something meaningful, whatever the prevailing ethos.

At the same time, it is important to acknowledge that the writing process – especially the 'first time around' – can be mysterious, and we might not know where it is going. Once we get into the 'zone' all kinds of unexpected material might rise to the surface, disturbing us in the night.

Whatever the conscious narrative of our project is – what we actively deal with in our plot, characters, themes, and title, there is always a subconscious narrative – one below the surface, one we may not be aware of. I am not talking about sub-plots and sub-text here. I mean what is just below your own radar. Whatever your main characters symbolise – one might be a 'voice-piece' character, mirroring your own world-view – you need to represent the opposite. A diametrically opposed character to your protagonist will make a fine antagonist, and give voice to the 'Other'. If you do not factor it in – it will be flagged up in good feedback, hopefully circumventing the negative reviews (because, guarantee by then, the telling absence – the unheard voice – will be noted). Those bad reviews, ripping your lovingly crafted masterpiece to shreds will seem like Grendel's mother. Avoid this traumatic experience, by giving voice to the critic inside the narrative – letting the 'Other' be heard, be it the voice of the heretic, the dispossessed, the right-winger to your left-field character, the believer to your atheist protagonist, the sceptic to the romantic, and so on.

Let the darkness speak.

Before we can move on, the 'lurker in the lake' must be faced – the absent presence of this void is an inevitable part of the quest. Like a black hole in the heart of the book – it will suck everything into its point of singularity.

And the only way is through.

A Dish Served Up Cold questings:

- What values does your main character represent?
- What are the opposite of these?
- Are these antithetical themes represented/given voice in your narrative?
- If not, could you create a character/a situation where these will be addressed/dramatised?
- What other qualities are not present in your project, e.g. Humour? Sacredness? The contemporary? Diversity? How could you give voice to these, without letting them 'take over' the story?
- What would the voice of the heretic say about your project? Imagine being the boy in the 'Emperor's New Clothes' – what is the one obvious thing you are not allowing yourself to see? Too serious? Too long? Too indulgent? Too rambling? Too short? Too fragmentary? Too similar? Too clichéd? Speak the unspeakable.
- Are you representing a cross-section of opinion within the story fairly? If not, how would the 'other voices' feel? Write a monologue, imagining their perspective. Let them speak. Were you surprised by their vehemence? Could you bring this energy into the story? How could you 'show' it?

- Consider the major actions of your characters? Are there any consequences that are not being shown or dealt with? These are plot-holes – how do you intend to fix these?

8

The Lurker in the Lake

Beowulf travels to the mere, which seethes with loathsome creatures. He slays one as the rest flee. His warriors await on the shore, as he swims to its bottom where he finds a cave – here he confronts Grendel's mother. In the heat of battle Unferth's sword fails; but Beowulf manages to overcome his opponent and slays her with another blade, a giant's sword, snatched from the hoard. Exhausted, he returns to the surface with proof of his victory: Grendel's head and the jewelled hilt of the giant's blade – the rest melted away by the hell-dam's blood.

The lonely mere where Grendel's mother dwells is vividly evoked by the poet of Beowulf, ('the lonely mere/Where trees firm-rooted and hung with frost/Overshroud the wave with shadowing gloom.'[203]) grimly setting the scene of this perilous encounter – the second of the hero's three mighty battles with the monstrous. The lake is a symbol of the subconscious; the realm of the feminine – fathomless, mysterious and possibly perilous ('no man so wise/ Who knows the bound of its bottomless depth.'[204]). Its depths have never been 'sounded by the sons of men' – no one knows how deep it is. It is the ultimate 'rabbit hole' – that is, a portal to the Underworld. How far down the rabbit hole do you want to go?

This sense of depthlessness is a crucial phase of the creative process. We enter this 'inner zone' in a Cloud of Unknowing – not certain how long the 'ordeal' will take, or even if we will succeed and come out the other side. John Steinbeck, on embarking on his King Arthur project in his later years[205], described it as 'I am now going into the darkness of my own mind.' In a letter to his friend Chase Horton, in relation to his deepening research into the Matter of Britain, he writes: 'A curious state of suspension has set in, kind of a floaty feeling like the drifting in a canoe on a misty lake while ghosts and winkies, figures of fog, go past – half-recognised, and only partly visible.'[206]

It is the classic 'Belly of the Whale' experience that many heroes undergo – in spiritual terms it is the Dark Night of the Soul; in alchemical, the *nigredo* phase – the blackening, when the dross rises to the surface, as a precursor to the true ore being revealed. Jung saw it as an important part of the patient's recovery. As a student of alchemy, he (and his followers) 'compared the "black work" of the alchemists (the nigredo) with the often highly critical involvement experienced by the ego, until it accepts the new equilibrium brought about by the creation of the self.'[207] WB Yeats described it as: 'to struggle again with the shadow, as with some older night.' [208]In terms of writing, it is time to turn that 'bloody stump' of a first draft into something more complete. It is time to sort out 'unfinished business'. It is essential to remember that the first draft is *never* the finished draft. Beginner writers are often dismayed by this realisation, that it is only the start of the journey, and there is an awful lot more work to be done. If we have received constructive feedback – perhaps from a writing tutor, or good writers' circle – we would have been given some clues: often to go more deeply into the process (as Lindsay Clarke advocates in his essay 'Going the Extra Inch' [209]). Our first attempt has only scraped the surface. Now we must fully commit. There is a Ndebele saying from Africa: *Zidele Amathambo* – which means literally 'give yourself up, bones as well', that is, take a chance – go for it. Nothing is gained from being half-hearted. Yet, it is understandable if you have a few qualms at this stage. By plunging in, we fully commit – we go beyond the point of no return. We leap into the unknown: 'Not yet have you tempted those terrible reaches,/The region that shelters that sinful wight'/Go if you dare!' [210]The considerable investment of time, energy, sheer life-force, that goes into a major writing project (years of your life) means, once we are in we have perhaps too much invested to pull out. We simply must keep ploughing ahead. This is admirable, but it takes a certain strength to realise something just isn't working, that it's dead in the water – and the project must be abandoned. That's a tough call. But assuming this project is 'the one' and we want to make it work with all of our heart, then we must be prepared to enter the lake – and go all the way. And that is what will make you a 'hero'. What have we to lose? 'Let him who may/Win glory ere death',[211] the poet says. Carpe Deum!We have to be careful not to lose our head – a fate which literally befell Hrothgar's steward, Aeschere, who was taken by Grendel's mother. The hero and his party track the beast – and make a grisly discovery: Aeschere's head at the foot of the cliff. There might as well have been a sign: Abandon hope, all who enter here. Also, a sign that we are entering a non-rational place, beyond words and consciousness.When we are on the trail of our dark muse – embodied by Grendel's mother, the ultimate Shadow feminine – we follow her tracks with skill. Sometimes her spoor is not hard to spot – she had left a trail of destruction behind her. Perhaps she wants to be followed. In her rage and grief she cares not:

> 'The tracks lay clear where the fiend had fared
> Over plain and bottom and woodland path
> With the lifeless body, the best of thanes' [212]

The mere is an abode of dragons, of chthonic energy. It is a simmering cauldron of potential:

> 'Their eyes beheld
> The swimming forms of strange sea-dragons,
> Dim serpent shapes in the watery depths,

> Sea-beasts sunning on headland slopes;
> Snake-like monsters that oft at sunrise
> On evil errands scour the sea.' [213]

These slippery devils could be plot-serpents – always waiting to entangle the unwary writer. They lurk below the surface, a hazard to any who 'roam the sail-road'. But Beowulf-the-wordsmith is continent – firm of purpose and his potent form contained with a tight structure ('Well could that corselet defend the frame/Lest hostile thrust should pierce to the heart' [214]).In a modern idiom, this would be the time the superhero dons his costume – Bruce Wayne slips into his bat-suit; Tony Stark, his cyborg exoskeleton. Clothes maketh the man – perhaps, but here it represents a 'strong container'. The writer's discipline. His 'hand-braided byrny' [215] (a coat of ring-mail) could be the words themselves. Wrought with skill, they are 'water-tight' and able to withstand the most ferocious of critics. For the writer, his word is his sword, so it is fitting that Beowulf is gifted Unferth's magical blade, Hrunting, 'an ancient heirloom, trusty and tried'. This 'blade (of) iron, with etched design,/Tempered in blood of many a battle.' was a reliable weapon in the hand of a bold warrior: 'Never in fight had it failed the hand/That drew it daring the perils of war,/The rush of foe.' [216] This could be a metaphor for the Writer's Craft. By picking up a pen, you are inheriting the mantle of a long tradition. Many others have attempted what now you attempt. You are not alone in your endeavour. You stand on the shoulders of giants. When you go into the dark – you do not go empty-handed. Although you must face the Wrath of the Furious Mother by yourself – the Kali, the Cailleach, the Washer at the Ford, here given the wonderful kenning of 'Tarn-hag', the crone of the deep, cold lake – you go advised by the wisdom of elder writers (if you heed them).

Bottoming Out

When embarking upon a novel or an equivalent major writing project – it might feel like we will never make headway; that we will keep discovering more material, more ideas, and be unable to land this beast – the fish keeps getting bigger and bigger:

> 'Many a sea-beast, strange sea-monsters,
> Tasked him hard with their menacing tusks,
> Broke his byrny and smote him sore.' [217]

But eventually, against all odds – something miraculous occurs – we bottom out. We reach the end of our research, or the depths of our despair, and ... survive: 'Nigh unto a day he endured the depths/Ere he first had view of the vast sea-bottom' [218]. And, incredibly, when we reach this dark place – we discover it is endurable:

> 'Then he found himself in a fearsome hall
> Where water came not to work him hurt,
> But the flood was stayed by the sheltering roof.' [219]

If the idea is strong enough (the 'hall-roofing') and the structure which contains it, then the project will not be overwhelmed by material, autobiographical freight, and outside forces. And in that 'dark place', true illumination can occur – an unexpected epiphany ('There in the glow of firelight gleaming...' [220]). This is a foretaste of the light which returns after Grendel's mother is defeated:

> 'She sank in death; the sword was bloody;
> The hero joyed in the work of his hand.
> The gleaming radiance shimmered and shone
> As the candle of heaven shines clear from the sky.' [221]

This 'breakthrough' does not come easily. It may take several attempts. Hrunting, the sword of magic gifted by Unferth, fails Beowulf – it does not harm his opponent ('The sword-edge failed at his sorest need.' [222]) The hero will need another approach. The rational, the linear, will not work here. In the hoard of the monster he spies a mighty blade, 'An ancient war-brand of biting edge,/Choicest of weapons worthy and strong,/The work of giants, a warrior's joy.'[223] This sword is 'So heavy no hand but his own could hold it,/ Bear to battle or wield in war.'[224] To defeat his enemy, Beowulf must strike a 'resolute blow'. Brute strength is not enough. The warrior goes into a berserker frenzy – but the angrier he gets, the tighter the grip his enemy has upon him. Grendel's mother 'grappled him tightly in her grim embrace.' And so the berserker Beowulf wears a different kind of 'bear-shirt' – the Bear could be seen as symbol of the smothering, overly-protective mother, such as the stifling Communist regime of 'Mother Russia'. Sheer force will not work against this shadow. Beowulf's mail-shirt saves him from a fatal blow – but his final salvation comes through a combination of divine providence and being able to 'pull himself up'.

> '...holy God,
> The Lord all-wise, awarded the mastery;
> Heaven's ruler gave right decree.
> Swift the hero sprang to his feet...' [225]

Beowulf strikes a blow which fells his opponent, and then finishes the job, cutting off her head. Hrothgar's retinue see the waters of the lake boil with blood and assume the worst. They turn to leave, assuming the Geat had been slain by the 'wolf of the deep'. He had been under the surface for a full nine hours – a solid day of working. Often we can spend this long, and sometimes longer, sat at our computers, laptops, tablets, or paper, engrossed in our writing – completely focused, forgetting to eat, drink and rest – until our bodies ache from the effort. Yet, still we continue – tasting imminent victory, knowing that we have to stay with it. That we need to see this thing through until it is done, until our dark muse is purged from our system. Finally, Beowulf emerges from the depths, wielding the hilt of the giant's sword (the blade melted away by the monster's blood – his phallic power overwhelmed by the menstrual, if we want to get Freudian) and the head of Grendel's mother. It takes four of his men to carry it back upon their spears:

> 'From the sea-cliff's brim the warriors bore
> The head of Grendel, with heavy toil;
> Four of the stoutest, with all their strength,
> Could hardly carry on swaying spear
> Grendel's head to the gold-decked hall.' [226]

This is the solid structure which is required to handle such potentially hazardous material – and the critical distance needed to do justice to it. Writing, especially when based upon our own lives, can be too 'raw' or too 'close'. We need to keep it at spear's length. This is echoes the notion of the 'Ten Year Rule'[227] in life-writing – allowing enough time for critical distance to do a powerful experience justice.The lurker in the lake has been defeated and the hero returns with his men, 'his mighty thanes came forward to meet him,/Gave thanks to God they were granted to see/Their well-loved leader both sound and safe.' [228]

In world myths and legends the lake is a place of testing, of choice. Most famously, King Arthur encounters the Lady of the Lake and from her receives Excalibur – but he is initially offered a choice between the sword and the scabbard. To protect his people he chooses the former, but he has 'chosen unwisely'. If he had chosen the latter, he would never come to harm. But he who lives by the sword, dies by the sword ... as he discovers. In Welsh legend, a farmer must choose his future wife from identical lake-maidens at Llyny Fan Fach in the Black Mountains. In the epic of Gilgamesh, the hero journeys to the otherworld to find the flower of life that will resurrect his friend, Enkidu. On the journey home, he falls asleep by a lake and a snake issues forth to eat his priceless, irreplaceable prize. There are countless other cautionary tales of 'Lake-lurkers' – all saying the same thing. The subconscious must be acknowledged, the greater mystery must be embraced, the feminine must be given sovereignty.Only then will the hero succeed.

The Lurker in the Lake questings:

- Visit a body of water – a pond, pool, lake, tarn, or estuary. Sit and observe. Open the senses. Make notes. Record any reflections.
- What hasn't been resolved in your life? What is lurking beneath the surface of your current situation?
- What treasures from the shadows can you bring up and out into the light? Wisdoms? Lessons?
- Create a 'lake' space in your daily life – a regular 'down-time' of stillness, silence and solitude. Sit by a running stream, your garden's water feature, or the village pond … gazing, being, and busily 'doing nothing'. Run a bath, take a long soak, play some 'oceanic' ambient music. Or in your daily 'swim' spend some time just floating.

9

Hrothgar's Riches

Beowulf's men, relieved to see their leader return from the depths, help him carry the head of Grendel. They march back to Heorot where their victory is celebrated. Hrothgar showers them with praise and a great feast is held. On the morrow, the King gifts the champion twelve treasures as the Geats depart, victorious. Hrothgar senses he will never lay eyes upon Beowulf again.

Beowulf returns from the mere, wielding evidence of his successful victory – the head of Grendel and the hilt of the giant's sword. He is greeted as the hero is undoubtedly is. Hrothgar, as good as his word, showers him with treasure – but this moment of glory has a bittersweet quality to it, as the Danish king offers Beowulf some cautionary advice about how such heady moments are underpinned by mortality. This is dramatised vividly by Beowulf's arrival:

> 'And Grendel's head by the hair was carried
> Across the floor where the feasters drank –
> A terrible sight for lord and for lady –
> A gruesome vision whereon men gazed!'[229]

Such memento mori (one of many the poet offers up) are the leitmotif of the epic – a constant note of fatalism running throughout the poem. In it every piece of treasure is a reminder of the way of all things. Beowulf describes his ordeal in the lake, and then hands over the blood-melted blade to the 'gift-lord' Hrothgar, echoing how it must have been passed down the ages:

> 'Into the hand of the aged leader,

The gray-haired hero, he gave the hilt,
The work of giants, the wonder of gold.'[230]

Hrothgar examines it remarkable workmanship – intricate designs depicting 'how war first came into the world/ and flood destroyed the tribe of giants'. Even the Mighty are not immune. Yet the sword-hilt, inscribed with runes, although incredibly ancient (as the markings suggest) has survived. The runes state for whom the sword was made – this was common practice. In the city of Bath, Somerset, a blade was discovered bearing the legend in Old English: 'Wolf-breath made this'. Yet it turned out to be a piece of Danelaw designer forgery – bearing the name of a popular sword-maker of the time. 'The Ruin...' poem, written by an Anglo-Saxon cleric possibly visiting the remains of the Roman temple of Aquae Sulis, survives on only two burnt leaves of parchment, epitomising the fragility of civilisation, and an Ozymandian sense of 'how the mighty have fallen'. Hrothgar, although clearly delighted at his retainer's success, offers him some salutary advice – using the example of a fellow countryman of the Geats, 'Heremod', a poor king despised by all, as a foil to Beowulf's potential greatness. Hrothgar sees king-material in the Grendel-slayer, and his speech seems to be preparing him for this mantle:

'Learn from his fate!
Strive for virtue! I speak for your good;
In the wisdom of age I have told the tale.'[231]

Beowulf is basking in his summer, but eventually he must prepare for the winter of his maturity. It would seem to a man in his prime that 'the whole world conforms to your will,' but a 'killer stalks him,/an archer who draws a deadly blow.' When this deadly archer strikes, it sours the man's heart: 'his old possessions seem paltry to him now.' Lost in his own selfish misery, 'he ignores the shape of things to come.' But Hrothgar's advice, how experienced 'a hard reversal' of fortune, is to consider the Long Game – celebrate achievement, but 'do not give way to pride.' This is wise advice for any writer to follow. You have held your nerve and completed your project – probably through blood, sweat, and tears. Well done! Let the feasting and the ring-giving begin: 'our treasure will be shared and showered upon you.' But now is not the time to rest on your laurels. Now, in earnest, the hard work begins. A feast is held in Beowulf's honour. Heorot is healed of its woes – yet even on such a night, the poet does not let us forget the darkness at the edges of things. In one remarkable section he seems to light the feast-torches and snuff them out:

> 'Once more, as of old, brave heroes made merry
> And tumult of revelry rose in the hall.
> Then dark over men the night shadows deepened…'[232]

This chiaroscuro continues in the next section, following swift on from the hero's much-needed rest:

> 'The lofty building, splendid and spacious,
> Towered above him. His sleep was sound
> Till the black-coated raven, blithesome of spirit,
> Hailed the coming of Heaven's bliss.'[233]

After the victory feast, Beowulf and his men are filled with longing to be on their way ('Our homes are far, and our hearts are fain/To seek again Hygelac over the sea.'[234]). Having undergone two great ordeals, Beowulf is ready to return to a place of safety. Yet, he is a 'considerate man', attending to details – returning Hrunting to its owner, Unferth, in a gracious act. Having set forth on his quest with a bold heart and a true purpose Beowulf met with success. Hrothgar's final speech observes how: 'That man fares best to a foreign country/Who himself is stalwart and stout of heart.'[235]This chimes with Cavafy's advice in 'Ithaka' – warning of the 'Laistrygonians, Cyclops/Wild Poseidon', the adventurer might meet he adds the caveat: 'You won't meet things like that unless your soul sets them up in front of you.'Beowulf clearly had the right attitude, as must the writer.As a result, the hero is gifted twelve treasures – a solar number, suggesting he has won the sun in a metaphorical way. He has brought light back to the benighted realm. He has brought full awareness to his own project – now he can look back on it with hindsight, and redraft it accordingly. What was initially written in the dark, is now written with the lights on. Bedecked in his golden bling, Beowulf becomes sun-like himself: 'Beowulf, glorious in gold regalia, stepped the green earth'. He has grounded his vision. As they depart, Hrothgar embraces Beowulf – who has become like a 'son' to him – and has two forebodings. The first is clear: 'nevermore would they meet each other/face to face.' The other is inchoate, but perhaps is a presentiment of Beowulf's own doom.The watcher on the shore, ordered to guard the boat, earns his own reward by the now kingly and magnanimous Beowulf:

> 'A battle-sword Beowulf gave to the boatwarden
> Hilted with gold; and thereafter in hall
> He had the more honour because of the heirloom,
> The shining treasure.'[236]

This could be seen as paying professionals to cast their gimlet-gaze over your manuscript – a keen-eyed editor or proof-reader, the shipwards of the craft – but also the attention we must pay to our own ship of dreams. Look after it, work on it – and it shall carry you far. Like Beowulf's trusty ship, it will take you on many adventures and bring you many enriching experiences. And so Beowulf returns to his homeland, carrying the hard-won treasure, among them a 'torc of gold'. Although a torc is sign of chieftainship, here perhaps it could be deliberately misheard as 'talk of gold' – the writer has forged the gift of the golden speech and with it won renown.

'Truly, these words has the Lord of wisdom
Set in your heart, for I have never harkened
To speech so sage from a man so young.
You have strength, prudence, and wisdom of word!'[237]

As you return with your hard-won manuscript take heed of Hrothgar's harsh but well-meaning advice – think on, to the Long Game.The journey has just begun.

Hrothgar's Riches questings:

- What reward can you offer yourself for completing your project? Small ones for shorter projects (a bottle of wine; book; DVD of your favourite series; or a massage); bigger ones for major projects (a holiday; a motorbike; jewellery; a spa weekend). It is satisfying to have something tangible to show for our efforts – whatever becomes of the MSS (which is in the lap of the gods). Gift yourself a personal gong.
- What still needs to be done? Create a plan of action to 'follow-through' and seal the deal.
- What will sustain you on this long journey (the second marathon)? Pace yourself. Keep something in reserve.
- Identify 'the shipwards of the craft' who will help you on your journey. Ask for their aid.

10

Homecoming

Returning to their ship, the Geats sail homeward. Here they are welcomed as returning heroes by King Hygelac and Queen Hygd. Of formerly low esteem, Beowulf's status shifts considerably through this act which brings honour to the countrymen. The court hears of Beowulf's great deeds, and the treasures won are offered to his liege and lady. In return, Beowulf is offered substantial lands, a hall, and a high position.

The hero-writer, supported by his well-tended craft, will eventually reach his or her destination. The exhilarating description the Beowulf poet gives captures the feeling of being borne along by your writing ('stiff winds kept the wave-crosser/skimming ahead.'). Sometimes it glides along – the Muse breathes wind into your sails – and being lost in this grace is one of the great pleasures. One feels like it could be sustained for days at a time, that one could simply go on and on until the book is finished.

Yet even if it feels effortless, there is a substantial amount of work to get to this point. It has been estimated that a professional athlete or musician needs to put in 10,000 hours of practice to get to their topflight competitive level[238] – this '10,000 hour Rule', as it's become known, is merely a matter of practicing a specific task that can be accomplished with 20 hours of work a week for 10 years. This level of dedication soon cuts the will-dos from the wannabes. It is a serious commitment – a life-time path really, because once you have got to that level you need to keep practicing and keep developing. No wonder Beowulf swaggers – he has followed his star, and is shining like one upon his return. As he and entourage return home, striding along the shore, the poet describes how: 'the world-candle shone,/The hot sun hasting on high from the south.'[239] There is nothing more empowering than when you follow your light – when you fulfil your potential, doing what you are born to do. This is the true homecoming – to your self.Beowulf, the returning hero, is warmly welcomed. His kinsmen are glad to see him back home alive. The glorious warrior relates his adventure and his status is assured. This is a volteface, as we discover that he was not always held in such high esteem:

'He had long been scorned, when the sons of the Geats
Accounted him worthless; the Weder lord
Held him not high among heroes in hall.
Laggard they deemed him, slothful and slack.'[240]

It is hard to imagine the muscle-bound Beowulf as a 'weakling' – yet such a dramatic transformation makes him even more superhero-like – a puny Peter Parker turned Spiderman; or a weedy comic-book reader transformed into a Charles Atlas, as the old ads claimed. No one will kick sand in Beowulf's face anymore, that's for sure.By our art, we can transform people's perceptions of us – but this should not be our motivation; only a pleasant byproduct. All we can do is behave with honour and integrity in our work – not following the whims of commerce, or popularity.Beowulf, destined to become king of his people, begins to display kingly qualities upon his return. He offers his hard-won treasures to his uncle, Hygelac – who has raised him like a father. He offers his liege: 'the battle-topping helmet, the mail-shirt grey as hoar-frost/and the precious war-sword.' Beowulf even makes tribute of the four war-horses and the 'priceless torque'. Thus, by sharing his treasures the homecoming hero is enriched even more, for Hygelac responds to the gesture with rewards fit for a king, starting with a highly-prized gem-studded sword, then: 'Gave him a hall and a stately seat/And hides seven thousand. Inherited lands/Both held by birth fee, home and estate.'[241]As a writer, if one's work is received with acclaim, all our efforts seem vindicated. A literary prize can place the seal of approval upon our work, and provide a useful marketing hook, boosting sales and interest. There might follow interviews, reviews, festival appearances – the whole media circus. Of course, this is something only experienced by the lucky few. However, with a book in print – be it self-published or by a small press, we can organise our own book launch celebration, readings, talks, even interviews and features – by being pro-active, and focused in our efforts. We have to be careful not to be 'eaten up' by this. Marketing can be a bottomless pit – there is no end to it. As soon as we stop pushing our book, it falls off the radar. With so many titles being published (with e-books and self-published works, the figure has gone through the roof) we need to be increasingly ingenious and industrious to get our work 'out there' and noticed. And yet, it is akin to Grendel's dragon-bag – an additional detail revealed in Beowulf's account to Hygelac's court:

> 'Wide and wondrous his huge pouch hung
> Cunningly fastened, and fashioned with skill
> From skin of dragon by devil's craft.
> Therein the monster was minded to thrust me
> Sinless and blameless, and many beside.'[242]

The dragon-bag could be seen as the 'food-chain' of literature – a metaphor for the insatiable market place. Many titles pass through the system without even being digested, ending up in the literary middens of remainder bookstores.

All we can do is write from the heart, and make our actions count – putting our all into projects that we believe in whole-heartedly, rather than cynical money-chasing efforts. Our time on this Earth is finite, as the poet of Beowulf keeps reminding us –

and we have to live well, and write well. Like Beowulf and his uncle, as fellow writers we should support each other – collaborate, rather than compete: 'each was concerned for the other's good'.An ethos of 'every man for himself' will get us nowhere. The journey is hard, and any help we can get along the way, or good company to cheer the road, should be cherished. Our fellow writers are 'kinsmen', in spirit – a community of intent. A writer who looks out for other writers will be appreciated, widening his luck. By being generous and warm-hearted, he improves his own lot, as well as enriching his or her writing community:

> ''Tis the way of a kinsman,
> Not weaving in secret the wiles of malice
> Nor plotting the fall of a faithful friend.'[243]

Homecoming questings:

- It is said that 'home is the place where your heart does not have to hide'[244]: in writing terms, when are you being most yourself? Where do you feel most 'at home'? In what medium, genre or style of writing?
- Identify your writing community: is it a community of intent (e.g. online or through a journal); or a physical community (a local writers' group; a creative neighbourhood)?
- What 'treasures' can you bestow upon your 'home'/your community? Could you write a poem, praising them or the genre? An article? A profile of an admired author? Supportive reviews of up-and-coming writers? Could you create a prize to encourage new writing in the field, or put together an anthology of your favourite writing?

11

The Long Road

When Hygelac dies in battle, Beowulf assumes his mantle and rules the Geats for half a century.

Writing a long project like a novel is like running two marathons. One in the execution of it – the sheer graft of writing it, day after day, until it is done; the other in 'getting it out there': the endless round of submissions, editorial, design, marketing, distribution, reviews, readings, signings and interviews (presuming you are fortunate enough to land yourself a deal, or have enough skill and chutzpah to 'go it alone'). Beowulf, inheriting his uncle's mantle, ruled his land for half a century. As writers, we are 'wardens of the land' – both of our own writing, and in a bolder sense, of our communities, our cultures – whatever we choose to represent in our stories. We should have a sense of responsibility for our characters, and for the authenticity of the drama, its depiction. What we choose to dwell on, what we choose to 'bring into' the world – these are decisions of the highest moral responsibility. Not that we should only dwell on the virtuous and the beautiful – often truth is found in the amoral and unglamorous. Yet, we should make each word count. Write with all of our heart, about our deepest beliefs – and not squander the gift of life on the trivial, the cynical, the puerile. Beowulf, the poet notes, grew 'aged and wise with the wisdom of years.'[245] He did not cling onto the heady and foolhardy life of a young warrior. His Spring matured to Winter. Writers worth their salt are in it for the love of the craft – and this will keep them going, long after the contracts and media coverage fade away. The cliché in the music business is the 'difficult second album'; sometimes the same applies to young writers whose debut has been received with acclaim, or a massive advance. How do they live up to the hype, the pressure of expectation? Some don't, or choose not to. Harper Lee, having written the iconic book, *To Kill a Mocking Bird* (1960), which won the Pulitzer Prize, never wrote another. Murray Lachlan Young, having received a famous million pound record deal from EMI, went into Cornish obscurity. Storyteller Martin Shaw, offered a substantial record deal, lived on the land for four years[246]. At the other end of the scale, authors in their 'autumnal years' often experience their own difficulties – to do with failing sales, waning interest, health, lack of inspiration, vices, (Kingsley Amis and his booze; Beryl Bainbridge and her cigarettes), rivalry, bitterness, depression, and so on.John Steinbeck spent the last ten years of his life working on a retelling of Mallory's *La Morte D'arthur*[247]. He was so consumed by the Arthurian bug that he moved to Somerset to 'live and breathe the same air as Arthur and his knights'. He set about his project with diligence, but lack of discipline – continually finding 'reasons' not to work on the actual drafts. He felt the need to learn Medieval English and study rare manuscripts in libraries across Europe before putting pen to paper. When he did, he laboured over each draft and was never able to make much progress. He said if he ever finished the project he 'may as well break his brushes'. He failed to finish it, but six acts were edited and published by his friend Chase Horton. The letters written during this period make for more exciting reading than the actual main text – an insightful analysis into the creative process.

One fears Steinbeck had a Casaubon complex – like the pedantic scholar in George Eliot's novel of provincialism and frustrated ambitions *Middlemarch* (1874), who struggled with his magnum opus, 'A Key to all Mythologies', all of his life. Plagued by ill-health and irritability, he fails to complete his work. The spectre of Mr Casaubon haunts all writers embarked upon major projects. In Michael Chabon's comic novel, *Wonder Boys* (1985), hapless creative writing professor Grady Tripp struggles to complete his two thousand page eponymous novel. It becomes a continuing source of embarrassment and shame for him – an albatross about his neck. When he is asked about its progress by his wife's family, Tripp uses this analogy to describe the feeling:

> 'For as long as they could remember, I'd been making vague and confident assurances that any day I would finish the thing. If and when I ever did, they would probably feel an almost physical sense of relief. I was like a massively incompetent handyman who'd been up on their roof now for years, trying to take down a gnarled old lightning-struck tree trunk that had fallen against the house, haunting every gathering, all discussions of family business, any attempt they made to sit down together and plan for the future, with the remote but ceaseless whining of my saw.'[248]

Writing a novel, or worse, a novel-series, is one of the ultimate acts of folly or madness – requiring a great deal of effort with little guarantee of success. Yet despite this, we feel that we simply must. That we have no choice – like Steinbeck who was compelled by chthonic motives ('There are voices in the land'[249]). The Long Road stage of the Writer's Quest sorts the men from the boys, the women from the girls. Only those serious in their commitment to being a writer will stay the distance. This is where you discover if you are a marathon-runner, a long distance walker – or someone who wishes for success without being willing to work for it. Maybe you discover you are more enamoured by the glamorous illusion of being a writer than the actual act (and craft; and practice) of writing. In which case, back to the sofa of sloth for you! But here's hoping you show your mettle, step up to the mark, and shine. If you are committed to being a writer, then the hoary and possibly annoying advice that creative writing teachers give about 'it's the journey, not the destination' rings true. You must learn to love the act of writing for its own sake: selecting and shaping words on the page, day after day. Akin to walking a long distance footpath, in terms of stamina and the hypnotic effect of a continuous rhythmic action, writing is solo endeavour of sustained effort: the pen on the page or digit on the keyboard like a solitary figure, perpendicular in a landscape spreading out as a page or screen. Robert Macfarlane captures the mirror act of writing and motion with typical stylistic élan:

> 'As the pen rises from the page between words, so the walker's feet rise and fall between paces, and as the deer continues to run as it bounds from the earth, and the dolphin continues to swim even as it leaps again and again from the sea, so writing and wayfaring are continuous activities, a running stitch, a persistence of the same seam or stream.'[250]

No one will do it for you. It is a long haul and a real test of stamina and character. Reading accounts of those who have embarked upon such odysseys and succeeded will help provide inspiration and guidance. How did they keep going? How will you?

If Beowulf was a real king, alive today and ruler of a country for half a century, he would undergo regular health checks. A writer who is in it for the long game should consider the same. Try out this writer's health check every now and then – it will help you to take stock and gauge your progress.

The Long Road: Writer's Health Check

- How do you feel your writing is going?
- What are your strengths?
- What are your weaknesses?
- What are you trying to achieve as a writer?

- What do you want to achieve as a writer
- …in one year?
- …in five?
- …in ten?
- What is your lifetime's writing ambition?
- As a writer, how do you want to be remembered?
- How will you achieve your literary ambitions?
- What prevents you?
- What are your fears as a writer?
- What are your hopes?
- What keeps you going?
- Write 3 writer's affirmations (pin above your desk & repeat often)

12

A Dragon Called Destiny

A runaway thrall stumbles upon a dragon's hoard in an ancient barrow. He steals a gold cup, which rouses the serpent from its centuries of slumber. Enraged by this theft, the dragon sallies forth to wreck havoc on the surrounding country.

For half a century Beowulf rules in glory – but all things must end – and the doom foreshadowed throughout the poem manifests fully now. Beowulf, slayer of Grendel and his mother, is about to meet his match – the third monster of the poem is the deadliest of them all; nothing can defeat it, for it is in fact his destiny, his wyrd (the Anglo-Saxon concept of fate). Seamus Heaney in his introduction to his translation says of the dragon: 'he lodges himself in the imagination as *wyrd* rather than *wyrm*, more a destiny than a set of reptilian vertebrae.'[251]It is as though Beowulf's death was made flesh – and waited, coiled on its hoard, for the hero to find it. In fact, it is an accidental treasure-seeker who disturbs the slumber of the dragon, a 'guilty fugitive fleeing the lash.'[252] Looking for a hiding place, he stumbles upon a 'stone barrow lofty'. It is filled with a glittering hoard of treasure. The light-fingered slave makes off with a 'flagon all fretted with gold,'[253] but like an Arthurian grave-robber, disturbing the once and future king and his sleeping knights, this barrow-raider gets more than he bargained for. Unfortunately, this ancient tomb is the abode of a dragon, asleep on top of its golden bed. The slave slips away, but not scot-free. Sensing the integrity of its hoard has been broken, the dragons stirs in wrath and flies out to lay waste to the land thereabouts – scorching the earth. Outwitted, the dragon 'cozened in sleep' is 'roused to wrath'[254]– for dragons are, by many accounts, fiercely intelligent and like nothing less than being made fools of. The dragon's treasure is described in vivid detail – with the trademark melancholy tinge. A warrior of ancient times, seeing his race was doomed, placed the hoard ('the countless wealth of a princely clan'[255]) within the tomb, as a writer must with his 'word-hoard', offering it up to the future.

'Keep thou, O Earth, what men could not keep –
This costly treasure – it came from thee!'[256]

The treasure is returned to the earth, from it first was mined – and in a similar way, we 'borrow' the alphabet to convey our stories – and offer it back into the collective 'word-hoard' of humankind. Hard won, the bitter irony is – it (whether gold or words) does not bring happiness if held onto. It must be passed on. A book is only as good as its reader.The hoard-giver's speech is charged with poignant fatalism:

'Now I have no one to wield the sword,
No one to polish the plated cup,
The precious flagon – the host is fled.
The hard-forged helmet fretted with gold
Shall be stripped of its inlay; the burnishers sleep
Whose charge was to brighten the battle-masks.
Likewise the corselet that countered in war
Mid clashing of bucklers the bite of the sword –
Corselet and warrior decay into dust;
Mailed coat and hero are moveless and still.'[257]

The treasure seems to be a symbol of the accoutrements of life – rendered meaningless without usage. Words are to be read or heard, spoken or sang. Without other ears, other mouths – they become sterile treasures. A book is just a bundle of dead leaves otherwise. The poet captures this in exquisite language:

'No mirth of gleewood, no music of harp,
No good hawk swinging in flight through the hall;
No swift steed stamps in the castle yard;
Death has ravished an ancient race.'[258]

This echoes the medieval story of the 'Sparrow in the Hall'. The Venerable Bede (c. 673-735) recorded the story of King Edwin of Northumberland at the hands of the missionary bishop Paulinus. Edwin was willing to hear the preaching of Paulinus and to convert at once, but he called together a meeting of his council of elders, which included his pagan high priest, Coifi. Paulinus presented the gospel to him, and one of the chief advisors replied with this observation:

> 'Your Majesty, when we compare the present life of man on earth with that time of which we have no knowledge, it seems to me like the swift flight of a single sparrow through the banqueting-hall where you are sitting at dinner on a winter's day with your thegns and counsellors. In the midst there is a comforting fire to warm the hall; outside the storms of winter rain or snow are raging. This sparrow flies swiftly in through one door of the hall, and out through another. While he is inside, he is safe from the winter storms; but after a moment of comfort, he vanishes from sight into the wintry world from which he came. Even so, man appears on earth for a little while; but of what went before this life or of what follows, we know nothing. Therefore, if this new teaching has brought any more certain knowledge, it seems only right that we should follow it.'[259]

Whether the poet of Beowulf knew of this anecdote, who can say, but the whole of the poem is charged with this sense of transience – of fleeting glory. The leitmotif of this in the poem is gold – the way it passes from vanquished to victor, from father to son, from king to champion, from ancestor to descendant, seems to symbolise the life-force itself. Heaney describes it as a metaphor of upheaval, as experienced in the Dark Ages – the dramatic paradigm shift from the pagan world to the Christian, from the old order to the new:

> 'It is *laene,* transitory, passing from hand to hand, and its changed status is registered as a symptom of the changed world.'[260]

And in another sense, the hoard is a symbol for the hoard of words – passed from poet to listener, writer to reader. An author's oeuvre is his or her 'wer-gild', blood-price of words, by which they are measured. You are only as good as your last movie, actors are told – and a writer is so, in terms of their last book. A writer's 'market value' goes up or down – and many are 'remaindered' when they fall out of vogue. Swathes of mid-list authors have been filleted out of publishers' lists – who now focus on a few stars, and the odd token break-through talent. Out with the old, in with the new. It is easy to see why an author might feel like the older Beowulf, living on former glories – sensing his end is near – desperate to make the comeback, or stoic in the face of oblivion.

Much is made of 'making it' – but little is written about, concerning 'what happens next'; or how you keep going, even in the face of repeat rejections ... even a lifetime of 'career neglect'. Sometimes, it is wise to accept we haven't got what it takes, and it's not a good idea to give up the day-job, whatever the self-help books optimistically tell us. When faced with a chorus of disapproval – a consensus critique of your writing as being dire (and I'm only talking about worst-case scenarios here) then perhaps the best thing to do is to give up and move on – rather than flog a dead horse. However, if we've experienced some modest success – and had a few positive responses from people – then we might find ourselves, years down the line, wondering 'what has it all been for?' Cue – the dragon. The monster in the night returns – deadlier than ever:

> 'Then the goodly treasure was found unguarded
> By the venomous dragon enveloped in flame,
> The old naked night-foe flying in darkness,
> Haunting the barrows; a bane that brings
> A fearful dread to the dwellers of earth'[261]

We might wake up one day to feel something is missing – like the 'gem-studded cup'. Grail-like, this missing quality – if rediscovered – will heal our 'wounded king' and restore the 'Wasteland' of our life. We might not be able to put our finger on it – but it can have a huge impact upon one's quality of life. It can lead to depression or worse – an existential longing which overshadows everything – like the hoard-giver:

> 'So sad of mood he bemoaned his sorrow,
> Lonely and sole survivor of all,
> Restless by day and wretched by night
> Till the clutch of death caught his heart.'[262]

This deep longing or yearning is summed up in the German concept of *Sehnsucht* (see **Sehnsucht and the Art of Writing Fantasy**), or the Welsh term, *Hiraeth*. It is a certain restlessness and dissatisfaction with life – what has been called the 'Divine Malcontent' by Colin Wilson in *The Outsider* (1956). It can manifest in anger, or in a fey-ness – a withdrawing from the world, and a longing for the beyond. The many descriptions of those taken to Faerie echo this – often it is triggered when music of the Fey is heard, or fairy fruit is tasted, or a fairy lover wooed. Things are never the same again, and the 'victim' is lured beyond, like the child in WB Yeats', 'The Stolen Child':

'O come away, human child to the water,
O come away, human child to the water, and the wild,
For the world's more full of weeping,
Than you can understand.'

The transgressive eater of fairy fruit in Christina Rossetti's 'Goblin Market' (1862), sweet-toothed Laura, experiences this:

'She pined and pined away;
Sought them by night and day,
Found them no more, but dwindled and grew gray...'[263]

as do the characters in Hope Mirrlees' *Lud in the Mist* (1926).

Upon hearing of the devastation caused by the fire-drake, Beowulf is shaken – a sun, eclipsed:

'The heart of the hero was heavy with anguish ...
Dark thoughts stirred in his surging bosom'[264]

The great warrior-king perhaps intimated that his end was near. His success came at a price – and now it was time to call in the debt. In Indian mythology and Buddhist tradition, it would be called his karma.

'The stalwart hero was doomed to suffer
The destined end of his days on earth'[265]

The symptoms of this chronic malcontent could manifest as Writer's Block – every writer's worst nightmare. There are many examples of this in literature... This is perhaps the real dragon – obliterating all attempts to create.

'Then the baleful stranger belched fire and flame,
Burned the bright dwellings – the glow of the blaze

> Filled hearts with horror. The hostile flier
> Was minded to leave there nothing alive.'[266]

The writer who is blocked feels impotent – and this can lead to severe depression. The enriching life-forces of creativity have been blocked in some way. The spring has been capped.

Alternatively, the dragon could be your magnum opus – which will demand everything you've got to achieve. It is your ultimate challenge as a writer. Will you rise to this challenge? Will you pass this final test, or will it overcome you?

> 'now with the sword,
> with hand and hard blade, I must fight for the
> treasure.'[267]

Time to hone that sword and don that armour one last time.

A Dragon Called Destiny questings:

- What 'hoard' do you sit upon? What untold stories are waiting to be shared? Make a list of all the ideas you have 'on the backburners' waiting for 'one day' to be made manifest: short stories, novels, collections of poems, plays, memoirs.
- Pick one 'gem-studded goblet' from this pile. Brainstorm it (cluster; free-write). Begin a work-book, incubate your idea in it: add to it whenever you have flashes of inspiration concerning the project – characters, scenes, plot-lines, titles, research, detail, world-building texture, backstory, etc.
- Complete the following phrases:

  When have you 'breathed fire', and been angriest?
  When have you felt most passionate?
  When have felt most sorrowful?

When have you felt most joyous?

If you truly lived up to your potential you would be…?

- What is your deadliest 'weapon'? your biting wit? your venom? your cold silence? your baleful stare? the blue pencil of the editor? the red claws of revenge?
- What is your greatest point of vulnerability?

13

Of Boasts and Beasts

The dragon scorches the land and exacts a heavy toll with his fiery breath – on villages, farms, and finally Beowulf's own hall. The catalyst of this calamity – the stolen cup – comes to Beowulf, who decides to act, despite his years. With a company of eleven men, he ventures forth to face the dragon, reflecting on former deeds and feeling his own mortality in the wings. He realises he must face this dragon alone.

This is the stage of the story when the old gunslinger is bested by some sharpshooting upstart – or allows himself to be, knowing his glory days are over. The 2007 film, *The Assassination of Jesse James by the Coward Robert Ford* (directed by Andrew Dominik) plays it as such. Jesse James even obligingly positions himself by a picture frame, so when his brains get blown out the splatter-pattern is preserved for posterity. Looking down the barrel of the gun, the director suggests James had an eye on immortality. Fear not, dear writer – your final bow need not be so fatal! There are other, more graceful, exit strategies.

In the Writer's Quest it is the stage of one's career when – you know you are past your best, and must defer to younger talent (presuming you have got that far). It is an inevitable part of the creative cycle – like Autumn is to Spring (you can't really have one without the other). That is not to say you just give up. Follow Dylan Thomas' advice and 'Do Not Go Gently Into That Good Night' – go out, all guns blazing. Perhaps you've saved your best until the last act, as Beowulf does – going out with a bang, not a whimper. Rage against the dying of the light, if that indeed is what is happening. Yet it takes a certain wisdom – it used to be called 'grace' – to acknowledge when it is time to 'hand on the baton', as visionary film-maker George Lucas has done with his *Star Wars* 'universe', paving the way for new directors and writers to reinvigorate the franchise. It takes dignity to do this – on whatever scale – and avoid rehashing old shtick, to the point where you parody yourself and potentially undermine former achievements (which the once-great actor Robert De Niro has done in his later career, with the odd notable exception). There can be one too many 'comeback tours' – fading rockstars in spandex are sad to see. Nobody likes to see their heroes become mediocre. Some seem to get better and better with age (Bob Dylan; Leonard Cohen; Robert Plant). But for every Clint Eastwood (the rare exception of an artist who has excelled in maturity) there is an Arnold Schwarzenegger. Put that Governator away! Books on creative writing rarely discuss this stage of the cycle – when you have passed through the 'food chain' of publishing and out the other side; when your successful creative career peters out. Many mid-list authors, with a few books under their belt – even successful ones – flounder in their later career. It depends when you start of course. If you are a prodigy, this might happen sooner (you have 'peaked' too soon). Some are late developers. A writer friend, Moyra Caldecott, did not get her first novel published until she was 54, then wrote 30 books – published internationally. But then found, as New Age became 'old news' that she had fallen out of favour and could no longer get a deal – and so had her books published by a small press – her life as a writer 'winding down' in her autumn years (her extraordinary career arc is charted in her 2007 memoir, *A Multi-Dimensional Life*). Some authors get a couple of books out – but the sales don't live up to the expectations of the advance – and their bubble bursts prematurely. They fall out of favour with hyper-cautious publishers, twitchy in the headlights of the Double-dip Recession and the Digital Revolution.

Beowulf has overcome two monsters – Grendel and his monstrous mother. He has ruled his kingdom for fifty years – but then it is time to face his final challenge, the fire-drake. He knows this will be his last fight – he must be in his seventies, after all – but he faces the music with courage.

Cue music as he dons his old armour one last time (perhaps a bit tight around the waist). Yet, he does not go to his death alone.

He sets off to face his doom with eleven comrades – making a solar twelve. All to the good. But, they recruit the barrow-thief (whose theft of the cup triggered the dragon's wrath) to guide them to the lair, making a fatal thirteen. With this ominous number, the final plot-cog falls into place – locking the endgame of the narrative into motion.

The dragon's cave has a suitably doom-laden Underworld feel to it – a veritable entrance to Hades:

> 'Where the earth-hall stood near the breaking billows
> Filled with jewels and beaten gold.'[268]

There is no doubt that this is a place of reckoning. No one here gets out alive: 'no easy bargain/would be made in that place by any man.' At this mortal threshold, Beowulf sits down on the cliff-top to brood over his demise:

> 'Sad was his spirit, restless and ready,
> And the march of Fate immeasurably near;
> Fate that would strike, seek his soul's treasure,
> And deal asunder the spirit and flesh'[269]

With his end near, Beowulf reflects on his former years – his early days as a ward at King Hrethel's court. At this point of the Writer's Quest – perhaps you have come to the end of a major project – it is wise to review, and look back on your process. What have you achieved? What have you learnt?

Contemplating an accidental killing and its effects on the

king, the poet uses the powerful analogy of a father mourning the loss of his son:

> 'Even so sad and sorrowful is it,
> And bitter to bear, to an old man's heart,
> Seeing his young son swing on the gallows.
> He wails his dirge and his wild lament
> While his son hangs high, a spoil to the raven.'[270]

In a metaphorical sense, the death of a son is like the death of one's younger self – in this case, Beowulf in his prime. There comes a point when we have to let go of our youth, of 'childish things' – of clinging to looking a certain way, or being into certain things. This realisation might be accompanied by a sense of grief – we will, in effect, by suffering the bereavement of this younger version of our self; a feeling that might leave us dissolute, even inconsolable:

> 'In the house of his son he gazes in sorrow
> On wine-hall deserted and swept by the wind,
> Empty of joy. The horseman and heroes
> Sleep in the grave. No sound of the harp,
> No welcoming revels of old!'[271]

'What was, is no more', is a poignant mantra at this stage. Rather than be in denial – about our career, our success or lack of it – it is wise to acknowledge the reality of things, draw a line under the past, and move on. The actor who knows he will never play a romantic lead again; a novelist who knows he will never get another major advance. It is a time for turning away from the world, for turning inward, as Beowulf reflects:

> 'He left life's joys for the heavenly light…'[272]

Eyes fixed on eternity, the old warrior puts his house in order, passes on his worldly goods, and goes to face the music.

There was a time when Beowulf was unconquerable in battle – a true champion of his people:

'in the press of battle
I was always before him alone in the van.
So shall I bear me while life-days last'[273]

To read this in a metaphorical way, imagine a Beowulf-like energy in your writing – 'at the front of the line' – driving it forwards. A good writer should never lose their edge, although *perhaps* it is inevitable with the onset of old age (with the apparent debilitation of the mind and body). In some, it seems to sharpen their mind, and refine their very purpose – as with Terry Pratchett, suffering a rare form of Alzheimer's, he has become an ambassador for euthanasia, while continuing to write witty and imaginative novels like *Snuff*.

The determined writer might feel this final challenge is his or her defining moment, and will go down fighting – firing on all cylinders, enervated by their cause:

'Then the lord of the Geats in the grip of his fury
Gave shout of defiance; the strong-heart stormed.'[274]

With your 'blade' in hand – go into the dark, knowing you are doing what you are born to do.

As Beowulf prepares to do this, he delivers a final formal 'boast', this is his 'My Way' moment, his swansong:

'I came in safety through many a conflict
In the days of my youth; and now even yet,
Old as I am, I will fight this feud,
Do manful deeds, if the dire destroyer

Will come from his cavern to meet my sword.'[275]

He declares that this is 'his fight alone' – as it will be when our 'time has come'. He is 'resolved':

'Not yours the adventure,
Nor the mission of any, save mine alone,
To measure his strength with the monstrous dragon
And play the part of a valiant earl.'[276]

Even at this stage, Beowulf trusts in his strength entirely. He steps into the mouth of the dragon's lair in his mailshirt and helmet, wielding his trusty sword – like Luke Skywalker going into the dank darkness deep in the swamps of Dagobah, light-sabre probing forwards.

Beowulf lets out a shout – his voice summoning the dragon from the dark:

'His voice rang out with the rage of battle,
Resounding under the hoary stone.'[277]

The description of the fight between Beowulf and the dragon is a tour-de-force of poetic art. It is moment of heightened emotion – we know the warrior is fighting a losing fight, which makes him even more the hero. When his trusty sword fails him (a final, cataclysmic case of writer's block) we know he is doomed. And yet, what an ending he will 'write' for himself with his deeds.

His warriors flee in his hour of need – all except one, young Wiglaf, in whom 'the claims of kinship cannot be denied'. He plays a pivotal role – as the one who survives, who lives to tell the tale, the essential witness. He is related to Aeschere, bringing the karmic symmetry right into the scene. Beowulf had slain Grendel's mother after she had slain Aeschere – now he will receive aid from one of Aeshere's kin; but meet his comeuppance by another monster, a metaphorical cousin of the tarn-hag.

The description of Wiglaf rallying to his leige's aid is thrilling and heartening:

'Wiglaf, the lad,
Was to face with his lord the first of his battles,
The hazard of war. But his heart did not fail
Nor the blade of his kinsman weaken in war;
As the worm soon found when they met in the fight!'[278]

Wiglaf's defence of Beowulf is echoed in every young artist who has stood up for their hero, or even befriended them and helped them out in their elder years – rekindling their belief in themselves. A young Samuel Palmer was among a small group of artists who were drawn to the elderly William Blake – neglected and under appreciated in his lifetime except by this coterie. In *Finding Forrester* (Gus Van Sant, 2000) the young writer stumbles upon the veteran Pulitzer-prize winning author – grumpily played by Sean Connery – hiding in a tenement in obscurity, resurrecting his spark and receiving the gift of inspiration in return.

'Let us haste to succour his sore distress
In the horrible heat and the merciless flame.
God knows I had rather the fire should enfold
My body and limbs with my gold-friend and lord.'[279]

Loyal Wiglaf is now in the position of inspiring his hero, Beowulf, to live up to his legend in an edifying speech – the equivalent of the coach's pep-talk between rounds; or in the locker room at half-time.

'Beloved Beowulf,
Summon your strength, remember the vow
You made of old in the years of youth
Not to allow your glory to lessen

As long as you lived. With resolute heart
And dauntless daring, defend your life
With all your force. I fight at your side!'[280]

The older world-weary writer can be restored by a young person's enthusiasm or belief in them – not that we should draw sycophants and fans to us, to shore up a flagging ego – but if we have inspired people with our writing, then why not let it come full circle? If your writing has motivated somebody to start on their path, to write, then honour their achievement. Take time to read their work and offer encouraging feedback – as JRR Tolkien did with a young poet who corresponded with him, sending him her first poems. The professor kindly wrote back, offering no-nonsense advice about their merits and faults. He took her endeavour seriously – she went onto work in publishing.

Let us honour those who have inspired us – and support them in any way we can, either by simply buying their books, attending their talks, or by befriending and perhaps even caring for them in their 'twilight' years:

'So they felled the foe and wrought their revenge;
The kinsmen together had killed the dragon.
So a man should be when the need is bitter!'[281]

Working as a team, they defeat the dragon – Wiglaf drawing first blood, and Beowulf administering the coup-de-grâce – but the deed takes a heavy toll. When Beowulf is mortally wounded, Wiglaf washes the battered warrior's wounds:

'In his hands bore water and bathed his leader,
And loosened the helm from his dear lord's head.'[282]

Despite all the boasts, all the machismo, at the end of the day, it comes down to simple acts of human kindness; to a deep sense of camaraderie with one's fellow writers – who share the journey, who endure the ordeal of attempting something challenging with no guarantee of reward. Salute them. Support them. Pass on the opportunities. Share your hard-won wisdom. Hand on the torch. Don't let the fire die.

Of Boasts and Beasts questings:

- Make a list of those who have inspired and influenced you. Is there a way you can honour them (if alive), or their memory (if not)?
- Has there been a point when the wave of your ambition 'broke' against the sea-wall of reality? How did it feel? How have you responded to this 'wake up and smell the coffee' moment? Or how will you respond when it does happen (as inevitably it will)?
- Is there a young writer you could 'take under your wing' and mentor in some way (if they wish it)? Could you pass on advice, resources, contacts?
- What is your greatest fear in old age? Dementia? Loss of bodily functions? Loss of independence? Loneliness? Do some research and write about it in a creative way (e.g. imagine a cantankerous, geriatric writer). Offer some personal support to someone in that predicament (e.g. simply listening to them, to their story); run a writing workshop in a care home; or support a palliative care charity (e.g. create a fundraising anthology for a hospice).

14

Grave Goods

Beowulf goes into battle alone. All but one of his company have fled – but young Wiglaf rallies to his lord's aid. Together they overcome their adversary, but the price of victory is high. Beowulf is mortally wounded. Dying, he asks Wiglaf to show him the hoard he has won with his life. The champion of the Geats casts his fading gaze upon its gold. He offers loyal Wiglaf reward and dies.

You have completed your major project – there it sits: a pile of manuscript pages, perhaps a couple of inches high; or a modest shelf of books. Not much to look at for a life's work. Yet you should be proud. It is an achievement. Look upon it for a while, and reflect upon all the experience, all the hard work, that has gone into it. Beowulf, mortally wounded, wants to gaze upon the treasure he has paid for with his life's blood. He says to his loyal retainer, Wiglaf:

'Make haste that my eyes may behold the treasure,
The gleaming jewels, the goodly store,
And, glad of the gold, more peacefully leave
The life and the realm I have ruled so long.'[283]

Wiglaf quickly obeyed his dying lord's wish and entered the barrow, where he beheld: 'glittering jewels and gold on the ground'[284]. It had remained hidden for centuries – although much of it remained glorious, glittering in the gloaming, there were also 'many a helmet ancient and rusted.' The poet observes dolefully: 'Many an arm-ring cunningly wrought,/Treasure and gold, though hid in the ground,/Override a man's wishes, hide them who will!'[285] There are many creative endeavours that sadly remain undiscovered, unappreciated. Unread manuscripts, gathering dust in drawers. Unseen canvases, rolled up. Unheard poems. Unsung songs. Unperformed plays, and unbuilt buildings of exquisite design. Many others, destroyed (as the MSS of Beowulf nearly was) or lost, a museum of What Ifs...? This is the cruel reality of the creative mainstream – for every book published, untold thousands will never get that book deal. With digital publishing it is possible to self-publish these days, but the chances of many people reading it are slim – with the odd exception that 'goes viral'. So many people are self-publishing that it almost makes it meaningless – and the true gems get lost in the crowd, like the real Grail hiding amongst many other chalices, goblets and false cups. Nevertheless, we should always honour our muse and write it 'because we have to', until the fire in the head peters out, the midnight disease is extinguished – like the dragon slain by Beowulf:

> 'The ancient sword with its edge of iron
> Had slain the worm who watched o'er the wealth,
> In the midnight flaming, with menace of fire
> Protecting the treasure for many a year
> Till he died a death.'[286]

Wiglaf carries out what treasure he could – into the cold light of day, bitter with the sea air – and showed it to his stricken lord. The sight of it brings a strange satisfaction to his face:

> 'aged and sad,
> Beowulf spoke, as he gazed on the gold.'[287]

This is what he had fought for, struggled for, journeyed towards – for so long. It was his wer-gild, his blood-price – his death, waiting for him, in a cold barrow, underground:

'I gave my life for this golden hoard'[288]

Was it truly worth it? Well, Beowulf – locked into his warrior culture and his character – had little choice it seemed. It had his name 'written on it'. Strangely poignant then, that his wish is to be buried with it – it had only just seen the light of day – and a 'stately barrow' raised over him on the headland, visible to all:

'It shall be for remembrance among my people
As it towers high on the Cape of the Whale,
And sailors shall know it was Beowulf's barrow.' [289]

Is there a sense in which this is a hidden desire of all writers – to create a lasting legacy, something that will survive of them into posterity – a kind of immortality? And as such, is every such project a rehearsal of death – a preparation for 'going away', an extended suicide note, or 'letter to be read in the event of my death'? With his magnum opus complete, the artist/author may well feel like 'breaking his brushes' like Steinbeck. His 'antagonist' – that which had defined him – lay defeated:

'The monster that slew him, the dreadful dragon,
Likewise lay broken and brought to his death.' [290]

Their respective fates – the warrior and the monster – are intertwined. The Higher and Lower Self, the Avatarian and Atavistic Impulses, have been reconciled and have cancelled each other out – the creative charge has been neutralised, or perhaps consummated in this fierce coupling – the ultimate sex magic – and now both lay, mortally wounded by this post-coital *majeure morte*:

'Beowulf bartered his life for the treasure;
Both foes had finished this fleeting life.' [291]

Wiglaf, after reprimanding the ten 'battle-dodgers', foresees strife and ruin befalling his nation. He arranges for the funeral pyre of Beowulf to be made and piled high with grave goods:

> 'The Geat folk fashioned a peerless pyre
> Hung round with helmets and battle-boards,
> With gleaming byrnies as Beowulf bade.' [292]

Once the pyre cooled sufficiently, a barrow is raised over it. No one will wear Beowulf's treasure – no son or wife will continue his line. The warrior-king, in obsessive pursuit of his quest, has left this world alone – but not unloved, for his people hold him in high regard, as the magnificence of his barrow attests. The dragon is pitched over the cliff-top into the waves; and the treasures are once more consigned to the soil:

> 'They bore to the barrow the rings and the gems,
> The wealth of the hoard the heroes had plundered.
> The olden treasures they gave to the earth.' [293]

So, all must be let go of. We offer up our treasures. The final creative act is often the hardest – one of letting go. A project which has possessed us for perhaps years, has become such a huge part of our life – must now be forsaken. It can trigger significant grief – and leave us feeling empty: a hollow victory. Sometimes, authors do not want to finish their project, do not want to let go. It seemed Tolkien experienced something of the sort – with his Middle-Earth becoming his 'precious'. But eventually, we have to drop the One Ring of our magnum opus into Mount Doom – it is only healthy. The gold forged in the fires of Mordor, must be melted:

> 'The precious hoard
> Shall burn with the hero. There lies the heap

Of untold treasures so grimly gained,
Jewels and gems he bought with his blood
At the end of his life. All these at the last
The flames shall veil and the brands devour.' [294]

This is the hard truth of the creative process. The final phase seems like one of destruction. We must be prepared to cut our ties to it – snip that umbilical cord – for it to live on, to have a 'life' of its own. It is in other hands now – for them to make of it what they will. Our words are our offering to the 'void' – a message in a bottle. We cast it out into the great unknown – wish it well – and walk away, perhaps heeding William Blake's wisdom:

'He who binds to himself a joy
Does the wingèd life destroy;
But he who kisses the joy as it flies
Lives in eternity's sunrise.'

The crucial question here is – to paraphrase the father and son dialogue from Cormac McCarthy's post-apocalyptic novel *The Road* (2006): 'are you a carrier of the fire?' Are you prepared to keep it alight and pass it on? That is all we can do:

We're going to be okay, aren't we Papa?
Yes. We are.
And nothing bad is going to happen to us.
That's right.
Because we're carrying the fire.
Yes. Because we're carrying the fire.[295]

When I complete the last book of *The Windsmith Elegy, This Fearful Tempest* (2012), in a castle in Scotland, I went out to the loch and howled my catharsis across the water. For ten years I had been carrying this. Now I was unburdened. Afterwards I felt hollowed out, weightless, and in a limbo. In the months that followed, I had something of a meltdown. So often in our culture, when we suffer bereavement we try and 'keep it together', to put a brave face on things? Why? This will not aid your recovery. Instead of burying your grief, exhume it and dance with its corpse like some mad person. Kiss the skull lovingly. Rub ash into your face and tear out your hair – whatever you need to, to acknowledge your inner hurt, your inner wasteland. Then, when you are broken in the rubble, when you have nothing left, no more tears to shed and your voice is raw from howling – then, the healing can begin. Then, you will spot a tiny bud emerging from a crack in the ground.

Grave Goods questings:

- When you have reached the end of a major project, create a 'parting rite' – a small ceremony to honour its completion and to let it go. Acknowledge its presence in your life, what it has meant to you, what you have put into it. When did it start? When were you first struck by inspiration, that 'love at first sight' feeling, with your project? How did you 'woo' it? What trials and tribulations did you face? How did you overcome them? How do you feel now? Perhaps you feel some form of grief – if so, give it voice.
- Clear your desk, put away your pile of research books, file away any documents, recycle the manuscript, valet your PC. Enjoy the Zen-like aesthetic. For a while stay with the emptiness – don't launch straight into a new project. Give yourself a month or two at least. Use your journal to explore your feelings, but resist the temptation to start on something else – until the itch becomes unbearable. When the time is right, you will not have a choice. But for now, simply 'be'. Stillness, silence, solitude, and doing nothing seem to be frowned upon in the West. Concerned friends

might ask, 'is there something wrong?' as you sit there, Buddha/slob-like. You could reply like John Lennon: 'I'm just sitting here watching the wheels go round and round…' Busy, doing nothing.

15

Wiglaf's Legacy

Wiglaf berates the craven warriors who fled their lord. A messenger sent to the Geatish host awaiting nearby relates how Beowulf bravely met his fate, and broods on what this betides for the future of their land when their enemies hear of their champion's demise. Their conscience stirred, the band of warriors return to the fateful place, where they raise a funeral pyre. Beowulf is buried with the treasure in a barrow high upon the headland. The dragon is cast into the sea. Beowulf's retainer reflects on his lord's legacy. The poet reflects on the themes of his tale.

Wiglaf – Beowulf's loyal retainer – serves the plot purpose of the 'one who survives', the witness, who relates the hero's glorious ending – often playing a key role in it. In the Matter of Britain it is Bedwyr who must cast Excalibur into the lake – he cannot bring himself to do it the first two times, but finally he follows his lords wishes. When he returns, to bear the news – The Lady of the Lake has taken the sword back – his Lord is gone, borne across the waters to Avalon on a dark ship by three queens. In Beowulf, it is Wiglaf who must arrange for the dragon to be cast into the water, for the pyre to be made and his lord and his hoard to be placed upon it, and then a barrow raised. He attends to practical matters, as well as metaphysical – declaiming a psychopompic eulogy for his King, appeasing his spirit and enshrining his memory. He ties up the final plot threads and introduces the final note of doom – that Beowulf's demise will create a power vacuum, which will result in bloodshed and chaos. The enemies of the Geats will be at the gate – and old feuds will flare up once more, without the protection of the mighty Beowulf. In effect, Beowulf himself was the 'dragon' of his people (as King Arthur was the Pendragon, inheriting the title from his father, Uther) – slaying the 'hoard-guardian' he became the guardian of the hoard.

The fallen king is buried with his hard won treasure – a poignant end to this tale, leaving a gloomy sense of futility: what was it all for?

'The gold to the ground, where it still remains
As useless to men as it was of yore.'[296]

After completing a major writing project there can often be a sense of anti-climax. In story terms, as soon as the line of tension of the central protagonist has been achieved/defeated for good, the tension evaporates – the elastic of the narrative snaps. It is time to finish off quickly. Wise advice for all writers is to 'arrive late, and leave early' – avoid protracted endings. Certainly in modern narratives it is popular to end snappily, that is why the epic register of Peter Jackson's treatment of *The Lord of the Rings: Return of the King* (2003) – with its sense of structural overture – jarred with some, not used to this slow 'pulling back', a symphonic fadeout. Despite the satire it attracted for this it won Best Film in the Oscars (Academy Awards 2004) and a slew of other awards. Jackson held his nerve, and it paid off. He didn't play to the crowd, he played to the mythic, if not literal, integrity of the story.

Peter Jackson perhaps wisely decided to leave out 'The Scouring of the Shire' chapter from his treatment, but taken metaphorically, this is a crucial part of the 'final stages' of any project. All vestiges of 'Mordor' must be riddled out – that is, full consciousness must be brought to every nook and cranny of one's 'domain' (i.e. manuscript).

The writer 'keeps faith' with his material, and, keenly watches over its final stages – a critical, vulnerable stage – seeing things through properly, like loyal Wiglaf, keeping vigil over the body of his fallen lord. When the mound is raised, the warriors ride around it, twelve in numbers, like the hours of the day:

> 'Then round the mound rode the brave in battle,
> The sons of warriors, twelve in a band'

And, so, sometimes grimly, we must remain 'a-wake', alert to every tiny nuance – encircling our work with full omniscience. We should review our work with the full perspective of hindsight.

Yet, there is no escaping, this sense of 'hollowness' after completion. I have experienced it as a sense of weightlessness. The millstone or cross you have been carrying – for possibly years – has been lifted away. That which defined us, which drove us on, consumed us and all of our energies is ... no longer there. Our 'antagonist' has been slain. Where does that leave us?

Well, in Beowulf's case – pushing up the daisies, but it need not be so final, you'll be relieved to know! Here are a few suggestions for coping with the aftermath:

Wiglaf's Legacy questings:

- Firstly, like Wiglaf you have a hard-won sense of perspective, the long view. You have the 'tidings of the eagle' – able to look back across the whole of your 'Quest', and the whole of your manuscript with the benefit of hindsight. Take advantage of this to reflect, to review. How do you feel about the project? What worked? What didn't? What were the highlights? The lowlights? The mountain peaks and abysmal troughs – the eagle soars above them all.
- Let your 'baby' have a life of its own. The worst thing a creator can do is smother their creation. Let it breathe. Step back and allow others to discover its treasures – avoid pointing them out, or apologising, justifying or defending. Allow it to stand or fall on its own merits.

- Allow yourself to have the 'fallow, before the fertile'. This is sometimes called the Fertile Void. It might seem unbearable, just to simply 'be', but maybe that is exactly what you need to do right now. Let it be.
- Rest, replenish the well – experience and enjoy the creativity of others; go on a stimulating holiday; catch up with old friends; or visit 'soul places' from your past – and inspiration will come.
- Follow Wiglaf's example and 'put your house in order'. Arrange to have your writings, library, journals, etc, put into a literary archive – not out of egotistical sense of your importance in the canon, but just for posterity. You have existed. You expressed your dream. By doing so, you have provided a role model to others. You never know who you might inspire. It might seem premature to consider Literary Estates, but it is wise to plan what will happen to your works when you're gone – clarify matters of copyright, royalties, bequests, etc – for the sake of your loved ones. You never know – you might become famous and successful when you're dead! In which case, your living relatives or chosen causes can benefit (e.g. Great Ormond Street Hospital have benefited from the royalties of JM Barrie's 'Peter Pan' for over a century).
- Manage your expectations. The sad truth is your 'legacy' might end up as a stack of unsold copies in the spare room; on a pile in a remainder bookstore; or shoved in a shelf with Mills and Boons and Dan Browns in a charity shop. The essential thing is to have 'enjoyed the journey' and savoured the honing of your craft. Anything else is the icing on the cake. Always remember Cavafy's immortal coda from his poem, Ithaka:

  'And if you find her poor, Ithaka won't have fooled you.
  Wise as you will have become, so full of experience,
  you'll have understood by then what these Ithakas mean.'

- Avoid 'Beowulf syndrome' – that is, the seeking after fame, which was his fatal flaw, the classic trait of the tragic hero:

  'Mildest, most gentle, most eager for fame.' [297]
- Beowulf's character arc was like the flight of an arrow – he 'held to his high destiny' and 'The shaft hit home.' The Champion of the Geats had no choice – he was compelled to act within the parameters of his character – but *we do*. Vainly seeking after fame and fortune will not produce great works of literature. It is the wrong motive. Glory will come (or a warm sense of satisfaction of a 'job well done') if you are good enough.

Change is as good as a rest. Try something different. A short, comic novel. A radio play. Lighten up. This magnum opus would no doubt have carried a lot of 'baggage'. A lifetime's wisdom, perhaps. Give yourself a break. How about something less serious and worthy? You might find it flows – with a lightness and grace missing from your weighty tome. Perhaps you just had to get that out of your system, and learn your craft – and now … you can dance. The result, an elegant and pithy novel which becomes an instant best-seller. You go 'viral' and your 'overnight success' seems 'effortless', when in fact it has come about through years of apprenticeship, through undertaking the Writer's Quest.

On Dragon Hills

Beneath soil, curved into landscape
Ancient bone rock, hatched to these shapes
Before time knew to count itself,
Wrapped into sleeping form,
Grown into land and hill, tree scaled
Spine ridge, curved belly melts to fields,
Wings out there lost in hedgerows
Tailing down from the heights,
Mound of a head, suggestive, subtle.

Underneath, the deep, unconscious
Occupies your long centuries
As mud slides into new shapes,
Cultures rise and fall, at breath pace,
Your slumber untroubled,

Rich with the fertile soil of your dreaming,
Rising in wisps and tendrils of unseen smoke
Through earth and bark, touching any
Who pause long enough to inhale
All that you exhale.
Each one gifted different visions
From the depths.

Nimue Brown

Part Three

The Dragon's Hoard – Other Essays

1

A Wilderness of Dragons

In the eponymous essay, reprinted in *The Monsters and The Critics* (2006), Tolkien cited the Beowulfian critic Professor Chambers' phrase 'a wilderness of dragons.'[298] Tolkien, punctilious as ever when it comes to language, queries the 'Shylockian plural', and yet it is clear he would prefer such a hazardous place to the bleak territory of the unimaginative critic. It clearly stuck in his mind, and perhaps acted as grit in the oyster for his creation of the 'desolation of Smaug', in the map for *The Hobbit* (1937) – a blasted wasteland on the edge of the cosy world of the hobbits.

This is a deliberate striking out into unchartered zones.

On the borders of medieval maps, where human knowledge ran out and reason slept, monsters stirred: 'Here Be Dragons' the legend read. This is the direct descendant of the primal fear which lurked outside the circle of firelight for our most ancient ancestors. Of course, some fears were very real, when ferocious predators roamed the world with early man. And the fear sometimes remains even when the threat has gone – or wasn't even there in the first place – the glass ceilings of the mind that keep us prisoners.

A map is a snapshot of available knowledge. It says 'this is where we are', 'this is how much we know'. It is a circle in the sand with man at the centre. This cartographical solipsism has continued well into the 21st Century, with OS postcode-centred personalised maps; and, on a larger scale, world maps which manipulate the landmass, showing the continents of the Northern Hemisphere far bigger than they should be: the classic North/South divide. A Peters projection depicts the landmasses in correct proportion to the surface of the Earth, and consequently Africa, South America and South East Asia dominate.

Other maps depict our 'Antipodes', Australia, as the centre of the world, the Pacific Rim, or one of the Poles – a healthy shifting of perspective. Indeed there is no reason why North should be 'up' on our maps – we are living on a sphere after all, which doesn't say This Way Up on it. But we feel, especially in the West, the world revolves around us.

There is nothing new in this.

The miraculously preserved 12th Century 'Mappa Mundi' ('Map of the World') in Hereford Cathedral, rendered on vellum with its hand-drawn detail looks, to modern eyes, like something out of a Fantasy novel that Tolkien & Sons might have fashioned. The world as we know it is virtually unrecognisable. Like many maps of the Middle Ages, it depicted the Holy Lands at the centre, and Jerusalem at the centre of those. This was and still is for many, the *axis mundi* of the human universe. The map depicted the whole of Christendom – then, the most successful of religious franchises – what lay outside that belonged to the Devil, that greatest of serpents. In Norse mythology it is the World Serpent who encircles Midgard, the Middle World, biting its own tail like Ouroboros. The dragon dwells where the known becomes unknown: the edge of the conscious world. It is the ultimate threshold guardian – often guarding untold riches, as in the Anglo-Saxon epic *Beowulf*, or in Sigurd and Fafnir, where the monstrous worm – once a covetous brother cursed for slaying his kin – guards a great treasure, Glitaheid: the glittering heath.

Tolkien had this to say on the subject:: 'I find 'dragons' a fascinating product of the imagination. But I don't think the Beowulf one is frightfully good. But the whole problem of the intrusion of the 'dragon' into northern imagination and its transformation there is one I do not know enough about. Fāfnir in the late Norse version of the Sigurd story is better; and Smaug and his conversation obviously is in debt there.' [299]

Dragons have haunted the human imagination for centuries –

resolutely defying all probability of their existence. They are the kundalini serpent of the Collective Unconscious; our suppressed desires, lurking in the shadows of the Id; the Smaug Within, grafted to our own reptilian brain. We can no more banish the dragon than we can shake off the coils of our DNA.

These ancient and canny beasts loomed large in Tolkien's febrile imagination, yet they seem hard-wired into the British psyche – certainly the Welsh and English soul – appearing on the Cymric flag and starring in many folk tales and legends (60 recorded in England[300]). The most well known, George and the Dragon, about England's national saint, is only the wing-tip of these, and to this exotic import we shall return, but first let us consider his native cousins.

Merlin, Myrddin Emrys, famously beheld a red and white dragon locked in combat beneath Vortigern's Tower: he explained that the former were the British, the white, the Saxon – and while they fought no peace would be in the land. Merlin gave his name to the British Isles: Clas Myrddin, Merlin's Enclosure – he is our tutelary guardian.

In another tale, 'Ludd and Llevelys', from the 13th Century Welsh cycle of ancient British oral tales, *Y Mabinogi*, a terrible scream is heard over the land every May Eve, which blights cattle, causes mares to drop their foals early, women to miscarry and milk to curdle. Llevelys tells Lludd, his brother, how to dispatch them: measure the land, and in its exact centre (which they decide is Oxford – X marking the spot) dig a pit and fill it with mead, covered with silk. This will lure the dragons down, they will drink, get drunk, fall asleep, wrapped in the silk. Then he needs to gather them up, (as they are now in the form of sticky pigs), lock them in a stone chest, and bury them in a hill near Snowdon called Dinas Emrys – where Vortigern's tower was said to have been and Merlin beheld his two feuding dragons. Thus the stories overlap, biting each others' tails.

The Lambton Worm and other similar folk tales seem to be

morality tales, regardless of their claims to authenticity. There are often local features which 'prove' the veracity of the story, as in Worm Rock in Lambton. Beneath the highly stylised chalk figure in Oxfordshire, the White Horse of Uffington, which some interpret as a dragon, there is a conical shaped hill called Dragon's Hill. It is claimed that the bare patches of earth found upon it were caused by the slain dragon's blood – highly toxic, like that of the serpentesque *Alien* in Ridley Scott's 1982 tech-noir film, which is essential a dragon-in-space horror movie with the message: we take our demons with us.

These, and many others, seem to create a British Dreamtime, with the equivalent of the windings of the Rainbow Serpent – as with the topographical narratives of Aboriginal Australia. Perhaps the large-scale legacy of glaciers in the British Isles suggested this, as they gouged out the valleys and shaped the rocks that stick out like the skeleton of a great land behemoth. With the last glacial period known as *Wurm*, it is tempting to link this to the being old English for serpent: 'wyrm'.

Our most famous dragon culture tale is Saint George and the Dragon of course – the 'pin ups' of many eponymous pubs, which bear his sign. The dragon had, by this time come to represent the chthonic forces of the unChristian, be they Pagan, Muslim or heretic. The irony is Saint George seems to have started off as a pork butcher from Cappadocia, in what is now modern day Turkey. His grave is situated in Lydda, Palestine – near the area where the story of Perseus, Andromeda and the great Kraken played itself out. Our Saint George similarly rescued a damsel in distress who was going to be fed to the local dragon. Yet lately he gets martyred: forced to walk in red hot iron shoes, broken on a wheel, and immersed in quick lime by none other than Gevya Garsa, the 'Serpent King'. Saint George's grave was discovered by Crusaders who adopted him in their campaigns against the Saracen. He was brought home and his Feast Day was chosen as April 23rd, and this eventually became

England's national day of celebration, a reassertion of collective identity. In recent years the English flag – the very same colours the Templar Knights wore – has been re-appropriated as a positive image, out of the hands of the hooligans.

Tolkien's folk hero 'Farmer Giles of Ham' – another kind of 'pork butcher' – shows how the chaos-dragon can be subdued by good old English commonsense and stubbornness. In essence, the dragon is any disruption to the status quo. For a full decade from 9/11 the world's modern Grendel or Chrystophylax was Osama Bin Laden and his Al Qaeda: a useful amorphous bugbear, with countless splinter cells. Like the Hydra of Leda which Herakles fights in one of his Twelve Labours – cut one head off and two more grow in its place: thus, a regenerating supervillain to keep the world's Stars-and-Stripes-spandexed 'Superpower' and his weedy sidekick (e.g. his 'special friend', Britain) busy, and feeding the Culture of Fear, for as long as people swallow it. In this way 'dragons' can stop the populace from straying too far the white-picketed enclosure and for justifying draconian measures. We live in the Age of the Dragon it seems.

Emblematic of their genre (once used in libraries as a symbol to designate that category) in their overused *unlikeliness*, dragons have been a staple of Fantasy fiction since the earliest stories, and it looks like there's no diminishing their popularity: Tolkien relaunched them in modern fiction and they haven't gone away since – what with the endless Tolkien pastiches (even the anti-Tolkienian, ultra gritty, brutal, and massively popular series 'Song of Ice and Fire', by George RR Martin, has them – a whole dragon dynasty). The roleplaying system from TSR, *Dungeons and Dragons*, have allowed participants to bait dragons in their lairs, and even play them: they come in all shapes, sizes, colours and elements: earth, air, fire and water, bronze, silver and gold dragons. Some have portrayed dragons more positively. German author Michael Ende, in his Fantasy classic *The Never-Ending Story* (translated into English in 1983) has a luck-dragon (similar to the oriental species – long-necked and whiskered) help the boy hero. American author Anne McCaffrey has made them the key *novum* of her long-running *Dragonriders of Pern* series (initiated in 1967, and comprising 22 novels in 2011); a new kid on the block – mega-hyped wünderkind Christopher Paolini – has resurrected them yet again with *Eragon,* 2003 (first of the Inheritance Cycle): joining the long list of its movie cousins on the big screen: Fritz Lang's silent double-bill *Die Nibelungen* (1924); Disney's *Pete and the Dragon* (1973); and *Dragonslayer* (Robbins, 1981); *Dragonheart* (Cohen, 1996); *Shrek* (Adamson/ Jenson, 2001) and its sequels; *Reign of Fire* (Bowman, 2002); *Harry Potter and the Goblet of Fire* (Newell, 2005); the *How to Train a Dragon* animation (Deblois, 2010); and the *Merlin* BBC TV series (2008-2012). The second part of Peter Jackson's extended Hobbit 'trilogy', *The Desolation of Smaug* (2013) is the latest to flap its wings and breathe fire over the heads of movie-goers.

No doubt more will be on the wing.

It seems many people still desire dragons. We simply cannot take our eyes off of them…

The Spell of the Dragon

A dragon's gaze was said to be mesmeric – once we fell under it, we were hypnotised and at its mercy. Those who 'desire dragons' had better watch out! Dracophilia can become an all-consuming passion, a burning obsession, which can cloud our judgement and drive us to extremes. Tolkien, who knew this fever more than most, describes the hero of *The Children of Hurin* (2007), falling under the spell of the Fāfnir-like fire-drake, Glaurung:

> 'Then Turin sprang about, and strode against him, and fire was in his eyes, and the edges of Gurthang shone as with flame. But Glaurung withheld his blast, and opened wide his serpent-eyes and gazed upon Turin. Without fear Turin looked in those eyes as he raised up his sword: and

> straightway he fell under the dreadful spell of the dragon, and was as one turned to stone.' [301]

Dragons could be interpreted as symbols of the chthonic forces of the subconscious, which we *should* bait in their lairs. It is far healthier to assimilate the Shadow than deny it. Jung, who wrote extensively on the Shadow, referred to it as: 'the thing a person has no wish to be'.[302] Jung defined the Shadow as: '...that hidden, repressed, for the most part inferior and guilt-laden personality whose ultimate ramifications reach back into the realm of the animal ancestors...' [303] Failure to recognise, acknowledge and deal with it led, in Jung's mind, to problems in the individual, in groups, and organisations. Yet the influential psychoanalysist believed it had positive spin-offs: 'If it has been believed hitherto that the human shadow was the source of evil, it can now be ascertained on closer investigation that the unconscious man, that is his shadow, does not consist only of morally reprehensible tendencies, but also displays a number of good qualities, such as normal instincts, appropriate reactions, realistic insights, creative impulses, etc.' [304] By embracing the energy of our 'animal ancestors' we can tap into deep springs of creativity.

The classic images of a knight struggling in the coils of a serpent seem to represent the armoured identity of the Ego fighting for dominion over the Lower Self: this crops up time and time again in world myths, e.g. Apollo and Python. The serpent is often depicted as being impaled by a spear or lance – in geomantic terms this is the 'fixing the spot' of the earth dragon energy. This seems to have been done quite deliberately within Christian temples on pagan sites (the prevalence of St Michael – the dragonslayer – churches on hilltops has been noted by the likes of John Michel, Paul Broadhurst, etc). St Patrick was said to have cast out all the serpents in Ireland from the top of Croagh-Patrick, a mountain on the West coast originally named after Crom-Croagh, the bent-backed one, a chthonic deity vanquished by the usurper priests. The lance, the standing stone, the cross or the spire acts like an acupuncture needle and channels the telluric currents. It is a way of conducting chaos.

There is a sense in which a writer does this every time he picks up a pen, or a musician his violin bow. We tap into the field of potential, give voice to it, craft it. This lateral approach has proved to be very effective, from the Dadaist automatic drawings and writing, to popular self-help books on creativity such as *Drawing from the Right Side of the Brain* (Betty Edwards, 1983) and *The Artist's Way* (Julia Cameron, 1992). It is a rich repository of creativity.

Similarly, the serpent can be seen as the libido, which can be channelled positively – as in the Tantric practice of raising the Kundalini, the serpent energy which dwells in the lowest chakra and snakes up the spine during lovemaking. In the East, the dragon is seen as a positive force, in the human body, in the land. It is worked with in acupuncture and in feng-shui. The Imperial Dragon in Chinese dynasties, and the presence of it in Oriental astrology (as one of the 12 zodiacal signs) shows a qualitatively different status than in the west.

Ophialatry, the worship of serpent deities is prevalent in several ancient cultures. In India the serpent is especially important in Hindu and Buddhist mythology – in the form of the snake god, *Nāga*; in Voudou the serpent is very important also. Serpent Magic seems to be regaining popularity in the occult circles. As with any sacred knowledge, however, it can be misappropriated, e.g. the Nibelungen Hall (built in 1913), an astonishing serpent temple at Konigswinter, North-Rhine-Westfalia, at the foot of the Seibengebirge range – the seven hills said to have been created by the thrashings of Fāfnir's tail – depicts a giant serpent interwoven with a pentacle on the floor of a dark shrine to the myth of Seigfried and Fāfnir (the temple is built near the 'Drachenfels' – Dragon Rock, the site of a former castle associated with the legend – where Siegfried was said to have slain the dragon and bathed in its blood). Made world famous (and notorious) by Wagner, it was used by the Nazis in the Second World War – a perverted symbol of national pride. These days, it has become a creepy tourist attraction with a reptile zoo, and a 'Dragon's Lair', complete with a long stone serpent, built in 1993 to celebrate the 50th anniversary of Wagner's death.

Generally in the West the idea of the serpent being the Evil One, the seducer, the tempter, is hard-wired into us from an early age. Many people have unnecessary phobias of snakes – exploited by such low-grade schlock as *Snakes on a Plane!* (Ellis, 2006); and *Q*, the 1982 monster flick directed by Larry Cohen – a spurious spin on the ancient icon of the Winged Serpent (the Meso-American Feathered Serpent, Quetzcoatl, transposed improbably to New York, in *King Kong*-like fashion). Yet fear and desire are often closely linked, and what is forbidden often becomes more appealing. The much maligned dragon has gained new fans over the years, and some feel protective towards such unlikely creatures as though they were endangered species. Their very 'existence' challenges the consensus reality. And a world which can accommodate dragons can also accommodate heroes, heroines, villains and a whole cast of magical beings. Suddenly the world seems less lonely. The mysterious is possible, and not everything is explained away or tidied up.

Jorge Luis Borges, in his preface to *The Book of Imaginary Beasts* (1967) calls dragons 'a necessary monster': 'We are ignorant of the meaning of the dragon in the same way that we are ignorant of the meaning of the universe, but there is something in the dragon's image that fits man's imagination, and this accounts for the dragon's appearance in different places and periods.' [305] The Mappa Mundi is like a retinal scan – around its periphery strange creatures flicker, as in Robert Holdstock's *Mythago Wood* cycle (1984-2009). Monsters and wonders await at the edge of consciousness, at the edge of knowledge, at the edge of the known.British Fantasy author Alan Garner, argues that it is intrinsic to our nature to explore these littoral zones: 'Man is an animal that tests boundaries. He is a 'mearcstapa', 'boundarystrider', and the nature of myth is to help him to understand the boundaries, to cross them and to comprehend the new; so that, whenever Man reaches out, it is myth that supports him with a truth that is constant, although names and shapes may change.' [306] Garner dramatises this concept most directly in his extraordinary 1996 novel *Strandloper.*

Author Moyra Caldecott, in her memoir, *A Multi-Dimensional Life* (2007) describes this process: 'In writing a novel one can play with ideas and concepts that hover on the edge of one's belief and, while doing so, consider seriously one's attitude to them.' [307]

This is the liminal territory the Fantasy writer explores. The twilight threshold, where humanity meets the unknown, the Fey, the divine or diabolic – a place we travel to every night in our dreams. Yet the Fantasy writer must be fully awake in this world of dreams, so as not to miss anything. He or she is the lucid dreamer, a Neo of *The Matrix* (Wachowski Bros, 1999), the one-who-is-awake. In his haunting classic *Voyage to Arcturus* (1920) David Lindsay has his protagonist Maskull say: 'I dream with open eyes … and others see my dreams, that is all.'[308]

In his robust defence of dragons in his influential essay on 'Beowulf', Tolkien wrote: 'A dragon is no idle fancy. Whatever may be his origins, in fact or invention, the dragon in legend is a potent creation of men's imagination, richer in significance than his barrow is in gold.'[309]

The dragon is, if nothing else, a potent symbol of the human imagination. The glittering treasure that it hoards could be seen to be the treasures of the subconscious, waiting to be unearthed. By tapping into our own creativity, we are disturbing our own dragon from its slumber. Something old and noble inside us is stirred. Something that has the memory of the Earth and fire in its belly.

2

Lines of Desire

(Writing for Imagination, University of Bath, 2005)

Each character in a story has a line of desire – the one thing they most desire in the world. This will govern their actions and drive them through the story, creating narrative traction. Odysseus wanted to get home; Hamlet wanted revenge; Juliet wanted love across the tracks; Emma wanted to match-make; Gilgamesh wanted to atone for his friend's death by bringing him back to life. Once the line of desire is established, the author's job is to thwart it as much as possible – through character, setting and incident – thus creating conflict and drama. In the fulfilment of that line of desire hangs the tale – it may or may not be achieved, and may or may not bring happiness, but the reader is on tenterhooks as they watch the protagonist struggle to complete their own 'quest'.

Critically, the writer's *own* line of desire needs to be acknowledged. By embedding our own secret dreams into the narrative, we are writing about what deeply moves and inspires us. We are coming from a place of authenticity – and that has power and sustainability. What pushes our buttons and pulls our levers will create convincing characters and engage the reader.

Here are a list of LoDs to consider, acting as catalysts for creating your own Worlds of Desire (the chief driving force of all imaginative fiction). Use them as prompts for short creative writing activities. Dream on the page:

- Imagine a character/person (real or imaginary) you would love to be. Write a monologue in their voice. Try to inhabit their way of seeing the world.

- Imagine a person (real or imaginary) you would love to meet. Describe the encounter.
- Imagine a special ability that you would love to have.
- Imagine a gesture or conversation you wish you had made.
- Imagine an incident which might have turned out differently if you had acted otherwise.
- Imagine and describe the life you would be leading now if you had made different choices.
- Imagine the one thing in the world you most desire.
- Imagine/consider/list the things you most dread.
- If you could only say/convey 10 important messages to the world, what would they be?
- Imagine the world you would love to live in.

3

Mythic Literacy

Before a writer embarks on the writing of yet another Fantasy novel, I recommend not only that they familiarise them self with the best in the field, classic and modern, but also, essentially, learn 'mythic literacy' – that is, cultivate a deep familiarity and understanding of world myths and legends. By doing so, one imbibes key elements of narrative and a treasure-house of tropes and creative possibilities. Further, myths and legends can provide a 'ready-made' structure which can underpin a narrative and give it added depth – what I call mythic resonance – amplifying its impact and universalising the content.

As a storyteller I've been performing myths and legends for a number of years and have noticed how these ancient tales still resonate with modern audiences. Not surprising considering two things: these stories have been told and retold since the year dot (their longevity proving their success); and all stories, however Byzantine on the surface, ultimately deal with the human condition (even though ostensibly the cast may be a Greek, African, or Norse Pantheon, various semi-divine heroes, talking animals, elementals, spirits, etc).There is something universal and timeless about them. Dealing with fundamental themes, they push our buttons. And, thus, they prove very effective structural underpinning for modern narratives. By giving a contemporary story an underlying myth or legend it acquires mythic resonance. It amplifies the whole thing – its particularity acquires universality.

This approach has become very common in Hollywood now thanks to the huge influence of Christopher Vogler's *The Writers Journey: mythic structure for storytellers and screenwriters* (1998). In his book, Vogler takes a discovery of mythographer Joseph

Campbell and applies it to film structure. Campbell in studying world myths and legends discovered common themes running throughout, which he collated, calling it the Monomyth, or The Hero's Journey. Vogler showed how, time and time again, this crops up in films – at one point intuitively, but now, in a conscious way, as screenwriters apply the template of The Hero's Journey to their film scripts. Of course, good writers take a more original approach. The ingenuity of a film is largely due to how these tropes are subverted, rearranged, etc – but bear in mind, they have worked for millennia, they satisfy us on a deep level, and, unless you can improve, best to stick to classic formulae ... at least as a starting point.

Fairy stories offer excellent templates – they tap primal childhood fears, and are also efficiently plotted with clear characters, setting and structure. They are often over in a couple of pages, but within them is contained the embryo of all fiction. Understand what is going on in a fairy tale, master it by emulation, and you would have 'learnt the ropes' – the fundamentals of story. And many contain powerful material. Many writers have drawn inspiration from them, perhaps best of all Angela Carter – in particular her 'Bloody Chamber' sequence, from which writer/director Neil Jordan took *The Company of Wolves* and adapted it for film (with Carter as co-screenwriter) to haunting effect.

In my novella *The Sun Miners* I took The Hero's Journey and used it as my structure – to see how it would work. The story flowed (I wrote the first 50,000 word draft in a month). Ideally, though, you should only use the Hero's Journey as a kind of 'literary MOT' – to check your story afterwards, or to help if you get stuck. Are all the ingredients there? Does the story have a sufficient dramatic rise, confrontation and resolution? To try and fit your story into a given structure is a little like putting a cart before the horse. Your characters should be in charge – but it's good to give the story parameters, to stop yourself getting overwhelmed by narrative possibilities. Without a direction, the story can just meander in a shapeless way. Permissible for a first draft; but not acceptable after. The more shapeless your story to begin with, the more times it will have to go to the 'writer's gym' to burn off the flab. Using a tried-and-tested structure, such as the triadic arc of beginning, middle and end (Complication; Crisis; Resolution) can help keep the narrative buff.

Raymond Carver, in his typically lean and mean way, says there are only two kinds of story: Man goes on a journey; or, Stranger walks into town. Think how much can be conveyed by the first one (e.g. *The Odyssey*); or the second (e.g. *Stranger in a Strange Land* [310]). A whole plot in a short sentence. Most soap operas are based upon the second – a fixed location with new arrivals every week or so. Of course, there are more than this. Christopher Booker, suggests there's 7 in *The Seven Basic Plots* (2005):

- Overcoming the Monster
- Rags to Riches
- The Quest
- Voyage and Return
- Comedy
- Tragedy
- Rebirth

Although there's lots of interesting stuff in Booker's 728 page tome, I feel these kinds of pigeonhole theories are too convenient, too neat. The received wisdom is that 'there's nothing new under the sun', but that might just be a consoling fiction for the intellectually lazy. The human imagination is limitless. The human condition offers infinite permutations and variations. And even if there is only a fixed number of 'ingredients' think how only the 26 letters of our alphabet can create the canon of English Literature.

The vast treasure hoard of myth and legend is yours to plunder.

By choosing carefully and using discerningly, your writing will really shine with an archetypal gleam.

By fostering 'mythic literacy' (familiarising yourself with world myths, legends, folk tales and fairy stories) your writing will be considerably enriched. Even if you don't utilise tropes consciously (as I did in my novel, *The Long Woman*, where I used the Egyptian myth of Isis and Osiris to provide mythic resonance) you will find they will 'bleed' through from your subconscious – in the same way a tree is fed from nutrients in the soil. The richer the soil, the deeper the roots, the healthier the tree.

So, consider how you could use mythic structure in your stories & scripts.

Suggested Activity: Pick an ancient myth or legend, folk tale or fairy story. Now update it. Consider transposing it into a contemporary setting. Be imaginatively lateral in your 'translation'. The more ingredients you change, the more the story becomes yours. You can alter much of the cosmetic detail – names of characters, appearances, period, minor plot details – but keep the basic structure and you can't go far wrong. You have a story that 'hits the buttons'. Eventually you may feel restricted by this story scaffold, but that's okay – see it as a starting point, a blueprint. Go as far as your imagination and skill will allow you.

4

Creativity and Well-being

(First published in *Resurgence* magazine, Issue 267, July/August 2011)

There is a saying from Ghana, one that I often share with my writing and storytelling students, which goes: 'Until the lion learns to write the hunter will always tell the story of the hunt.' This profound wisdom sums up, for me, why creativity is essential to well-being. We all deserve to be heard, to be seen, to be witnessed. When we are not, we can suffer, sicken, even die. Creative expression is essential for the health of individuals as well as their communities – soul hygiene, if you will. The greatest tragedy when a loved one is taken from us suddenly and prematurely by death, is not the cold fact of their extinction, but that a life has been somehow unfulfilled – that it has failed to live up to its promise; its narrative has been arrested.

So many of us postpone our happiness, through apparently practical, 'realistic' reasons, until retirement – only then do we learn how to paint, to sing, to travel, to write, to manifest our dreams – but that retirement might never come. *This moment* is all we have – there may not be another. The received wisdom is that creativity is for the 'gifted' – the virtuosos and geniuses – but life is a gift we all receive, and it is an insult to that gift, to the sacredness of life, to squander it, for even a single second. To not to at least strive to achieve our potential, as human beings, is anathema to the matrix of Creation, that ever unfolding field of potential of which we are all participants, not by-standers.

Yet, however 'active' we are in awakening our creative impulse, we can enjoy creativity in small, mundane ways and this author advocates random acts of art on a daily basis. Always and ever the here and now. Tomorrow is another canvas. But creativity is first and foremost, an act of perception – of appreciating what is right in front of you, with your senses fully engaged in the miracle of being alive on this amazing planet. So, it is about waking up, being fully present, and playing with an open heart and mind in the joy of the moment.

Creativity is intrinsic to well-being. We do not need the latest research to tell us this. Listen to your body (it is wiser than you think). How often has a piece of uplifting music, a beautiful painting or sculpture, a heart-stopping poem, or dazzling film made you feel better? Movies are especially sold on their 'feel good factor', but this 'side-effect' is not unique to cinema. I would argue that the origins of art are entwined with this principle – it might even be its raison d'etre. From cave paintings to cathedrals, iconic art has been used as a form of sympathetic magic to manifest 'luck' for the tribe or community it represents. For millennia humans have prayed to icons to bring good fortune, a change of circumstance, for re-assurance, strength to continue, or a shift of consciousness.

Yet creativity is not just something we can benefit from by enjoying as viewers, listeners, audience or readers with our senses and intellect; enormous benefits can be reaped in the creation and in the sharing. Artists continually receive the direct benefit of their art – in the pleasure of working with their materials, with forms, colours, textures, sounds, concepts, light, spaces, movements and so on. And who has not felt the pleasure of sharing something we enjoy – a favourite book, film, play, poem, image, object, place? In the giving is the receiving. Creative expression is empowering – for an individual, for a group or a community. It is when such channels are blocked that dis-ease occurs – when our creative spark is suppressed, when we are not 'heard' or 'seen', when a person or a place loses touch with its story and has one imposed upon it. William Blake wrote: 'I must Create a System, or be enslav'd by another Man's; I will not Reason and Compare: my business is to Create.' So, by being creative emancipate ourselves from other narratives – we stop being consumers and become participants. We take charge of our own narrative, and, in doing so, feel our soul has been expressed, that 'we matter' in some way, our presence on Earth has not been in vain. By being creators, not consumers, it is better for our planet and for our communities. Of course, we cannot excel or specialise at everything, so other people's creativity is just as important – we can appreciate others' talents by being creative in our lifestyle choices – buying the local, the hand-made, the beautiful and well-crafted. We empower through our conscious purchasing – talk to the producer/stall-holder direct and make a human connection.

Farmers' Markets are a shining example of this, but also Small Press Book Fairs, Open Studios, festivals, local celebrations, etc. Spend some time simply appreciating another's creative presence. The experience of being heard can be enough – some spend their whole lives not being listened to. Being able to stand up and perform a poem, tell a story, paint one's dreams and fears, mime, dance or sing – from the heart – can be one of the most powerful sensations. Creativity can lead to self-knowledge – as one journeys deeply inwards. It is a tool for personal development. It can transform one's life, relationships, work, home, and community. Incrementally, small acts of creativity can change the world.

Imagination is a spiritual vitamin – with it, another world is possible. By giving ourselves permission to dream, by entertaining the aesthetics of difference, exploring alternative modalities, we widen the parameters of what is possible. Creative play leads to 'happy accidents' – Eureka! moments of discovery, of break-through. Thought experiments can lead to real changes, as, with skill and compassion, we manifest them on Earth. The best artists enrich our existence on this planet – after the solitude of their 'vision quest' they bring their healing vision down from the 'mountain' and 'perform' it for the benefit of the tribe. The artist-shaman sings the soul back into the body, re-enchants matter, reminds us of the wonder of being alive. Their art celebrates the miracle of our existence, and helps us to see Creation anew – our place within it restored.

We can tap into creativity in many ways – it is not exclusively the province of the 'artist or poet in the garret' – we can all enjoy playing with colour, forms, textures, words, movement, sound... In gardening, in cookery, in the clothes we wear, the homes we live in, the relationships we nurture, our work and our play, we can honour and manifest our creative self on a daily basis, re-enchanting the mundane with continual acts of imagination and discovery. And in doing so we feel better about where we live and who we are. We feel engaged with the world in a positive way, with those around us. Monochrome monologues become rainbow dialogues – celebrating the joyous dance of life.

Decrees & Quotes on Creativity

Creativity is our birthright: 'Creativity, an integral element of the simple life, is our birthright, intrinsic to our nature and, according to the biologist Brian Goodwin, an underlying biological and evolutionary need.' John Lane

Creativity connects us with our natural state: 'What writing practice, like Zen practice, does is bring you back to the natural state of mind, the wilderness of your mind where there are no refined rows of gladiolas. The mind is raw, full of energy, alive and hungry.' Natalie Goldberg

Creativity connects us with our sense of our identity: 'I was in a queer mood, thinking myself very old: but now I am a woman again – as I always am when I write.' Virginia Woolf

Creativity gives voice to our inner life: 'There is no greater agony than bearing an untold story inside you.' Maya Angelou

Creativity returns us to a sense of belonging: 'Each of us brings something alive in the world that is unique. There is a profound necessity at the heart of individuality. As we awaken to this sense of destiny, we can begin to live a life that is generous and worthy of the blessing that is always calling us.' John O'Donohue

Creativity consoles us and keeps us sane: 'You must stay drunk on writing so reality cannot destroy you.' Ray Bradbury

Creativity keeps us plugged into something greater than ourselves: 'I can very well do without God both in my life and in my painting, but I cannot, suffering as I am, do without something which is greater than I am, which is my life, the power to create.' Vincent van Gogh

Creativity connects us to the dance of Creation: 'If you think of the universe as a vast electrical sea in which you are immersed and from which you are formed, opening to your creativity changes you from something bobbing in that sea to a more fully functioning, more conscious, more co-operative part of that ecosystem.' Julia Cameron

Creativity can heal our sense of self and self-worth: 'Not just this line I write but the innocence of an earned forgiveness flowing again through hands made new with writing.' David Whyte

Creativity is an organic impulse: 'Creativity is our true nature, that blocks are an unnatural thwarting of a process at once as normal and as miraculous as the blossoming of a flower at the end of a slender green stem.' Julia Cameron

Creativity returns us to meaning: 'Creativity is a central source of meaning in our lives... [and] when we are involved in it, we feel that we are living more fully than during the rest of life.' Mihaly Csikszentmihalyi

5

Dancing with Ghosts: notes on genre

(additional notes written for A215 Creative Writing, The Open University, by Kevan Manwaring)

Genre (n. a style or category of art or literature) in some ways is only something booksellers and critics need to worry about. Fantasy; Science Fiction; Erotica; Crime; Cookery … convenient pigeon-holes to place things in. In a bookshop this is practical – where should this or that title go? For critics, it provides a convenient frame of reference: this is like 'such-and-such'. Yet it also works for the reader: 'I'll buy this book because it's in my favourite genre.'

However, as writers should we worry about genre?

We certainly shouldn't write to fit into pigeon-holes. The blank page or screen should be just that – a tabula rasa, as limitless as your imagination. See what comes out. Don't limit yourself. Creative writing is perhaps one of the only areas in life where we can have true freedom – value that, defend it, dance with it.

All that said, certain caveats need to be considered: *all* writing fits into a genre, or sub-genre, whether we like it or not. There's no such thing as genre-less writing (writers often have blind-spots as to the genre of their own writing – for them it is simply 'telling the truth' – this is reality as they see it). Considering the root of the word 'genre' is the same as 'gender', perhaps similar problems assail both. Writers unsure about what genre they write in might find themselves with an existential 'genre-anxiety' akin to confusion over sexual identity. Hermaphrodite Lit might be an intriguing notion, but it could so easily become a Curate's Egg. Even if your writing is an exotic hybrid, it's good to decide, so as not to neuter the potency of your work. Establish a genre-identity (for marketing purposes at least).

If it's hard to put a finger on, then it might just be 'Contemporary Fiction', or it may be more Family Saga, even Aga Saga, than we realise or would care to admit. Some genres are easier to spot – Westerns, Ghost Story, Lad Lit, Historical Romance. If you're writing in a certain genre it's normally because you are fond of it yourself – perhaps it is your guilty pleasure. Comfort reading. That's okay. If that's what you want to produce then utilise the genre conventions. Play along with the 'rules' – the aesthetics, the tone, and plot devices – of that genre. Failure to do so can create a jarring slippage of tone. Sometimes we may want to do this to wake the reader up, but more often than not it will simply annoy them. If a novel fails to live up to its genre expectations (as suggested by the cover and blurb) then it will probably frustrate and lose readers.

That's playing it safe anyway.

Yet the daring author tries to push the boundaries of their genre (skilfully subverting its conventions and parameters). We should always try to raise the bar as writers.

Push the envelope, and shatter the glass ceiling. Be the iconoclast, the heretic, the literary anarchist with your Molotov cocktail of an idea. Be the first to say what has never been said before.

But first we must walk before we can run – try writing a story successfully in a particular genre. If you manage to pull this off, well done – you are ready to move onto the next level. Once you know the rules, you can start to bend them – but first you need to understand and be able to utilise them, otherwise you'll quickly come a-cropper.

I believe original writing is produce when we 'widen the genre pool' – when we cross-fertilise different genres. This is how creativity works on a basic level – combine two or more hitherto disparate ideas or objects and create something that wasn't there before, a new combination – hopefully greater than the sum of its parts, and not just a Frankenstein's monster. Stitch too many ideas (tropes) or genres together and you can get an uneven, unsatisfying result. There needs to be some thematic unity – some reason why these things overlap. Anything is possible if you can justify it on the page – does it work with the narrative, or against it? Jasper Fforde, who writes very much in the vein of Douglas Adams, combines literary genres at breakneck speed in such comic cross-over novels as *The Eyre Affair* (2001) and *The Well of Lost Plots* (2004). Witty at first, after a while, such explicit inter-textuality can become exhausting – a relentless roller coaster ride. However mind-bending paradigm-shifting can be, it is a law of diminishing returns. Constant rug-pulling can sever the writer/reader contract. We no longer trust the narrator – our guide turns out to be a trickster.

However, what is now known as 'Fusion Lit', or the 'New Weird', is becoming increasingly popular – and seems to be the endgame of Postmodernism. Basically anything goes. The entire history of humanity, literature, theatre, cinema, etc, is up for grabs – to be quoted, used, exploited. These strange hybrids debunk the myth of the Grand Narrative (as in the Victorian realist novel when it was thought everything could be understood – all the characters actions explained by their social circumstances, etc – a vast clockwork universe, ticking along nicely like the Empire...). If the New Wave of the Sixties cracked the clock-face, the tragedy of 9/11 shattered that paradigm, and any future pretensions of mono-culture Imperialism for good. What has resulted since could be called Post-millennium fiction: exploring uncertainties; conflicting paradigms; moral ambiguities; multiple narratives; many voices. Basically, we're back to Babel – which could be seen as healthy diversity, depending on your point of view. What does this mean for genre? Is it realistic to dwell within the cosy microcosm of one genre in this day and age?

Ironically, genre seems more popular than ever as people seek consoling fictions – Fantasy, historical fiction, superheroes ... are hugely successful. You can capitalise on this – by playing with and subverting genre expectations – but don't try and cash in on it. The bandwagon is well and truly packed, the gravy train left the station long ago – publishers are always a few years ahead. What we think of as the New Thing is something they commissioned a couple of years ago. They are looking for the next big thing *after* the next big thing (due in your bookshops this Christmas, but marketed to the book trade last autumn).

So, as writers we shouldn't worry about such things which are out of our control. Genre may consist of little more than marketing tags when all's said and done, but as writers we can use its conventions in a creative way – working with or against them, blending them, breaking them. Don't write in boxes – write *outside* of the box, while being aware that it's almost impossible to escape them (imagine dancing in a straitjacket and summon your inner-Houdini). Someone will find a box for what you write eventually – it might even be a new one! Don't be disheartened – simply be mindful that generally every thing you write will stir one literary ghost or another. A piece of writing cannot exist in isolation. You can choose to dance with these ghosts, but it is unwise to ignore them.

6

Courting the Muses

(First delivered as a workshop at 'The Castle of the Muses', Loch Goil, Scotland, Bardic Equinox Weekend, September 2012)

In the 'Hymn to the Muses and Apollo' from Ancient Greece the poet says: 'If the Muses love you then you are blessed and sweet sound flows from your mouth.' This seems like a good reason to 'court' them – that is to woo them and invite their graceful presence into your life. Too often we take inspiration and eloquence for granted – as though it is our God-given right; when I would argue that it is our Goddess-given right. For time immemorial poets have personified inspiration in the form of a female figure, the Muse – classically as 'the girl in a white gown', as Flaherty wittily puts it[311]. This *could* be because the male poet connects with his feminine side and gives it voice in the creative process in the arts of embodied introspection: connecting with and expressing one's feelings; feeling empathy for others; a receptivity to other people's opinions and a certain permeability of spirit can be thought of as 'feminine' qualities (of course, that does not mean they are gender-prescriptive).

How do women writers fit into all of this? If they feel the need to have a 'Muse' at all, then it can be imagined in any way they wish, but in the British Folk Tradition they are clues that suggest the shadowy figure of the 'demon lover', often a devilishly handsome young fellow awaiting to lead wayward women 'astray' across the fluid threshold of the Otherworld, a zone rich in imaginative possibilities. In truth, with any such 'demon lover', is it is *your* daemon, *your* inner genius. Whatever you see this as, and however you tap into it, it is worth connecting with.

Such a proposition might seem wilfully archaic and unsimpatico with the materialist zeitgeist, but at one time, the invocation of the Muse at the beginning of a creative endeavour (e.g. epic poem) was *de rigueur*.

Although the Muse manifests in many aspects across culture and time, it is in the mythos of Ancient Greece that we are most familiar with them. Traditionally, they are thought to be 9 in number, each presiding over a particular art or science. Like a litany of old lovers fondly recollected, it is worth citing these for the alluring paradigms they evoke:

- Calliope (Epic Poetry)
- Clio (History)
- Erator (Love Poetry)
- Euterpe (Music)
- Melpomene (Tragedy)
- Polyhymnia (Hymns)
- Terpsichore (Dance)
- Thalia (Comedy)
- Urania (Astronomy)

Mother of the Muses was Mnemosyne, originally Mnemosune (literally, the 'House of the Moon') – she was the very embodiment of the Palace of Memory. She presided over a pool in Hades, counterpart to Lethe – the difference being if a draught from *her* pool was taken one would remember, rather than forget. Daughter of Gaia and Uranus, she gave birth to the nine Muses after sleeping with Zeus, the Father of the Gods on one of his many wayward adventures. Lying together for nine consecutive nights, the nine daughters were conceived – an interesting number, a multiple of three, sacred of many cultures. The Muses are aspects of the Triple-Aspect Goddess (the Goddess^3 squared, so to speak). An echo of this triple-aspect can be seen in Athena, the Hellenic Goddess of Warfare, Wisdom and the Arts. In the Celtic Tradition the Goddess Brighid is patron of Poetry, Smithcraft and Healing. Awen is sometimes thought of as the Welsh goddess of inspiration, and the three rays which symbolise the awen again seem to allude to the three-in-one quality of the goddess.

The awen is a good place to start, if one wishes to invoke the Muses. Here are some suggestions for 'Courting the Muses':

1. Raising the awen. Chant the awen three times, sounding each syllable slowly, the Welsh 'w' being an 'oo' sound. The fourth syllable is the most important – the silence – inbetween each chant. If we wish to speak, first we must listen.
2. Meditate in the silence and let words and images float to the surface.
3. Afterwards, make a note of them, draw, compose. You have asked for inspiration – now respond to it.
4. You are going to visit the Palace of Memory. In turn visit each room, dedicated to the 9 Muses. Experience its atmosphere. Notice any details. Commune with the Muse. Converse with her. Receive any gifts. Ask for her blessing. Thanking her, leave in peace, and move onto the next. Return and record your impressions.
5. Write a 9-line poem, with one line for each Muse. Perhaps choose a regular line-length, e.g. 9 syllables or words per line, to create an elegant structure.
6. Choose one of the Muses, and write 9-line poem, dedicated to Her alone.
7. Imagine 9 modern Muses. Invent and describe them. Be playful. Create your own personal Muse. Imagine him or her in vivid detail. Bring them alive.
8. Choose 9 women who have been influential to you (e.g. mother; grandmother; aunt; sister; partner; colleague; old friend; teacher; author, etc). List them. Write a poem in praise of each, in turn – perhaps preparing them for birthdays, anniversaries, etc.

9. Honour the Muses in your daily life – create a shrine for them in your house, with flowers, poetry, incense, music, icons, candles, fruit and libations. Connect with them each day, asking for their blessing and guidance. Remember to thank them.

It was once thought that the wind blowing at the time of your birth defines the pathway in your life – the direction you will take. In some cultures, the winds have different presiding spirits. In the Celtic Tradition, the Muses are sometimes referred to as the 'Daughters of the Back of the North Wind':

> 'The winds are under the aegis of the Nine-fold Sisters also called the Daughters of Ocean, or the Daughters at the Back of the North Wind. As the gifting mothers of destiny, their breath impels each of us to find our gifts and use them.' [312]

Reading the Winds was a form of divination. The wind is thought to be synonymous with spirit – the breath of the Holy Spirit, moving across the Earth. Breath is seen as indivisible from one's spirit (*spiritus*). As Flaherty points out, 'inspiration' is etymologically connected to 'breath', and throughout the world life and language are connected by this:

> 'The word for "life force" means "breath" in Greek (*pneuma*), Hebrew (*ruach*), Chinese (*chi*), Japanese (*reiki*), Hindu (*prana*), Algonquin (*Manitou*), East Africa (*mulungu*), and many other languages.' [313]

In the Welsh poem 'Preiddu Annwn', The Cauldron of Plenty which King Arthur harrows the Underworld for was said to be 'warmed by the breath of nine muses'. This is the sacred breath which bestows life, the Word that called forth the Earth in Genesis, the primary utterance. By connecting with this magical quality of language we become Sub-creators, summoning new worlds into being, like Adam in Eden naming the animals.

By Courting the Muses we are courting our own creativity. Allow yourself to be a-mused.

The Muse need not be fair – the goddess comes in many shapes and sizes. The Nine Hags of Gloucester are cousins of the lissom Muses of Ancient Greece. The Three Graces are sisters of the three witches from *Macbeth*. Could they not be different faces of one and the same? The Muse can be cruel as well as generous, as Keats' knight discovered in 'La Belle Dame Sans Merci':

'Oh, what can ail thee, knight-at-arms,
Alone and palely loitering?'

This 'Beautiful-Woman-Without-Mercy', the ultimate femme fatale, is epitomised most memorably in Robert Graves' poem, *The White Goddess*:[314]

'Whose broad high brow was white as any leper's,
Whose eyes were blue, with rowan-berry lips,
With hair curled honey-coloured to white hips.'

She is the Queen of Elfland who bestows the Tongue That Cannot Lie upon Thomas of Ercildoune in the Scottish Border Ballad, 'Thomas the Rhymer' – yet the gift of prophecy is a mixed blessing:

'My tongue is my ain,' true Thomas said.
'A gudely gift ye wad gie to me!'[315]

She is Spenser's Faerie Queene; Dante's Beatrice; Lennon and MacCartney's Eleanor Rigsby; Van Morrison's Gloria; Eric Clapton's Laila, or any beautiful woman who catches a poet's eye. She has been there since the dawn of humanity, has appeared across the world in all cultures, in all races, and will continue to haunt us until the sun takes a bow, expiring in a catastrophic heat-death – and in that moment we will see her face. Her ghost will unnerve us across the universe and we will find her waiting at the end of time. Of course, all this might be poetic fancy. A neurological interpretation might see the whole shebang as 'carrot and stick' – a motivational trick of the mind, as Flaherty half-seriously postulates: 'Perhaps the feeling of inspiration is merely a pleasure by which your brain lures you into working harder.'[316] Yet that in itself is a miracle of biology (who designed our 'software' and 'hardware' in the first place?). Whatever the primary cause, we can see the results of such tricks of the brain all around us: 'From an evolutionary standpoint, it is not surprising that creative activity should be so intensely rewarding, given that the innovations that are its fruits have been so useful for human survival.'[317]

And so those wishing to write imaginative fiction would do well to woo the Muse, in whatever guise she/he/it 'does it for you'. Who knows, a real-life one might even step into your life.

7

Writing Magical Fiction

(First delivered as a talk to PF Wessex Conference, Stroud, April 2013)

Firstly, let's start by stating what magical fiction is not.... So much Fantasy fiction can have the ingredients of magic, but feel anything but magical. You can put in all the unicorns and dragons, vampires and werewolves, wands and broomsticks you like ... but that doesn't mean the end result will be necessarily magical – as the shelves of sub-standard rip-offs attest.

So, what *does* make fiction magical? Well, for my money...

It is well-crafted (poor punctuation, grammar, presentation, characterisation, or storytelling will always break the spell). Creative writing is a skill – it can be taught, but it rarely happens by itself. Having an idea for a good story is not the same as making it work on the page. There is often a painful gulf between concept and execution. Craft it with care and your readers will care.

It draws upon an authentic experience. The story is based up something 'real' – to anchor it in this world, to make it grounded, to give it grit. The best magical stories cross-fertilise with the mundane. They transform the familiar, and re-present reality in a fresh way.

It leaves room for the reader, i.e. doesn't 'spell' everything out. It avoids clunky exposition (telling, not showing) and creates subtext through use of what isn't said. It describes enough but not too much.

It alludes to genuine magical knowledge. Ancient traditions; esoteric alphabets; obscure shamanic practices; the magical laws of reality. It is not airy-fairy, or cobbled together through a poor understanding of Wicca, Druidry, Norse Magic or whatever thing it is a pastiche of. Fully imagined by the author, the narrative universe is coherent and convincing, with sufficient detail and depth – suggesting more than is revealed. Research is undertaken, but not completely shown. **It is lucidly visualised.** Each scene has a tangible quality to it. The world lives and breathes. It evokes the senses and provides telling details, bringing alive character and setting. Everything in frame, is in focus – perhaps even feels hyper-real like a Pre-Raphaelite painting. However, the balance has to be right. It invites the reader in, but doesn't suffocate them.

Examples of Magical Fiction:

Gilgamesh; The Odyssey; Beowulf; Gawain and the Green Knight; La Morte D'Arthur; Brothers Grimm; Hans Christian Anderson; the works of Dion Fortune; John Cowper Powys; David Lindsay; Fiona Macleod; George Macdonald; Hope Mirrlees; Mikhail Bulgakov; JRR Tolkien; CS Lewis; Charles Williams; TH White; Marion Zimmer Bradley; Angela Carter; Robert Holdstock; Charles De Lint; John Crowley; Lindsay Clarke; Alan Moore; Neil Gaiman; Susanna Clarke; Margaret Elphinstone; Graham Joyce... And the list goes on. Textual illustrations of these go beyond the scope of this paper, but they are easy enough to discover in any decent library, bookshop, or online archive.

My Methods

1. Summon the Awen (see **Courting the Muses**); light a candle; smudge/burn incense; invite in the Muse, the Goddess, Hermes, Taliesin...
2. Visit ancient sites: spend time there in solitude; wildcamp; dream; make notes, recordings, drawings; take photographs; collect a curious stone, feather, shell,

twig, flower, postcards, souvenirs ... Anything that might act as an aide memoire.

3. Research – novels, biographies, collected works, letters, photographs, museums, heritage sites/centres, documentaries, archives, interviews...
4. Embed a magical structure, e.g. the four cardinal directions; the five elements (Earth, Air, Fire, Water, Spirit); seven colours of the rainbow; the Chakras; the planets; the zodiac.
5. Use a real magical system, e.g. the Ogham, the Bardic Tradition, the Runes, I Ching.
6. Sleep on it – picture a scene just before going to sleep, dream on it, allow the subconscious to do its work. Record any vivid dreams.
7. Creative Visualisation – journey into your story, picture each scene like a frozen tableaux – explore it 3-dimensionally. Notice any details.
8. Use archetypes – work with the Tarot (major arcana for characters; minor for scenes; or do a spread and let that create a dramatic arc); commedia dell'arte; mummers plays; the works of Carl Jung, Joseph Campbell and Caroline Myss.
9. Work with the seasons and lunar cycles.
10. Give it life with breath – read it out loud, read it in situ, as a way of giving thanks.

Grounding It

So, have a go yourself... Get a pen and some paper. We're going to do some brief writing activities – write the first thing that comes to mind. You don't have to share these. Do them fast. Ready? Okay, here goes:

- List 5 things you desire.
- 5 things you fear.

- 5 places you love and know well.
- 5 people who have influenced you/inspire you.
- 5 animals you are drawn to.

You have the elements of a (possibly) great story here – fictionalising some of them, e.g. changing names, circumstantial details but retaining the core emotion, the same Level of Attraction or Repulsion. These will provide the Push/Pull Factors of your writing, what Hollywood screenwriters call the Fear/Desire Axis.

The real test of magical fiction is the reaction it elicits. Workshop your story in a small group. Listen to the feedback. Redraft, edit and proof-read exhaustively. The best spells take serious application of will, hyper-attention to detail, and the most refined ingredients – the same goes for writing. Pour some of your life-force into it. Sweat, bleed and weep and you will create something with a vital spark.

8

Imaginary Conversations

(A paper for BSU conference: Other Voices, Other Times; Corsham Court, Wiltshire; June 2012)

Controversial Victorian poet Walter Savage Landor (1775-1864) who lived in the city of Bath for many years – being a familiar figure with his beloved Bologna dog – created a series of poetic colloquies entitled 'Imaginary Conversations', (1824-1829) in which historical figures conversed with one another. The roots of the compositions lay in his childhood as he wrote later: 'When I was younger ... [a]mong the chief pleasures of my life, and among the commonest of my occupations was the bringing before me such heroes and heroines of antiquity, such poets and sages, such of the prosperous and unfortunate as most interested me ...[and e]ngaging them in conversations best suited to their characters.'[318]

Although Landor lacked the skill of the dramaturge, it was in his poetry he found the ideal form. It was to prove a fruitful project, giving birth to six volumes in which were recorded fictional dialogues between personalities of classical Greece and Rome: poets and authors; statesmen and women; and fortunate and unfortunate individuals. The odd bedfellows of Fantasy and history.

In this paper I explore this liminal space created in the collision of what Nathaniel Hawthorne called 'the Actual and the Imaginary'. Describing the effect of moonlight on a familiar domestic scene, Hawthorne says:

> 'A child's shoe; the doll, seated in her little wicker carriage; the hobby-horse – whatever, in a word, has been used or played

> with, during the day, is now invested with a quality of strangeness and remoteness, though still almost as vividly present as by daylight. Thus, therefore, the floor of our familiar room has become a neutral territory, somewhere between the real world and fairy-land, where the Actual and the Imaginary may meet, and each imbue itself with the nature of the other. Ghosts might enter here, without affrighting us.' [319]

This *unheimlich* (in a nutshell, the 'opposite of what is familiar'[320]) effect is quintessential to the disorientation that true works of the imagination require. Dickens termed a word for it: 'mooreeffoc'. He mentions it in a fragment of his abandoned autobiography, when he describes his poverty-stricken youth:

> 'In the door there was an oval glass plate, with COFFEE-ROOM painted on it, addressed towards the street. If I ever find myself in a very different kind of coffee-room now, but where there is such an inscription on glass, and read it backward on the wrong side MOOR-EEFFOC (as I often used to do then, in a dismal reverie,) a shock goes through my blood.'[321]

'A shock goes through my blood' – what could describe the *unheimlich* better? Surely, this is the effect that any writer would wish for in their readers (albeit, at certain points only. It is not an effect to be overdone, if you wish to avoid the law of diminishing returns).

Chesterton said of Dickens' term that it denoted 'the queerness of things that have become trite, when they are seen suddenly from a new angle.' Tolkien pursued it further in his essay 'On Fairy-stories': 'The word Mooreeffoc may cause you to realise that England is an utterly alien land, lost either in some remote past age glimpsed by history, or in some strange dim future reached only by a time-machine; to see the amazing oddity and interest of its inhabitants and their customs and feeding-habits.'[322]

Whatever the machinations of the plot, the ordinary world is transfigured by this act of perception. Reality is tilted – whilst retaining the all important ballast of truth.

In *The Windsmith Elegy* (2002-2012) I combine real and imaginary characters – Isambard Kerne, my Edwardian antiquarian; 30's aviatrix Amelia Earhart; French poet of the skies, Antoine de St Exupéry; explorer and scholar Leo Africanus... Many of these, whom I call the Lost of History, appear cheek by jowl with Morgen le Fay; Merlin; and other figures of myth and legend. The historical provides the 'grit in the oyster' for the imagination – one anchors/enriches the other. In the third in the series, *The Well Under the Sea* (2009) I imagine a wine-soaked conversation between Arthurian Poets in an Avalon-like idyll – arguing the meaning of the Holy Grail (a meeting of paradigms, in the spirit of Caryl Churchill's 1982 play, 'Top Girls', where powerful women from history hold a dinner party). Author of *The Once and Future King*, TH White, features alongside Welsh bard Taliesin; Sir Thomas Mallory; Wolfram von Eschenbach; Alfred, Lord Tennyson and others. White himself foresees this in his imagining of the ultimate posthumous plenary:

> '...I am inclined to believe that my beloved Arthur of the future is sitting at this very moment among his learned friends in the Combination Room of the College of Life, and that they are thinking away in there for all they are worth, about the best means to help our curious species: and I for one hope that some day, when not only England but the World has need of them, and when it is ready to listen to reason, if it ever is, they will issue out from their rath in joy and power.' [323]

Writer Alan Moore calls such narrative parlour tricks 'literary games'[324]. Iain Sinclair brought this conceit into the late 20th

Century with his 2002 novel *Landor's Tower* (subtitled 'the imaginary conversations'); Jasper Fforde does it in *The Eyre Affair* and its sequels; and Moore himself has done it in his ongoing graphic novel series, *The League of Extraordinary Gentlemen*. There are no doubt many other examples – inter-textuality, both extant and implicit. As soon as one picks up a pen, one is entering into a conversation with other works in the canon. It is impossible to do otherwise (a notion I explore in **Dancing with Ghosts: notes on genre**).

Novelist Lindsay Clarke in his essay 'Imagining Otherwise'[325] examines the fertile threshold created in the overlap between the conscious and the unconscious – using the venn-like symbol of the *vesica pisces*. Where the circles cross-over – in the almond-shape known as the mandorla – there is formed the doorway of the imagination. It is the writer's job to hold this door open – and to walk between the worlds. He says: 'it is through the meeting of opposites that something new appears,' and we, as human beings are the 'locus of their collision'. This creative tension is an essential ingredient in creating effective works of art. Without it – the crackle of static from opposing forces – the frisson evaporates. This is seen time and time again in volatile but extremely productive creative collaborations, friendships or partnerships: George Sand and Chopin; Rimbaud and Verlaine; Frost and Thomas; Hughes and Plath; Lennon and McCartney.

When worlds collide something beautiful can be born.

To extend the idea of 'imaginary conversations' one could argue that this can also take place in a meta-narrative sense between worlds (as in cross-over Fantasy such as the Narnia, or His Dark Material books); or genres (Stephen King's 'Dark Tower' series grafts the Western onto the Epic Fantasy). There are many other literary hybrids (most astonishingly, David Mitchell's multi-genre tour de force, *Cloud Atlas*, 2004). I suggest that such cross-fertilisation is healthy – what I call widening the gene pool is essential to avoid Nth generation pastiches – especially common in Fantasy (re: the countless Howard, Tolkien and Rowling rip offs). All the 'bandwagon' books aside (e.g. the numerous 'Harry Potter' and 'Twilight' clones, who should be culled at birth) – many commercial writers seem to be referencing TV and Cinema more than the literary canon: books reared on a junkfood diet of popcorn and TV dinners. Fiction that comes across as sub-standard screenwriting more than fully-fledged prose (what Le Guin called memorably 'McProse').

Yet, when handled well (and not with thumping crudeness of *Pride and Prejudice and Zombies*; or *Abraham Lincoln: vampire hunter*), the unlikely convergence of two or more disparate genres or paradigms can create something fresh (e.g. Douglas Adams' masterful *The Hitchhiker's Guide to the Galaxy* sequence).

I take this to the extreme in my (largely) Secondary World Fantasy – *The Windsmith Elegy*, which is set primarily in a place I consciously call Shadow-World – where things ... cross-over. There is a symbiotic relationship with Earth – what happens in one affects the other. Shadow World is a kind of Platonic Realm, although it's far from ideal. However, there is a suggestion that Earth itself might be the 'shadow' – a faded version of the gleaming original 'Otherworld' – an idea foreshadowed, if you excuse the pun, in the Ancient Greek notion of Antichthon, a twin Earth:

> The Counter-Earth is a hypothetical body of the Solar system first hypothesized by the pre-Socratic philosopher Philolaus to support his non-geocentric cosmology, in which all objects in the universe revolve around a Central Fire. The Greek word 'Antichthon' means 'Counter-Earth.' According to some Greek Mythology, Antichthon was placed between Earth and the center of the universe, the throne of Zeus, to stop man from looking at God directly. (Wikipedia)

Perhaps all fictional worlds are Antichthons – populated by shadow versions of us ... or vice versa? Are we *their* creation? Who is the 'Red King' here? The author, or is he or she just another character dreamt of by someone or something else?

There is also a Manicheaistic dialectic running through my series – an eternal feud between the forces of Darkness and Light, Chaos and Harmony, which might actually be my way of personifying the inner conflict in all writers – between what John Fowles called 'the wildman and the academic'. Is fiction born in an imaginary conversation between the Left and Right sides of the brain? Are we simply talking to ourselves? As Woody Allen joked: 'I love talking to myself – it's the only way of having a decent conversation around here.' Seriously, is the act of writing a kind of permissive madness? In other societies writers might have been burnt or forced into becoming a medicine man or woman. At its best, there is something shamanic about the storyteller's craft – when, in moments of ecstatic inspiration, the sham-manic act gives away to the real thing. Successful novelists are merely fakirs who make it.

Every writer knows the delight when characters take on a life of their own. It is even more thrilling, I have found, when historical characters do the same. It is somewhat daunting – trying to put words into the mouths of famous people – one feels it is not something to be undertaken until you have read everything written by or about them, yet time and time again I have found 'real' voices come alive – often with only a tentative 'steeping' in their works (Arthur Koestler: 'soak, and wait'). These extended acts of ventriloquism (akin to an actor's portrayal of a famous person – beyond, but not dissimilar to, the mimic's gift for an 'impression') seem to be in vogue: historical fiction and drama has become a mainstream phenomenon. The huge success of ITV period drama *Downton Abbey* is only the crest of a wave of what historian Simon Schama called 'nostalgic necrophilia.' Britain has made an industry out of its history –

English Heritage; re-enactment events; living history... Yet it is a game we can all play – as writers, as well as readers – of 'make-believe'; of dressing up (adopting different voices beyond gender, race, era); of playing in the sandpit of time, to extend Derek Neale's notion in his article, 'Being in Uncertainties, Mysteries and Doubts.'[326]

Perhaps one of the strongest motivations for a writer are the 'What ifs...?' of our own personal history: The Things You Never Said (or did) – hypothetical dialogues, driven by wish-fulfilment, regret, longing, desire... We revisit our own past, and take the roads less travelled:

> Two roads diverged in a yellow wood,
> And sorry I could not travel both
> And be one traveler, long I stood
> And looked down one as far as I could
> To where it bent in the undergrowth...
>
> Robert Frost, 'The Road Not Taken'[327]

We become quantum navigators – rerunning endlessly divergent versions of history. Every story (and not just Historical/Fantasy) is a System Restore point from where we can take a new path, install new software, create new files – modelling a better (or worse) version of ourselves.

To end with a tantalising notion: could writing itself be a form of time-travel – imagining other times, and even 'inhabiting' them for a while? These places feel real to me as I'm visualising them (it has been said that we do not 'write a novel', but we 'see and hear' it). Perhaps, then, the notion of clairsentience or clairaudience would be more apt an analogy, with the creative process as a kind of trance – John Gardner talks of 'the fictive dream' which the writer needs to immerse themselves in to create their work; a kind of 'willed hallucination the fiction writer needs to be able to foster' (see **Waking Up in the Fictive Dream**) – 'channelling' other voices, other worlds. To extend the metaphor, could the keyboard be a kind of ouija board, with the pen or digit as a planchette? Knock once for yes... You never know what might come through!

In *Beyond Black*, Hilary Mantel takes this to the comic extreme, in her tale of a mediocre medium. Perhaps the whole 'medium' of the novel is slightly fraudulent – with novelists as fairground mystics: in their mysterious narratives seemingly reflecting the reader's own individualist experience ('Reader, you will meet a tall, dark stranger ... and marry him.'). The novel becomes a scrying mirror – displaying whatever fears and desires we project onto it.

The ultimate 'imaginary conversation' happens, then, between the writer and the reader; and the reader and the characters. The former – in the writing of a piece; the latter as it is read. In the suspension of disbelief, both writer and reader walk the tightrope – meeting precariously in the middle – and engage in a death-defying conversation above the thundering waters of oblivion, cheating the Reaper of his prize: the silence of the scythe.

9

Cultivating the Write Habit

'The daily practice prepares and calms the artist, creating more fertile soil for whatever seed lands.' [328]
Alice W. Flaherty

Writing is many things – a craft, discipline, a means of expression, of therapy, of potential fame and riches – but before all this it has to become a habit you develop. In the same way our bodies (normally) expect to be fed, watered, washed and rested at certain times of the day and night you can make your 'writer within' expect to be attended to at a regular time each day – it doesn't matter if you're a night owl or an early bird, we all have different metabolisms, times when we're at our sharpest, and it's whatever works for you. The aim is to cultivate a state of what could be called 'creative preparedness'. If, every day, without fail, you sit down to write a certain number of words between, say, the hours of 9 and 10am, then your body and mind, after a while will come to expect it – and all your subconscious yearnings will find an outlet then, resistance will lessen each time and it'll become your default setting. In the same way we can train ourselves to become used to exercise (e.g. a morning run or swim) so we can with writing. At first it may seem painful – but the more you do it, the quicker those endorphins (or writer's equivalent) will set in. If it's a habit we do almost without thinking, there's also less chance for the 'excuses' to set in – also known as 'displacement activities'. Watch for those (sharpening pencils; tidying your desk; hovering, etc). Keep that writing muscle supple by writing every day, and it will no longer feel a strain to start writing. A major way of getting over the initial inertia, fear, doubts, etc, is to tell yourself: 'this doesn't have to be perfect the first time'. The first draft should never be the finished draft. Get some words down on the page/on the screen and then you have something to play with: that block of words is your *prima materia,* your raw material, your clay, your block of marble. So, just hammer out some words and see what happens. Julia Cameron's exercise 'the Morning Pages' is great for this – 20 minutes non-stop writing every day, or 3 A4 pages, whichever comes soonest. Write whatever's in your head, about the washing up, the kids, bills, a holiday, a loved one, a dream – don't edit, don't censor, just get it down. No one has to see it and you can even delete it all when you finish (although read through because sometimes you get the odd 'diamond of the dustheap': Virginia Woolf's memorable phrase for what can be unearthed through such a practice. The subconscious can produce some real gems – just think of the vivid dreams you may or may not remember having every night). The Morning Pages is an exercise that allows you to tap into that rich seam, but also provides a way of 'limbering up' in the same way an athlete warms up before training. Once you have done the Morning Pages, you have 'flushed out' your system and are ready to start. You have got the synapses firing and your brain should be up to speed.

To reassure you this cultivation of a writing habit is something of legitimate value – not just something that teachers make you do – I sat down at my desk this morning to begin work on a new novel. I didn't leave the desk until I had written a thousand words. This is my daily target. I will continue doing this until I have blocked out the first draft. Increase this target to 3000 and within a month you can have written a novel (approx. 90,000 words) which I have done previously, although with distractions, other commitments etc, this process can take up to say, 3 months (my novels average 120,000 words these days). This is only the 'dirty first draft' mind you – I believe it is best to 'block it out, then hack it back' rather than sweat over each word. Get over getting it perfect the first time – very few writers seldom do – that's why we have Word Processors (although try and save and print each subsequent draft). Masterpieces don't materialise fully-formed, they often are the result of numerous drafts, and blood, sweat and tears. A bad writer never revises, a true writer always does, but for now, it's not about 'getting it right', it's just about 'getting it down'. Create a block of words by the Morning Pages, or by a daily target – write, and you can call yourself a writer.

Alan Sillitoe talked about his writer's habit in the *Guardian's* Writers' Room feature: 'I'm usually at my desk by 9.30am. I have an hour's sleep in the afternoon and a couple of vodkas with supper, but I'm often still there at 10.30pm. I can't stand Radio 4 but have Radio 3 on most of the time. Sometimes I might just put in a comma in the morning, and take it out again at night. But that's the way it goes.'

So cultivate a healthy writing habit, and you will achieve that longest of journeys one word at a time. Fill the page and the rest will follow.

10

Waking Up in the Fictive Dream

(additional notes written for A363 Advanced Creative Writing, The Open University, by Kevan Manwaring)

John Gardner talks of 'the fictive dream'[329], which the writer needs to immerse themselves in to create their work – a kind of 'willed hallucination the fiction writer needs to be able to foster.'[330] This is indeed essential – so much writing fails because the writer has not sufficiently immersed themselves in their fictive dream – it has not been lucidly visualised. The result is like watching a film that is out-of-focus or with a poor soundtrack. We may be able to get the gist, but everything needs sharpening up. This is the function of the redrafting process.

This is the point when we need to wake up in the fictive dream.

In Lewis Carroll's *Through the Looking Glass* (1871) Alice encounters a cast of animate, sentient chess pieces. The whole narrative seems to be a game being enacted in the dream of a sleeping Red King…The existential idea is if he awakes, would they all vanish? In Chapter 8 of the book, subtitled 'It's my own invention', this fascinating but unsettling idea is expressed:

> After a while the noise seemed gradually to die away, till all was dead silence, and Alice lifted up her head in some alarm. There was no one to be seen, and her first thought was that she must have been dreaming about the Lion and the Unicorn and those still lying at her feet, on which she had tried to cut the plum-cake, 'So I wasn't dreaming, after all,' she said to herself, 'unless – unless we're all part of the same dream. Only I do hope it's *my* dream, and not the Red King's! I don't

like belonging to another person's dream,' she went on in a rather complaining tone: 'I've a great mind to go and wake him, and see what happens!'[331]

As writers, we may be the 'Red King', as Lewis might have been here – but we need to 'wake up' in the fictive dream we are trying to create. We may write it in a kind of trance – perhaps even in a half-waking/half-sleeping state if we write just before we go to bed or as soon as we wake up (the hypnagogic or hypnapompic state) – and we may want the reader to fall into a kind of trance as they read it, suspend their disbelief, be put under its spell. The collusive trance of make believe. But as writers we need to become conscious at some point and wake up in our self-willed hallucination – the equivalent of lucid dreaming, when the dreamer becomes conscious of the fact they are dreaming. They have woken up in their own dream and can start to manipulate it. This is the stage we want to reach as writers – with us controlling the writing (at least in the redrafting stage) rather than the writing controlling us.

Once, at the Bath Literature Festival, I asked Liz Lochead (poet of 'Dreaming Frankenstein') what her creative process was. She responded: 'A pen and a notebook'. This rather glib brush-off made the audience laugh, but perhaps masked either her unwillingness to divulge her 'trade secrets', or her own lack of awareness of how her poems come to be born – a nebulous process which is often intuitive, subconscious.

As professional writers you may get away with this lack of clarity, but as creative writing students of an accredited course you will not. In the commentary it is essential that the student shows they have indeed 'woken up in the fictive dream,' that narrative strategies have been employed consciously, techniques are being implemented discerningly. That we have shaken that Red King from his slumber – interrogated him vigorously with 'serious questions' (as below) before allowing him to return to his snooze – reconstructing the fictive dream, allowing it to cast its spell once more.

> ''Now, Kitty, let's consider who it was that dreamed it all. This is a serious question, my dear, and you should *not* go on licking your paw like that – as if Dinah hadn't washed you this morning! You see, Kitty, it *must* have been either me or the Red King. He was part of my dream, of course – but then I was part of his dream, too! *was* it the Red King, Kitty. You were his wife, my dear, so you ought to know – Oh, Kitty, *do* help to settle it! I'm sure your paw can wait!' But the provoking kitten only began on the other paw, and pretended it hadn't heard the question.'[332]

Further Reading

Mythology

A Short History of Myth, Karen Armstrong, Canongate, 2005

Greek Myths, The, Robert Graves, Penguin, 2011

Hero with a Thousand Faces, The, Joseph Campbell, Princeton, 1992

Kalevala, The, Oxford World Classics, Trans. Keith Bosley, 2008

Mabinogion, trans Jeffrey Gantz, Penguin Classics, 1976

Metamorphoses, The, Ovid, Penguin Classic, 2004

Monsters & the Critics and Other Essays, The, JRR Tolkien, HarperCollins, 1997

Myths & Folk Tales of Ireland, Jeremiah Curtin, Dover, 1975

Road to Middle Earth, The, Tom Shippey, HarperCollins, 2005

Saga of the Volsungs, Trans. Jesse L. Byock, Penguin Classics, 1990

Children's Writing

Alice in Wonderland; Alice Through the Looking Glass, Lewis Carroll, various editions

Borrowers, The (complete) Mary Norton, Puffin 2007

Chronicles of Narnia, The, CS Lewis, various editions

Dark is Rising, The, sequence, Susan Cooper, Red Fox, 2010

Earthsea Quartet, The, Ursula K. Le Guin, Puffin, 1993

Harry Potter Series, JK Rowling, Bloomsbury, 2001-2011

His Dark Materials, Philip Pullman, Scholastic Press, 1995-2000

Hobbit, The, JRR Tolkien, various editions

Holes, Louis Sachar, Collins, 2000

Howl's Moving Castle, Dianne Wynne Jones, HarperCollins, 2009

Skellig, David Almond, Hodder, 2009

Tales from the Perilous Realm, JRR Tolkien, HarperCollins, 2009

Watership Down, Richard Adams, Penguin, 1977

Weirdstone of Brisingamen, The, Alan Garner, HarperCollins, 2010

Where the Wild Things Are, Maurice Sendak, Red Fox 2000

Fairy Tales & Faerie

Brothers Grimm, The Complete, trans. Jack Zipes, Vintage, 2007

Caught in a Story: contemporary fairytales and fables, ed. Christine Park & Caroline Heaton, Vintage, 1992

Fairy Reel, tales from the twilight realm, ed Terri Windling & Ellen Datlow, Firebird, 2006

Fairy Tales and the Art of Subversion, Jack Zipes, Heinemann, 1983

Fairy Tales, Charles Perrault, Dover Publications, 2000

From the Beast to the Blonde: on fairy tales and their tellers, Marina Warner, Virago, 1995

Gossip from the Forest: The Tangled Roots of Our Forests and Fairytales, Sara Maitland, Granta, 2012

Hans Christian Anderson, Chancellor Press, 1985

Interpretation of Fairy-Tales, The, Marie-Louise Von Franz, Shambhala, 1995

King of Elfland's Daughter, The, Lord Dunsany, Ballantine, 2000

Kingdoms of Elfin, Sylvia Townsend Warner, Penguin, 1979

Uses of Enchantment, The, Bruno Bettelheim, Penguin, 1991

Fantasy

A Voyage to Arcturus, David Lindsay, Gollancz, 2003

Ash: a secret history, Mary Gentle, Gollancz, 2000

At The Mountains of Madness/Dagon & Other Tales/The Haunter of the Dark, (Omnibus editions), HP Lovecraft, Voyager, 1985

Brown Girl in the Ring/Midnight Robber, Nalo Hopkinson, Grand Central Publishing,1998/2000

Children of Hurin, JRR Tolkien, Harper Collins, 2007

Crown of Stars (series), Kate Elliot, Orbit, 1998

Daughter of the Forest, Juliet Marillier, HarperCollins, 2001

Dwellers in the Mirage, Abraham Merrit, Futura, 1974

Exiles, Melanie Rawn, Daw 1995

Farseer Trilogy (*Assassin's Apprentice, etc*), Robin Hobb, Harper Voyager, 2007

His Majesty's Dragon, (series) Naomi Novik, Ballantine, 2006

Jonathan Strange & Mr Norrell, Susanna Clarke, Bloomsbury, 2005

Kushiel's Legacy Trilogy (Kushiel's Dart, etc), Jacqueline Carey, St Martin's, 2002

Lilith; Phantastes, George Macdonald, various editions

Little, Big, John Crowley, HarperCollins, 2006

Lord of the Rings, The, JRR Tolkien, Harper Collins, various editions

Lud in the Mist, Hope Mirrlees, Del Rey, 1977

Mythago Wood, Robert Holdstock, Gollancz, 2009

Never-Ending Story, The, Michael Ende, Allen Lane, 1983

Nightshades (stories), Tanith Lee, Headline, 1993

Oxford Book of Fantasy Stories, Ed Tom Shippey, OUP, 2003

Realms of Fantasy, Edwards & Holdstock, Paper Tiger, 1983

Soldier of the Mist, Gene Wolfe, Futura Orbit, 1991

Stone and the Flute, The, Hans Bemman, Penguin, 1987

Tamir Trilogy (The Bone Doll's Twin, etc), Lynn Flewelling, Spectre, 2011

The Chronicles of Thomas Covenant, (omnibus) Stephen Donaldson, Collins, 1993

The Crystal Cave, The Hollow Hills, The Last Enchantment, Mary Stewart, Eos 2003

The Deed Of Paksenarrion (series), Elizabeth Moon, Orbit 2010

The Golden Key, Kate Elliot/Melanie Rawn/Jennifer Robertson, Tor, 1997

The Tears of Artamon (series), Sarah Ash, Bantam, 2004

The Wine Dark Sea (stories), Robert Aickman, Faber and Faber, 2008

Tigana, Guy Gavriel Kay, Harper Voyager, 2011

Time and the Gods, Lord Dunsany, Gollancz, 2000

Tough Guide to Fantasy Land, Diane Wynn Jones, Victor Gollancz, 2004

Treasury of Fantasy, A, Ed. Cary Wilkins, Gramercy, 1995

Weaveworld, Clive Barker, Harper Voyager, 2009

Wizardry & Wild Romance: a study of epic Fantasy, Michael Moorcock, VGSF, 1988

Storytelling

A Sampler of British Folk-Tales, ed. Katharine Briggs, Routledge & Kegan, 1977

Arabian Nights, trans Sir Richard Burton, Collins, 2011

Bardic Handbook, The, Kevan Manwaring, Gothic Image, 2006

Folk-Tales of the British Isles, Ed. Kevin Crossley-Holland, Faber 1991

Italian Folktales, Italo Calvino, Penguin Modern Classics, 2000

Little Black Book of Stories, AS Byatt, Chatto & Windus, 2003

Storytelling & Ecology, Anthony Nanson, Papyrus/SFS, 2005

Storytelling & the Art of the Imagination, Nancy Mellon, Yellow Moon Press, 2003

Storytelling for Life, Josie Felce, Floris, 2012

Way of Awen: journey of a bard, Kevan Manwaring, O Books, 2010

Way of the Storyteller, The, Ruth Sawyer, Penguin, 1977

Science Fiction

Consider Phlebas, etc (The Culture Novels), Iain M Banks, Orbit, 1987-2012

Cosmic Trilogy: Out of the Silent Planet; Perelandra; That Hideous Strength, CS Lewis, HarperCollins, 2005

Discworld series, Terry Pratchett, 1983-2013

Dispossessed, The, Ursula K. Le Guin, Gollancz, 1999

Doomsday Book/To Say Nothing of the Dog, Connie Willis, Gollancz 2012/2013

Drowned World, The, JG Ballard, Harper Perennial, 2008

Dune series, Frank Herbert, 1965-1985

Encyclopedia of Science Fiction, John Clute/Peter Nicholls, Orbit, 1999

Entropy Exhibtion, The, Colin Greenland, Routledge, 2011

Fahrenheit 451, Ray Bradbury, Harper Voyager, 2008

Left Hand of Darkness, The, Ursula K Le Guin, Orbit, 1981

Mammoth Enclycopedia of Science Fiction, Ed. George Mann, 2001

Oxford Book of Science Fiction, Ed Tom Shippey, OUP, 2003

Perdido Street Station, China Melville, Pan, 2011

Slaughterhouse Five, Kurt Vonnegut, Vintage, 1991
The Works of Philip K. Dick, various
Trillion Year Spree, The, Brian Aldiss & David Wingrove, Gollancz, 1986

Speculative Fiction

1984, George Orwell, Penguin Classics, 2013
40 Signs of Rain, Kim Stanley Robertson, HarperCollins, 2005
A Clockwork Orange, Anthony Burgess, Penguin, 2006
Bold as Love, Gwyneth Jones, Gollancz, 2002
Brave New World, Aldous Huxley,Vintage, 2007
Handmaid's Tale, The, Margeret Atwood, Vintage, 1996
Island, Aldous Huxley, Vintage, 2005
Lanark, Alasdair Gray, Picador, 1991
Neuromancer, William Gibson, Voyager, 1984
Pavane, Keith Roberts, Millennium, Gollancz, 2000
Sum: Tales from the Afterlives, David Eagleman, Canongate, 2010
Wind-up Girl, The, Paolo Bacigalupi, Orbit, 2010

Literary & Modern Classics

A Glastonbury Romance, John Cowper Powys, Penguin, 2000
After London, Richard Jefferies, Oxford, 1980
American Gods, Neil Gaiman, Headline, 2005
An Apple from a Tree, Margaret Elphinstone, The Women's Press, 1991
Astonishing the Gods, Ben Okri, Phoenix, 1999
Baudolino, Umberto Eco, Vintage, 2003
Beyond Black, Hilary Mantel, Fourth Estate, 2010
Book Thief, The, Marcus Zusak, Black Swan, 2008
Burning Your Boats, Angela Carter, anthology, Vintage 1996
Cloud Atlas, David Mitchell, Sceptre, 2001
Don Quixote, Cervantes, Wordsworth Classics, 1992
Dracula, Bram Stoker, Penguin, 2003
Frankenstein, Mary Shelley , Oxford World's Classics, 2008

Gormenghast Trilogy, Mervyn Peake, Mandarin, 1996
Jonathan Livingstone Seagull, Richard Bach, HarperCollins, 2005
Life of Pi, Yann Martel, Mariner, 2003
Lord of the Flies, The, William Golding, Longman, 1980
Riddley Walker, Russel Hoban, Bloomsbury 2012
Stardust, Neil Gaiman, Headline, 2005
The Chymical Wedding, Lindsay Clarke, Picador, 1990
The Limits of Enchantment, Graham Joyce, Phoenix 2006
The Little Prince, Antoine De St-Exupéry, Egmont, 1991
The Magus, John Fowles, Panther, 1981
The Master and Margarita, Mikhail Bulgakov, Penguin, 2007
The Storyteller, Mario Vargas Llosa, Faber & Faber, 1998
The Water Theatre, Lindsay Clarke, Alma, 2011
Wuthering Heights, Emily Bronte, Wordsworth Classics, 1992

Miscellaneous

Artist's Way, The, Julia Cameron, Pan, 1995
A Multi-Dimensional Life, Moyra Caldecott, Mushroom Books, 2007
Selected Poems, Rumi, translated by Coleman Barks, Penguin, 2004
From Elfland to Poughkeepsie, Ursula K Le Guin, Pendragon Press, 1973
From the Isles of Dream, Ed J. Matthews, Floris, 1993
JRR Tolkien: author of the century, Tom Shippey, Harper Collins 2000
The Book of Imaginary Beasts, Jorge Luis Borges, 1967
The Candle of Vision, A.E., Prism, 1990
The Child That Books Built, Francis Spufford, Faber, 2003
The Rhetorics of Fantasy, Farah Mendelhson, WUP, 2008
The White Goddess, Robert Graves, Faber, 1991
Words of Re-enchantment, Anthony Nanson, Awen, 2008
Wordsmiths of Wonder, (interviews with authors) Ed Stan Nicols, Orbit, 1993

On Writing

Steering the Craft: exercises and discussions on story writing for the lone navigator and the mutinous crew, Ursula K. Le Guin, Eighth Mountain Press, 1998

The Creative Writing Coursebook, Ed. Magrs and Bell, Macmillan 2001

The Gist: a celebration of the imagination, ed. Lindsay Clarke, The Write Factor/Arvon, 2012

The Midnight Disease: the drive to write, writer's block, and the creative brain, Mariner, 2005

The Writer's Journey: mythic structure for storytellers and screenwriters, Pan, 1998

Walking in this World, Julia Cameron, Rider, 2002

Writing Fantasy & Science Fiction, Brian Stableford, Hodder & Stoughton, 1997

Writing without a Parachute: the art of freefall, Barbara Turner-Vesselago, Vala 2012

Zen in the Art of Writing, Ray Bradbury, Joshua Odell, 1996

Acknowledgments

This book has had a long genesis. The initial essay, 'Desiring Dragons' was written in 2006. Thank you to students of my 'Writing for the Imagination' class at the University of Bath; the estate of JRR Tolkien; all the writers I have cited, plunded and adored; Anna Rubin, Nimue Brown and Adam Horovitz for their poems; Tom Brown for his fabulous frontispiece; Anthony Nanson and Kirsty Hartsiotis for giving me valuable feedback, and their great suggestions for further reading; Kevin Williams, for allowing me to stay at Dominion House in Wiltshire to finish it; Chantelle Smith for desiring this dragon; and you, dear reader, for staying the distance.

End Notes

1. George Orwell, *Why I Write*, Penguin, 2004
2. Orwell, ibid, p4
3. Letter to WH Auden, 7 June 1955, *The Letter of JRR Tolkien*, Ed. Humphrey Carpenter, Harper Collins, 1995
4. Alice W. Flaherty, *The Midnight Disease: the drive to write, writer's block, and the creative brain*, Mariner Books, 2005, p213-214
5. 'This is no case of petty right and wrong', Edward Thomas, *The Annotated Collected Poems,* ed. Edna Longley, Bloodaxe, 2008, p104
6. JRR Tolkien, *The Monster and the Critics and Other Essays,* HarperCollins, 1997, p16
7. JRR Tolkien, 'On Fairy Stories', (OFS) ibid
8. Letter to the Observer, printed 20 Feb 1938, *The Letter of JRR Tolkien*, p30
9. Kevan Manwaring, *The Long Woman (2004); Windsmith (2006); The Well Under the Sea (2009); The Burning Path (2011); This Fearful Tempest (2012),* Bath/Stroud, Awen Publications
10. James Branch Cabell, *The Music from Behind the Moon: an epitome of a poet,* John Day Company, 1926
11. John Clute & John Grant, *The Encyclopaedia of Fantasy,* St Martin's Griffin, 1999
12. Robert Silverberg, *The Fantasy Hall of Fame*, Harper Voyager, 1998
13. JRR Tolkien, OFS (cited in Edwards and Holdstock, *Realms of Fantasy,* p6)
14. Edwards and Holdstock, , *Realms of Fantasy,* introduction, p6
15. Edward and Holdstock, ibid
16. Tolkien, OFS, *The Monster and the Critics,* p139
17. Tolkien, ibid, p139
18. Tolkien, ibid, footnote, p139

19. Tolkien ibid, p143
20. Tolkien, ibid, p144
21. CS Lewis, *Surprised by Joy*, 1955, p179
22. Tolkien, to his son, 9 June 1941, *Letters*, p54-55
23. *The Book of Lost Tales*, p. 15
24. Lindsay Clarke, Green Spirit pamphlet No. 6, 2004
25. Clarke, ibid, p11
26. Fannie E. Ratchford, *The Brontës' Web of Childhood,* 1949
27. David Daiches, introduction, *Wuthering Heights,* Penguin 1965
28. Alain-Fournier, *Le Grand Meaulnes*, 1912, p148
29. Jung, *Man & his Symbols*
30. Robert Holdstock, *Lavondyss,* 1988
31. Farah Mendelsohn, *The Rhetorics of Fantasy,* Wesleyan University Press, 2008
32. Holdstock, *Wordsmiths of Wonder*, p100
33. JRR Tolkien, The Cottage of Lost Play, p15
34. CS Lewis, *Surprised by Joy,* 1955
35. 'I cordially dislike allegory in all its manifestations, and always have done since I grew old and wary enough to detect its presence' (Foreword, *The Lord of the Rings*, 2nd Edition, cited by Tom Shippey, *JRR Tolkien: Author of the Century*, p161)
36. 'Of course, Allegory and Story converge, meeting somewhere in Truth. So that the only perfectly consistent allegory is a real life; and the only fully intelligible story is an allegory. And one finds, even in imperfect human 'literature', that the better and more consistent an allegory is the more easily can it be read 'just as a story'; and the better and more closely woven a story is the more easily can those so mind find an allegory in it. But the two start out from opposite ends.' Letter to Rayner Unwin, 31 July 1947, *Letters*, p121
37. Richard Jefferies, *The Story of My Heart*, Bradford-on-Avon, Ex Libris Press, p124

38. Jefferies, ibid
39. Jefferies, ibid
40. as explored in *The Maiden King*, Robert Bly and Marion Woodman, Henry Holt & Co.,1998
41. Nick Drake, 'I was made to love magic', Time of No Reply, Hannibal,1986
42. Tim Buckley, Larry Beckett, 'Song of the Siren', Starsailor, Straight 1970
43. http://www.folktale.net/openers.html [accessed 13.06.2013]
44. Tolkien, On Fairy Stories, *The Monster and the Critics*, p119
45. Holdstock,*Wordsmiths of Wonder*, p100
46. The Piccolomini, III, 4. cited in Introduction, *The Uses of Enchantment*, Bruno Bettelheim, p5
47. EM Forster, *Aspects of the Novel,* p48
48. *From the Beast to the Blonde: on fairy tales and their tellers,* Marina Warner, introduction xix, Vintage 1995
49. 'Explaining to a child why a fairy tale is so captivating to him destroys, moreover, the story's enchantment, which depends to considerable degree on the child's not quite knowing why he is so delighted by it.' Bettelheim, p18
50. BBC News, Bogeymen: Five scary visitors in the night, accessed, 24 Dec 2012
51. *The Hero with a Thousand Faces,* Joseph Campbell
52. *Wordsmiths of Wonder,* p105
53. *Wordsmiths of Wonder,* p103
54. *Care of the Soul,* Thomas Moore, p13, HarperPerennial, 1994
55. Individuation: 'the process of self realisation, the discovery and experience of meaning and purpose in life; the means by which one finds oneself and becomes who one really is.' The Society of Analytical Psychology, www.theasp.org.uk/individuation [accessed 26.04.2013]
56. EM Forster, *Aspects of the Novel,* Penguin 1976
57. JRR Tolkien, *Tales from the Perilous Realm,* HarperCollins, 2009, p322

58. *Caught in a Story: contemporary fairytales and fables,* Vintage 1992
59. AS Byatt, *Caught in a Story,* ibid, p25
60. Bettelheim, *The Uses of Enchantment* p16
61. Warner, ibid, p21
62. Warner, ibid, p11
63. Warner, ibid, intro, xvi
64. Lindsay Clarke, fiction workshop, MA Creative Writing, Cardiff University, 2002
65. On the Gods and The World by Sallustius, Part I, Translation by Gilbert Murray in *Five Stages of Greek Religion,* http://hermetic.com/texts/on_the_gods-1.html [accessed 15/06/2013]
66. Clute, *Enyclopaedia of Fantasy,* p338
67. Clute, ibid, p338
68. Tolkien, OFS, p140
69. Tolkien, OFS, p140
70. Clute, p338
71. Tolkien, ibid, p144
72. *Realms of Fantasy,* Edwards and Holdstock, Paper Tiger, 1983, p6
73. Edwards and Holdstock, ibid
74. Tolkien, OFS, p143
75. Anthony Nanson, *Words of Re-enchantment,* Awen, 2011, introduction, p3
76. Nanson, ibid, p96
77. Tolkien, OFS, p143
78. Letter to the Houghton Mifflin Co., 30 June 1955
79. Tolkien, OFS, p143
80. AE, *The Candle of Vision,* Prism Unity, 1990
81. Term coined by Brian Stableford to describe the intrusion of a new invention, discovery, or alien being into a world not unlike our own.
82. Tolkien, OFS, p143

83. William Blake, letter to a Thomas Butts, dated 22 November 1802
84. Jack Zipes, *Fairy Tales and the Art of Subversion*
85. *Freud and the Non-European*, Edward W. Said, 2004, p68
86. Karen Armstrong, *A Short History of Myth*, Canongate, 2006, p35
87. ibid
88. ibid
89. Rumi, *Selected Poems*, translated by Coleman Barks, Penguin, 2004, p171
90. Tolkien, 'On Fairy Stories', p138
91. Tolkien, OFS, p122
92. ibid, p139
93. ibid, p139
94. ibid, p140
95. Mike Scott, 'Let it Happen', A Rock in a Weary Land, BMG Int, 2000
96. Tolkien, OFS, p155
97. 'If the doors of perception were cleansed every thing would appear to man as it is, Infinite.' William Blake, from 'The Marriage of Heaven and Hell', used by Aldous Huxley in the title of 'The Doors of Perception' (1954) which went on to inspire the name of the LA rock group, 'The Doors'.
98. Tolkien, ibid, p154
99. Clarke, Imagining Otherwise
100. Bruno Bettelheim, *The Uses of Enchantment*, p7
101. Bettelheim, ibid, p7
102. Bettelheim, ibid, p144
103. Bettelheim, ibid, p144
104. Thomas Moore, 'Wakening the Soul', from *Dark Nights of the Soul*, p220-221, 2011
105. Robert Holdstock, *Worlds of Wonder*, p106
106. Barbara Turner-Vesselago, *Writing Without a Parachute*, Vala 2012

107. cited in WG Sebold, *A Place in the Country*, trans. Jo Catling, *Guardian Review*, 20.04.13
108. Flaherty, p14
109. Moyra Caldecott, *Multidimensional Life: a writer on writing*, Mushroom, 2007, p19
110. Caldecott, ibid
111. David Lodge, *Consciousness and the Novel*, Secker and Warburg, 2003
112. 'Sense and Sensibility', *Guardian*, 2 Nov 2002
113. Freud, *Delusions and Dreams in Jensen's "Gradiva"*, 1907, p8, cited in *Art and Psyche: A Study in Psychoanalysis and Aesthetics*, Ellen Handler Spitz, Yale 1985
114. Caldecott, p26
115. Sara Maitland, *The Book of Silence*, Granta, 2009, p32
116. ibid, p32
117. *The Conference of the Birds*, Farid ud-Din Attar, trans. by CS Nott, Arkana 1985
118. Attar, ibid, p129
119. 'On Fairy-Stories', *The Monsters and the Critics*, p129
120. JRR Tolkien, *Tales from the Perilous Realm*, cited in Foreword, p3
121. Robert Kirk, *The Secret Commonwealth of Elves, Fauns and Fairies*, ed. Lang, 1893
122. Alice W. Flaherty, *The Midnight Disease*, p12
123. Bettelheim, p7
124. Elizabeth Sutherland, ed. *The Golden Key and the Green Life*, 1986, p1
125. Sutherland, ibid
126. John Moat, *The Gist: a celebration of the imagination*, 2012, p24
127. Lindsay Clarke, *Imagining Otherwise*, Green Spirit pamphlets, no. 6
128. Clarke, *ibid*
129. Lindsay Clarke, *The Water Theatre*, Alma, 2011, p184-5
130. Clarke, *Imagining Otherwise*, Green Spirit pamphlets, no. 6

131. *Introducing Romanticism*, D. Heath & J. Boreham, Icon 2010
132. CS Lewis, *Selected Literary Essays* 1969
133. Caldecott, p155
134. Karen Armstong, *A Short History of Myth*, p106
135. Nancy Mellon, *The Art of Storytelling*, Element 1998
136. Caldecott, ibid
137. In the summer of the year 1797, the Author, then in ill health, had retired to a lonely farmhouse between Porlock and Linton, on the Exmoor confines of Somerset and Devonshire. In consequence of a slight indisposition, an anodyne had been prescribed, from the effects of which he fell asleep in his chair at the moment that he was reading the following sentence, or words of the same substance, in Purchas's Pilgrimage: "Here the Khan Kubla commanded a palace to be built, and a stately garden thereunto. And thus ten miles of fertile ground were inclosed with a wall." The Author continued for about three hours in a profound sleep, at least of the external senses, during which time he has the most vivid confidence, that he could not have composed less than from two to three hundred lines; if that indeed can be called composition in which all the images rose up before him as things, with a parallel production of the correspondent expressions, without any sensation or consciousness of effort. On awakening he appeared to himself to have a distinct recollection of the whole, and taking his pen, ink, and paper, instantly and eagerly wrote down the lines that are here preserved. At this moment he was unfortunately called out by a person on business from Porlock, and detained by him above an hour, and on his return to his room, found, to his no small surprise and mortification, that though he still retained some vague and dim recollection of the general purport of the vision, yet, with the exception of some eight or ten scattered lines and images, all the rest had passed away like the images on the

surface of a stream into which a stone has been cast, but, alas! without the after restoration of the latter! Samuel Taylor Coleridge, preface to *Christabel, Kubla Khan, and the Pains of Sleep*, 1816

138. Beowulf: The Monsters and the Critics, Tolkien, p7-8
139. *The Letters of JRR Tolkien*, Harper Collins, 1995, p216
140. JRR Tolkien, cited in introduction to *The Book of Lost Tales*, George Allen & Unwin, 1983/1984
141. Alain-Fournier, *Le Grand Meaulnes*, 1912, p110
142. Tolkien, OFS, p139
143. 'Darest Thou Now O Soul', Walt Whitman, *Leaves of Grass*, Penguin 1981
144. George RR Martin: Barbarians at the gate, Guardian interview, Alison Flood, 13 April 2011
145. T.S. Eliot – 'Little Gidding' *The Four Quartets*, Faber
146. South Bank Show interview, Season 26, episode 13, 1st Broadcast 9 March 2003
147. Tolkien, On Fairy Stories, p137
148. Aldo Leopold, *A Sand County Almanac, with other essays on conservation*
149. Henry David Thoreau, *Walden: or, a Life in the Woods*
150. Robert Macfarlane, *The Wild Places*, Granta, 2007, p7
151. From interview in Guardian Family, 'Being Tolkien's grandson blocked my writing...' Joanna Moorhead Saturday Guardian 24.11.12
152. 'What big teeth you have...' BBC Radio 4 documentary, broadcast Christmas 2012
153. 'Es necesario hacer un mundo nuevo. Un mundo donde quepan muchos mundos, donde quepan todos los mundos', Subcomandante Marcos, of the Zapatista Army of Liberation, EZLN Mexico, 2000
154. Ben Okri, *A Way of Being Free*, Phoenix, 1988, p2
155. Ursula K Le Guin, *The Language of the Night: Essays on Fantasy and Science Fiction*, Putnam, 1979, p58

156. Hazelton Spencer, *British Literature from Beowulf to Sheridan*, DC Heath & Co., 1963
157. Seamus Heaney, trans. *Beowulf*, Faber and Faber, 2002
158. George Orwell, Why I Write, Penguin, p10
159. William Faulkner, cited in *The Midnight Disease*, p214
160. Michael Chabon, *Wonder Boys*, Fourth Estate, 2008, p20
161. John Cowper Powys, *Porius*, Duckworth & Co., 2007, p210
162. 'Comeback Man', *The Economist*, October 2006
163. Hazelton Spencer, translation, p20, 22-24
164. Alice W. Flaherty, *The Midnight Disease*, p13
165. Julia Cameron's *The Artist Way*, Pan 1999
166. Spencer trans., ibid, p17, 127-128
167. *Beowulf*, Heaney translation, Faber, 2002
168. Spencer trans., p16, 4-7
169. ibid, p17, 69
170. ibid, p17, 56-57
171. ibid, p15, 91-94
172. ibid, p18, 39
173. ibid, p17, 129-131
174. ibid, p12, 25-27
175. Shakespeare, *Hamlet*, Act II, Scene 2
176. Spencer, trans., p19, 133-137
177. ibid, p18, 15-17
178. ibid, p19, 15-17
179. ibid, p19, 21
180. ibid, p20, 29-33
181. ibid, p20, 75-80
182. ibid, p20, 91-95
183. ibid, p22, 122-126
184. ibid, p20, 1-6
185. ibid, p21, 72-74
186. ibid, p22, 133-135
187. *Linguarum Veterum Septentrionalium Thesaurus Grammatico-Criticus et Archaeologicus*, Oxoniae 1705

188. Finnsburgh fragment, *Beowulf,* trans. Michael Alexander, Penguin, 1973
189. ibid
190. Version by Kevan Manwaring, Bath, 1999
191. *Speak Like Rain: letters to a young bard,* Awen 2004
192. Heaney, *Beowulf,* intro
193. Spencer, ibid, p23, 107-111
194. ibid, p23, 112-113
195. ibid, p22, 20-24
196. ibid, p22, 39-40
197. ibid, p22, 13-14
198. ibid, p22, 57-58
199. ibid, p23, 75-76
200. ibid, p23, 80-81
201. ibid, p23, 96-97
202. ibid, p23, 98-99
203. ibid, p23, 117-119
204. ibid, p23, 121-122
205. John Steinbeck, *The Acts of King Arthur and his Noble Knights, 1976*
206. Steinbeck, ibid
207. Hans Dieckmann, Shadow (Analytical Psychology), http://www.enotes.com/psychoanalysis-encyclopedia/shadow-analytical-psychology
208. William T. Gorski, *Yeats and Alchemy* (1996) p. 85
209. *The Creative Writing Coursebook,* Ed. Magrs and Bell, Macmillan 2001
210. Spencer, ibid, p23, 133-135
211. ibid, p23, 4-5
212. ibid, p24, 21-24
213. ibid, p24, 42-47
214. ibid, p24, 64-65
215. ibid, p24, 61
216. ibid, p24, 77-82

217. ibid, p25, 19-21
218. ibid, p24, 4-5
219. ibid, p25, 22-24
220. ibid, p25, 25
221. ibid, p25, 77-80
222. ibid, p25, 32
223. ibid, p25, 67-69
224. ibid, p25, 70-71
225. ibid, p25, 62-65
226. ibid, p26, 17-21
227. Barbara Turner-Vesselago, *Writing Without a Parachute*, Vala, 2012, p28, 35
228. Spencer, ibid, p26, 9-11
229. ibid, p26, 28-31
230. ibid, p26, 57-59
231. ibid, p27, 104-106
232. ibid, p27, 168-170
233. ibid, p28, 180-184
234. ibid, p28, 17-18
235. ibid, p28, 35-36
236. ibid, p29, 13-16
237. ibid, p28, 38-41
238. Malcolm Gladwell, *Outliers*, Little, Brown, 2008, citing the research conducted by Swedish psychologist, K. Anders Ericsson
239. Spencer, ibid, p29, 45-48
240. ibid, p31, 23-26
241. ibid, p31, 233-235
242. ibid, p30, 123-127
243. ibid, p31, 205-207
244. Gabriel Bradford Millar, *Crackle of Almonds*, Awen 2012
245. Spencer, ibid, p31, 9
246. Martin Shaw, *Branches from the Lightning-Tree*, White Cloud, 2011

247. Steinbeck, ibid
248. Michael Chabon, *Wonder Boys*, Fourth Estate
249. Steinbeck, ibid
250. Robert Macfarlane, *The Old Ways: a journey on foot*, Hamish Hamilton, 2012, p105
251. Heaney, *Beowulf*, introduction
252. Spencer, ibid, p31, 23
253. ibid, p31, 16
254. ibid, p31, 17-19
255. ibid, p31, 30
256. ibid, p32, 41-42
257. ibid, p32, 46-55
258. ibid, p32, 56-59
259. Bede, Historia Ecclesiastica Gentis Anglorum, Book II, chapter 13, cited in Wikiquote, (http://en.wikiquote.org/wiki/Bede) accessed 21 June 2013
260. Heaney, *Beowulf*, intro
261. Spencer, ibid, p32, 64-68
262. ibid, p32, 60-63
263. Christina Rossetti, Goblin Market, http://www.poetryfoundation.org/poem/174262 (accessed 21 June 2013)
264. Spencer, ibid, p33, 22-23
265. ibid, p33, 32-33
266. ibid, p32, 1-4
267. ibid, p34, 188-190
268. ibid, p33, 98-99
269. ibid, p33, 106-109
270. ibid, p34, 130-134
271. ibid, p34, 139-143
272. ibid, p34, 153
273. ibid, p34, 178-180
274. ibid, p35, 40-41
275. ibid, p34, 2-6
276. ibid, p35, 23-26

277. ibid, p35, 42-43
278. ibid, p36, 113-117
279. ibid, p36, 135-138
280. ibid, p36, 149-155
281. ibid, p36, 192-194
282. ibid, p37, 10-11
283. ibid, p37, 32-35
284. ibid, p37, 41
285. ibid, p37, 47-49
286. ibid, p37, 60-64
287. ibid, p37, 72-73
288. ibid, p37, 79
289. ibid, p37, 84-86
290. ibid, p37, 104-105
291. ibid, p38, 118-119
292. ibid, p39, 26-29
293. ibid, p39, 52-54
294. ibid, p38, 62-66
295. Cormac McCarthy, *The Road*, Picador, 2006, p87
296. Spencer, ibid, p40, 55-56
297. ibid, p40, 68
298. Tolkien, *The Monsters and The Critics, Harper Collins* 2006, p11
299. letter to Naomi Mitchison, 18 December, 1949, *Letter of JRR Tolkien*, p134
300. A History of Dragons, Ronald Hutton, DruidCast: A Druid Podcast, Episode 49, April 2011, http://www.druidcast.libsyn.com/rss
301. JRR Tolkien, *The Children of Hurin* HarperCollins, 2007
302. Carl Jung, Collected Works 16, para 470
303. Jung, CW 9, para 422
304. Jung, CW 9, para 423
305. Jorge Luis Borges, *The Book of Imaginary Beasts*, Vintage, 2002
306. Alan Garner, *The Voice That Thunders*, Harvill Press, 2010, p108

307. Moyra Caldecott, *A Multi-Dimensional Life*, Bladud, 2007
308. David Lindsay, *Voyage to Arcturus*, Dover, 2005
309. Tolkien, The Monsters and the Critics, p16
310. Robert Heinlein, *Stranger in a Strange Land*, 1961
311. Metaphor, the Inner Voice, and the Muse, Alice W. Flaherty, *The Midnight Disease*, p236
312. John & Caitlín Matthews, *Celtic Wisdom Tarot*, Thorsons, 1999
313. Flaherty, *The Midnight Disease*, p252
314. Rober Graves, *The White Goddess: a historical grammar of poetic myth*, Faber and Faber, 1999, p3
315. 'Thomas the Rhymer', *The Oxford Book of English Verse: 1250-1900*, ed Arthur Quiller-Couch, 1919
316. Flaherty, ibid, p242
317. Flaherty, ibid, p242
318. Landor, Walter Savage, *Imaginary Conversations*, (1824-1829) Gutenberg Book Project (online)
319. Nathaniel Hawthorne, 'The Custom House': Introduction to *The Scarlet Letter* (page 14)
320. The Uncanny, Sigmund Freud, translation, 1919
321. Cited in John Forster, *The Life of Charles Dickens Complete*, Vol I-III, online, http://books.google.co.uk/ [accessed 20/06/2013]
322. Tolkien, OFS, ibid
323. White, TH, *The Once and Future King*, Penguin 1958
324. Alan Moore, Hardtalk interview, BBC April 2012
325. Green Spirit pamphlet no. 6, 2004
326. 'Being in Uncertainties, Mysteries and Doubts' (NAWE journal, Spring 2012)
327. Frost, Robert, *Selected Poems*, Penguin 1973
328. Alice W. Flaherty, *The Midnight Disease*, p256
329. *Creative Writing: a workbook with readings*, ed. Anderson, OU/Routledge, 2006
330. Anderson, ibid, p149

331. Lewis Carrol, *Through the Looking Glass and What Alice Found There,* Macmillan, 1871
332. Carrol, ibid

About the Author

Kevan Manwaring is a writer and storyteller who lives in Stroud, Gloucestershire. He teaches creative writing for the Open University and performs wherever his Triumph Legend motorbike will take him. He sometimes wanders into other worlds.

Selected Works

Fiction
The Windsmith Elegy:
The Long Woman
Windsmith
The Well Under the Sea
The Burning Path
This Fearful Tempest
The Sun Miners
Oxfordshire Folk Tales
Northamptonshire Folk Tales

Non-fiction
The Bardic Handbook
Lost Islands
The Way of Awen
Turning the Wheel
Storytelling for a Greener World (contributor)
An Ecobardic Manifesto (co-author)

Poetry
Green Fire
Wildblood
Thirteen Treasures

The Immanent Moment
Soul of the Earth (contributor)

For more information, performances and workshops, visit: www.kevanmanwaring.co.uk

COMPASS
BOOKS

Compass Books focuses on practical and informative 'how-to' books for writers. Written by experienced authors who also have extensive experience of tutoring at the most popular creative writing workshops, the books offer an insight into the more specialised niches of the publishing game.